MURDER AT MONK'S BARN

CECIL Waye was a pseudonym of Cecil John Charles Street (1884-1964), who, after a distinguished career in the British army, became a prolific writer of detective novels.

He produced two long series of novels; one under the name of John Rhode featuring the forensic scientist Dr. Priestley, and another under the name of Miles Burton. As Cecil Waye, Street also produced four mysteries in the early thirties: *Murder at Monk's Barn, The Figure of Eight, The End of the Chase* and *The Prime Minister's Pencil.* These works are now republished by Dean Street Press.

CECIL WAYE

MURDER AT MONK'S BARN

With an introduction by
Tony Medawar

DEAN STREET PRESS

INTRODUCTION

THE writer best known as 'John Rhode' was born on the 3rd of May 1884 in the British territory of Gibraltar at the southern tip of Spain.

His birth name was Cecil John Charles Street but to his family and throughout his life he was known as John. His mother, Caroline Bill, was descended from a wealthy Yorkshire family, and his father, General John Street, was a distinguished former commander of the British Army in what is now known as Sri Lanka. At the time General Street was serving in Gibraltar as colonel-in-chief of the second battalion of Scottish Rifles. He had joined the Army in 1839 and served in China and the Crimea, including at the battles of Balaklava and Inkerman, as well as at the siege and fall of Sebastopol. Shortly after the birth of their child John and Caroline Street returned to England where, not long after John's fifth birthday, General Street died unexpectedly. John and his widowed mother went to live with her father in a house called *Firlands* in Woking, England, and in 1895, John was sent to school at Wellington College in Crowthorne, Berkshire, recognised as the school for children of army officers.

John did well in his academic studies. Perhaps unsurprisingly, his strengths seem to have been in the sciences. In 1901 he was joint winner of the school chemistry prize, and he also won the Pender Prize for an essay on a natural history subject, his being "The Scenery of Hampshire from a Geological Point of View", a title strongly reminiscent of the geological scholarship of Dr. Thorndyke, the detective created by the great mystery writer Richard Austin Freeman with whom Street is sometimes compared. In 1901, Street was awarded the Wellesley Prize, and the following year the Talbot Prize; and he also won praise for his prowess in intermural cricket matches.

At the age of 16, John Street left Wellington to attend the Royal Military Academy at Woolwich as a "gentleman cadet", joining the Royal Garrison Artillery in August 1903. On passing out from the Academy he was awarded the Armstrong Memorial Silver Medal for Electricity and Magnetism, and prizes for his work in these subjects.

Around this time, John met Hyacinth Kirwan, who was descended from Irish gentry and the daughter of a major in the Royal Artillery. They became engaged in September 1905 and were married on 24 February 1906. In March, he resigned his commission as a second lieutenant and their daughter, Verena, was born later in the same year. The family moved to Lyme Regis in Dorset, where they lived in a beautiful house, *Summerhill*, and Street worked as the manager of the Lyme Regis Electric Light & Power Company. During his time in the town, Street also served as a special juror, gaining an experience of the work of juries that would come in useful when he came to write one of his most famous detective mysteries.

On the outbreak of what has become known as the first world war, John Street – then in his late 20s and possibly inspired by his father's military record – enlisted, initially as a second lieutenant in the Royal Garrison Artillery. On 8 August 1915, as part of the special reserve, he landed in France where three months later he was wounded for the first of what would be three occasions. In 1917 Street returned to Britain and joined MI7, a branch of British military intelligence, where he worked on the promulgation of allied propaganda "behind the lines", as he described it in a fascinating study on the work of the military intelligence sections in the territories occupied by Germany.

In the New Year Honours List for 1918, Street was awarded the Order of the British Empire and that January he was also awarded the prestigious Military Cross, an honour that is granted in recognition of "an act or acts of exemplary gallantry during active operations against the enemy on land".

Street went on to write three books about his war experiences, all of which were published under the pseudonym 'F.O.O.', standing for Forward Observation Officer. The first was *With the*

Guns, the story of "a siege battery involved in the battle of Loos, with chapters on artillery, its employment, evolution, observation, changing positions and communications." This was quickly followed by another book *The Making of a Gunner*, about the artillery, and a semi-autobiographical novel, *The Worldly Hope*. All three books remain highly readable, as does the short story that appears to be John Street's earliest published fiction. In "Gunner Morson, Signaller" – which was written, one imagines, for propaganda purposes – a British soldier saves a group of his countrymen from an unexpected German attack, disarming one of the enemy with a telephone and, consistent with what would become the hallmark of John Street's detective stories, killing another with a most unusual weapon, an earth pin, a pointed steel bar about two feet long used to establish an earth return for telephone circuits.

As the First World War came to an end John Street moved to a new propaganda role in Dublin Castle in Ireland, where he would be responsible for countering the campaigning of the Irish nationalists during the so-called war of Irish independence.

But the winds of change were blowing across Ireland and the resolution – or rather the partial resolution – of what Disraeli had defined as "The Irish Question" would soon result in a treaty and the partition of the island of Ireland. As history was made, Street was its chronicler, at least from the British perspective.

He wrote *The Administration of Ireland, 1920* under a new pseudonym, 'I.O.', short for "Information Officer", and then *Ireland in 1921*, the first book to appear under his own name. Both books were a success but, with the ink now dry on the Anglo-Irish Treaty, Street moved away from the promulgation of politico-military propaganda on behalf of the British state.

Other than making headlines for falling down a lift shaft, John Street would spend most of the rest of the 1920s at a typewriter. There were political studies of France, Germany, Hungary and Czechoslovakia as well as two biographical studies and English translations of a memoir of life in the French army and a celebrated biography of the Marquis de Vauban, the foremost military engineer of the late seventeenth century. His most popular book at this time was almost certainly a translation of Maurice Thiery's acclaimed biography of Captain James Cook.

As well as full-length works, Street continued to write short stories as well as articles for various outlets on an eclectic range of subjects including piracy, camouflage and concealment, Slovakian railways, the value of physical exercise, peasant art, telephony and the challenges of post-war reconstruction. He also found time to write three thrillers – *A.S.F.*, *The Alarm*, *The Double Florin* – and a First World War love story, *Mademoiselle from Armentières*. These were published under a new pen name – or should that be a pun name – 'John Rhode', which was also the name he used for a full-length study of the trial of Constance Kent, who was convicted for one of the most gruesome murders of the nineteenth century, at Road House in the village of Rode, then a village in Wiltshire.

However, while these early books found some success and *Mademoiselle from Armentières* was even filmed, the Golden Age of detective stories was well under way, and so John Street decided to try his hand.

The first challenge was to create a great detective, someone to rival the likes of Roger Sheringham and Hercule Poirot with whose creators he would soon be on first name terms. Street's great detective was the almost supernaturally intelligent Lancelot Priestley, a former academic who was, in the words of the critic Howard Haycraft, "fairly well along in years, without a sense of humour and inclined to dryness". From his first case, *The Paddington Mystery* (1925), Doctor – or rather Professor – Priestley was an immediate success, and Street was quick to respond, producing another six novels in short order.

Priestley appears in all but five of Street's 76 'John Rhode' novels – one of which is based on the notorious Wallace case – and they often feature one or both of two Scotland Yard detectives, Inspector Hanslet and Inspector Jimmy Waghorn who would in later years appear without Priestley in several radio plays and a short stage play.

*

So by 1930, John Street, a highly decorated former Army major with a distinguished career in military intelligence behind him, had written 25 books using four names. He was 45 years old but, astonishingly, he was just getting started . . .

By 1930, the Streets were living in North Brewham, a village in Somerset where John became vice-chairman of the local branch of the British Legion, sitting on its employment committee to help ex-servicemen find work. The village was located in the parish of Bruton and from this Street derived the first of two new pseudonyms – 'Miles Burton' as whom he wrote a series of what would eventually be 63 novels. These feature Desmond Merrion, a retired naval officer named for Merrion Street in Dublin, and – in all but two titles – Inspector Arnold of, where else, Scotland Yard. There also exists an unfinished and untitled final novel, inspired it would appear by the notorious Green Bicycle Case.

The 'Burton' and 'Rhode' detective mysteries are similar but while Priestley is generally dry and unemotional, Merrion is more of a gentleman sleuth in the manner of Philip Trent or Lord Peter Wimsey. Both are engaged from time to time by Scotland Yard acquaintances, all of whom are portrayed respectfully rather than as the servile and unimaginative policemen created by some of Street's contemporaries.

However, two pseudonyms weren't enough for a crime writer as fecund as John Street and, again adopting a pun on his own name, he *also* became 'Cecil Waye' although this was not revealed until long after Street's death. For the four 'Cecil Waye' books, Street created two new series characters – the brother and sister team of Christopher and Vivienne Perrin, two investigators rather in the mould of Agatha Christie's 'Young Adventurers', Tommy and Tuppence Beresford. Curiously, while three of the 'Waye' novels are metropolitan thrillers, the first – *Murder at Monk's*

Barn – is a detective story, very much in the style of the 'John Rhode' and 'Miles Burton' books.

With three series of crime books in hand, it is not surprising to find that John Street was also a founding member of the Detection Club, the illustrious dining club for crime writers founded by Anthony Berkeley in the late 1920s. In Street's words, the Club existed so that detective story writers might "dine together at stated intervals for the purpose of discussing matters concerned with their craft." Street played a lively part in the life of the Detection Club and his most important contribution was undoubtedly the creation of Eric the Skull which – showing that he had not lost his youthful technical skills – he wired up so that the eye sockets glowed red during the initiation ceremony for new members. He also edited *Detection Medley*, the first and arguably the best anthology of stories by members of the Club, and he contributed to the Club's first two round-robin detective novels, *The Floating Admiral* and *Ask a Policeman*, as well as one of the Club's various series of detective radio plays and the excellent true crime anthology *The Anatomy of Murder*.

Street was popular and he was happy to help other Club members with scientific and technical aspects of their own work. In the foreword to Dorothy L Sayers' Wimsey novel, *Have His Carcase*, she thanks Street for his "generous help with all the hard bits" drawn from his knowledge of code-breaking and ciphers. And Street also provided the technical input for *Drop to his Death*, a novel attributed to him as well as to his closest friend at the Detection Club, John Dickson Carr, writing under his 'Carter Dickson' pen name; the two were firm friends and Carr later made Street the inspiration for his character Colonel March, head of *The Department of Queer Complaints*.

Away from crime fiction, things were running less smoothly. At some point in the 1930s, Rhode's marriage failed, possibly because he seems to have had his hands permanently welded to a dictaphone – which he had come to use rather than a typewriter – but more likely because of the effect on the marriage of the loss of their daughter Verena who died in 1932 at the age of only twenty five.

During this decade, John met Eileen Waller, the daughter of an Irish engineer and a French mother, and the couple moved to Orchards, a house in Laddingford, Kent, where Street would set one of his Dr. Priestley novels, *Death in the Hopfields*, where a local journalist described Street as "the most jovial, 'hail-fellow-well-met' types of men I have ever had the pleasure of meeting" and revealed that Street owned a talkative parrot and collected pewter tankards, which will not come as a surprise to anyone who has appreciated the many, many, imaginatively-named public houses that pepper his novels. It was also revealed that, somewhat improbably, John Street and Eileen wove tapestries together on a large hand loom. While in Laddingford, Street also served as a school governor and he sponsored the village cricket team, acquiring for them a playing field and a pavilion.

In October 1943, John and Eileen let Orchards and moved to the remote village of Swanton Novers in North Norfolk. In 1949, after the death of Street's first wife, Hyacinth, John and Eileen married in 1949, in Yorkshire, and they moved to Stowmarket in Suffolk, where they lived in a beautiful 16th century thatched house with exposed timbers, original fireplaces and flooring.

However, John Street's extraordinary career was coming to an end. The couple moved to a bungalow in Seaford in Sussex on the south coast of England and his final novels – *The Vanishing Diary* by 'John Rhode' and *Death Paints a Picture* by 'Miles Burton' – were published in 1960 and 1961 respectively

John Street died on the 8th of December 1964 in Leaf Hospital, Eastbourne. He left nearly three quarters of a million pounds in today's money. Fourteen years later his wife Eileen also died, in a Seaford nursing home.

*

John Street wrote a large number – more than 140 – of what one Japanese fan, Yoshito Tsukada, has aptly described as "pure and clever detective stories". His approach to writing detective fiction was simple, as he explained in a letter he wrote to the author of a book on the subject, published in 1934.

"The first thing is to devise a suitable plot. Of which there is no lack. A perusal of the daily press, and of criminal records, will disclose an almost unlimited supply. Unknown correspondents are frequently good enough to send me ideas. The progress of scientific discovery naturally suggests fresh means of ingenious murder . . ."

He went on to explain how he would "complete the crime as though I myself were the criminal, trying to think of every possible precaution. I next take the opposite point of view, that of the investigator charged with inquiring into the death of the victim . . . I am myself the logician in Dr. Priestley, giving him the services of expert practising scientists where necessary."

That attention to detail led Street's friend, Dorothy L. Sayers, to describe him as "the kind of man who tries everything out on the dog in his own back kitchen (under proper safeguards, of course, for the dog)." His mission was simply to write books that invited the reader to pit their wits against him. This was exactly the kind of novel that Street himself enjoyed, as he described in an article published to accompany a radio series entitled "Thoughts of a Detective Story Writer".

"I want painstaking workmanship and accurate expression of fact. Given those two essentials, I can thoroughly enjoy myself in trying to unravel the problem before the author divulges it . . . in true detective fiction, the actual crime is of secondary importance. To the author, and therefore to the reader as well, it is merely a peg upon which to hang the subtlety of his criminal and the acuteness of his detective."

Clearly, the technique worked for, in the 1930s and 40s in particular, John Street was immensely popular and not only with the reading public. For the writer and reviewer E.R. Punshon, Street was "Public Brain-Tester No. 1" while Dorothy L. Sayers praised him warmly – here writing about *The Robthorne Mystery*: "One always embarks on a John Rhode book with a great feeling of security. One knows there will be a sound plot, a well-knit process of reasoning, and a solidly satisfying solution with no loose ends or careless errors of fact." And on the other side of the ocean, Ellery Queen included two novels by 'John Rhode' – *The Paddington Mystery* and *The Murders in Praed Street* – in a list of cornerstones of detective fiction, drawn up with Howard Haycraft. The list also included two titles each by Christie and Sayers (as well as four by Queen!) and while Street does not have anything like the same profile as these giants of the genre, he remains among the most sought after crime writers of the Golden Age. In an essential study of some of the lesser luminaries of the Golden Age, the American writer Curtis Evans described Street as "the master of murder means" and praised his "fiendish ingenuity" in "the creative application of science and engineering". And another writer on the Golden Age, Ian Godden, has suggested that Street's books were "often read until they fell to pieces, which is as good a tribute as any to their popularity and the reason why they are so hard to find today."

While Street is not without his critics, his books are thoroughly enjoyable, often humorous and consistently entertaining. He tackles impossible crimes – with murder in locked houses, locked bathrooms and locked railway compartments, even – with Carter Dickson – a locked elevator. And who else but Street could come up with the idea of using a hedgehog as a murder weapon, or conceive of dealing death by means of a car battery . . . or a marrow . . . or a soda siphon . . . or a hot water bottle. Even bed-sheets and pyjamas prove lethal in the hands of John Street. He often creates unusual and believable settings for his mysteries such as a motor show, or the work of the Home Guard, Britain's local defence force in the Second World War, or the excavation of a dinosaur, which forms the backdrop for the 'Miles Burton' title *Bones in the Brickfield*. Street also defies some of the expectations of the genre, with one novel in which Dr. Priestley allows a murderer to go free and another in which the guilty party is identified and put on trial . . . but acquitted. And his characters – though simply drawn – are engaging and at times display an emotional depth that is rarely found in detective stories of the Golden Age. As Curtis Evans has shown in his biblio-biographical study of Street's life and work, Street was in several respects far more modern in his outlook on life than many of his contemporaries, with libertarian anti-capitalist sentiments, non-judgmental references to adultery, illegitimacy, prostitution and homosexuality, and markedly different views to most of his contemporaries on Jewish people and the rights of women as well as credible working class characters that function as real people rather than stereotypes.

Today, around 60 years after his death and a century since they were first published, only a few of the 'John Rhode' and 'Miles Burton' books are currently in print but, thanks to Dean Street Press, the four 'Cecil Waye' novels – the rarest of the author's more than 150 fiction and non-fiction titles – are now available. John Street would be simply amazed.

Tony Medawar
Wimbledon
November 2020

CHAPTER I

THE main street of the little village of Fordington was completely deserted, as might have been expected at a little after seven on a cold winter evening. It was also very dark, since the bitter east wind that was blowing had extinguished the two solitary oil lamps placed one at each end of the street. The only light visible came through chinks in the curtained windows of the houses bordering it. And of these the most conspicuous was the big house known as Monk's Barn.

Cold and deserted though it appeared, it seemed to Constable Burden, the village policeman, as a haven of rest. It was market day in the neighbouring town, Yatebury, and he had been on duty all day directing traffic in the market-place. As he dismounted from his bicycle at the door of his cottage, nearly opposite Monk's Barn, he felt that his evening in front of the fire had been well earned.

"The wind's bitter enough to bite the nose off your face," he remarked to his wife, as he took off his helmet and laid it on the table. "It's blown them dratted lamps out again. I'll have to go out and see about them presently, I suppose. Hullo! what's that?"

A sharp report, plainly audible above the howling of the wind, had occasioned his exclamation. But Mrs. Burden, busily engaged in laying the tea-things, was quite unperturbed. "It's only one of them motor-bikes trying to start up," she replied; "sit down and have your tea, you must be starved."

"That weren't no motor-bike," said Burden. "'Twas a shot, if ever I heard one."

He went to the door and opened it. The wind swept in, threatening to extinguish the lamp on the table, and he shut it behind him hurriedly. He stood there for a moment or two, listening, but all was quiet and dark as before. Then, close at hand, he heard a door bang, and footsteps hurrying towards him. His lantern was at his belt, and he took it out and flashed it towards the sound.

It revealed the form of a tall man, with an overcoat hastily flung round him. "Hullo, is that you, Burden?" he asked. "Did you hear anything just now?"

Burden touched his cap. "Good evening, sir," he replied. "Yes, I could have sworn I heard a shot fired, not a minute ago."

"So could I, that's what brought me out. It sounded as though it were just outside, in the street somewhere, but there doesn't seem to be anybody about."

"No, that there doesn't, sir," agreed Burden.

"Mayhap it was over the wall there, in the garden of Monk's Barn."

The other shook his head impatiently. "Who'd be shooting there, at this time of night?" he asked. "I was over at Monk's Barn ten minutes ago, to see what time Mr. and Mrs. Wynter were starting. I'm going to a dance with them tonight. Wynter was just going upstairs to dress when I left, and his men will be gone home, long ago."

"Well, it's a very queer thing, sir—" Burden began. He stopped suddenly as the front door of Monk's Barn was flung open, shedding a beam of light across the dark street. In this beam appeared a female figure running rapidly towards them.

"Hullo! what's up?" exclaimed the man by Burden's side. "That's the Wynter's parlour-maid." He raised his voice slightly. "What's the matter, Phyllis?"

At the sound of his voice the girl uttered a gasp of relief. "Is that you, Mr. Cartwright?" she replied in distracted tones. "Will you help me find Doctor Palmer? A dreadful thing's happened. The master's been shot!"

"What!" shouted Cartwright, starting to run towards the open door. But Burden laid a detaining hand upon his arm. "I think that's my job, sir," he said. "You'll do better to get hold of Doctor Palmer and bring him along."

"Quite right," replied Cartwright. "I'll ring him up from my place; it won't take a couple of seconds. You'd better go back with Mr. Burden, Phyllis; you'll probably be wanted."

"Thank you, sir. Now, Miss Mintern, you show me the way. And hurry, there's a good girl."

She ran back to Monk's Barn, Burden following closely on her heels. Once inside the house, she mounted the broad oak staircase, and led the way along a corridor to a door, which she flung open, standing inside to let the policeman pass, then, with a stifled scream, she sank into a chair and buried her face in her hands.

Burden paid no attention to her, but advanced into the room. It was evidently Mr. Wynter's dressing-room, and had two windows, one looking out over the village street, and a second at right angles to it. Just in front of this second window was a dressing-table, with an electric lamp suspended above it.

So much Burden took in at a first glance. But these were merely trifles. For, lying in a huddled heap in front of the dressing-table was the form of a man half-dressed, his head a mass of blood, and by his side, a woman on her knees, vainly endeavouring to staunch the flow with a pocket-handkerchief.

The woman looked up at the sound of his approach. Her face was white and set, but she showed no signs of panic. "Where's Doctor Palmer?" she asked dully.

"He's on his way, ma'am," replied Burden. "Mr. Cartwright has just telephoned to him."

She made no answer, but bent once more over the huddled form of her husband. Burden, who had served in the war, and had considerable experience of death in its violent forms, took a pace forward. He saw at once that Mr. Wynter was beyond mortal aid. There was a bullet wound in the centre of his forehead, and the back of his head was shattered where the bullet had come out. One side of his face was still covered with soap, and a razor lay on the floor beside him. It was quite plain to the policeman that Mr. Wynter had been shot while in the act of shaving.

From the prostrate figure Burden's glance turned to the window behind the dressing-table. The heavy curtains were closely drawn, but in one of them was a neat round hole. He drew them aside, to find a similar starred hole in the glass of the window.

The bullet had clearly come from outside, and the shot which he had heard had been fired from the garden.

Burden was perfectly familiar with the outside of the house. One wall of it, in which was the front door, abutted upon the village street, and faced due east. To the north of the house stretched a lawn, screened from the street by a high stone wall. The lawn was about fifty yards long, and was terminated by a second high wall, against which stood a range of greenhouses and a few tall-growing shrubs. Behind this wall a short drive, at right angles to the road, led to the stables and garage.

It was far too dark for Burden to see any of this, but he was able to picture it vividly in his mind. It was clear to him, from the position of the hole in the window relative to where Mr. Wynter must have been standing, that the shot must have been fired either from the lawn, or from the shrubbery at its farther end. He could do no more for Mr. Wynter. His duty was to run to earth the person who had murdered him.

He was about to leave the room, where he felt decidedly uncomfortable and out of place, when he heard the sound of hurried footsteps mounting the stairs. A moment later Mr. Cartwright entered the room, closely followed by Doctor Palmer, an elderly man in glasses. The doctor wasted no time in preliminaries. He knelt down beside Mr. Wynter and stared at him fixedly for a few moments. He rose silently to his feet, and, glancing at Cartwright, shook his head. Then he looked meaningly at the immobile form of Mrs. Wynter.

Cartwright understood him, and laid his hand gently on her shoulder. "Come, Anne," he said gently, "we had better leave Doctor Palmer to do what he can."

His voice seemed to rouse her from the stupor into which she had fallen. She rose shudderingly to her feet, and stood swaying for a moment with staring eyes. Then, with a sudden hysterical sob, she burst into a passion of tears. "Frank!" she exclaimed. "He's dead, I know it!"

She would have fallen, had not Cartwright put out his hand to steady her. Once more she looked at the body of her husband, then, without a word, she allowed Cartwright to lead her from the room.

Doctor Palmer turned to Burden. "Bad business, this," he said gruffly. "There's very little I can do, but it seems to me it's up to you to get busy. Anyhow, take that other woman away, and leave me in peace for a bit, for heaven's sake."

He bent once more over the body, and Burden walked across the room to the chair on which Phyllis was still sitting, rocking herself slowly backwards and forwards. "Come along, Miss Mintern," he said. "Show me the way into the garden, quick."

She rose to her feet, and led him down the stairs and into the hall, where the rest of the servants were by now clustered in a frightened group. They passed through this and into the drawing-room, at the extremity of which was a wide french window.

This was all that Burden wanted. "Thank you, Miss Mintern," he said. "I can let myself out. Now, you must pull yourself together, you know. Mrs. Wynter will want all the help you can give her."

The only reply was a sob, but Burden had no time for further attempts at comfort. He drew back the curtains, disclosing the french window. It was locked, and secured on the inside by two bolts. He drew these back, and turned the key, noticing that all the fastenings worked easily. Then he opened the window, and stepped out on to the lawn. Right above his head was the window of the dressing-room, with the curtains drawn back as he had left them. A certain amount of light came from this, illuminating the nearer side of the lawn, but failing to penetrate the thick shadows under the wall at its end.

Burden cast the rays of his lantern on the ground in front of him. It was as hard as iron, and there was no chance of finding any imprint upon it. But something might have been dropped, something which would give him a clue to the individual who had entered the garden. However, search the surface of the lawn as he might, he could find nothing to help him.

As he looked up at the dressing-room window, a fairly obvious fact occurred to him. As Mr. Wynter was standing at the dressing-table, his head must have been about twenty feet above the surface of the lawn, and some little way back from the window. The hole in the window-pane had been a little below the level of Burden's eyes, and Mr. Wynter was about the same height as himself. It followed that the shot must have been fired from some little distance away. The most likely place for a murderer to conceal himself would be among the shrubs against the farther wall.

Whoever had fired the shot had crept away at once, favoured by the darkness. So much was pretty certain. But he might have left some clue behind him. Burden, who had a pretty shrewd idea that as soon as he informed his superintendent in Yatebury of the tragedy he would be relegated to the background, decided to investigate.

He entered the shrubbery, which was not more than two or three yards deep, and began to explore it with his lantern. It seemed to afford a convenient screen for things not immediately required in the greenhouses beside it. Against the wall at the back stood rows of flower-pots, some of which were broken, and piles of wooden boxes in various states of repair, together with other debris. The earth here, being sheltered from the freezing wind, was comparatively soft, and Burden searched it eagerly for footmarks.

But, in spite of his meticulous care, he found none, nor any trace suggesting that the shrubbery had recently been entered. He was about to desist from his search, when the rays of his lantern fell upon an object half hidden among the lower branches of an evergreen. Burden with difficulty restrained himself from shouting with delight as he made out what it was. Within a few minutes of the crime having been committed, he had, alone and unaided, found a clue of which the importance could not be overrated. For the object which lay before him was a double-barrelled gun.

His first impulse was to pick it up and examine it. But suddenly he remembered. Finger-prints! There was some old sacking lying among the flower-pots, also a piece of tarred twine, such as gardeners use. He wrapped the gun in the sacking, and secured it with the twine.

Then, carrying the precious bundle under his arm, he returned to the house. He was now ready to telephone to the Superintendent.

CHAPTER II

FOUR days later, a young and remarkably good-looking man alighted from a taxi in Hanover Square, and, after looking about him for a moment, entered an inconspicuous doorway, which was almost overshadowed by the imposing bulk of the adjoining facade. He climbed a steep flight of stairs, until he reached a door upon which was inscribed the single word "Perrins." After a moment's hesitation, he rapped softly on the door.

A pleasant voice bade him enter. He opened the door, and found himself in a large room, equipped as a library, with row upon row of bookshelves. At a table in the centre sat a middle-aged woman, surrounded by a sea of newspapers, which she was busily scanning, stopping every now and then to snip out a paragraph and lay the cutting in a tray by her side.

The young man stood looking at her for a second or two in silence. "Er, excuse me," he said at last, rather awkwardly "But—is this Perrins?"

"It is," she replied brightly. "What can we do for you?"

"I came to see whether your firm could help me in—er—a private matter," said the young man.

The woman looked at him narrowly for a moment. "I believe that Mr. Christopher Perrin is disengaged for a few moments," she said. "Will you give me your name, please?"

He fumbled in his pocket, and produced a card, which he handed to her. Having glanced at it, she disappeared through an inner door. In a minute or two she reappeared. "Mr. Perrin will see you," she said. "Do you mind coming this way?"

He followed her into a small room, which bore no resemblance to an office. The most conspicuous thing in it was the bright fire blazing in the grate, to which were drawn up three or four luxurious arm-chairs. In one of these was seated an athletic-looking man, who rose as his visitor entered.

"Sit down, Mr. Wynter," he said. "You'll find this the most comfortable chair. There are cigarettes in that box beside you. Now, then, how can we help you?"

Austin Wynter lighted a cigarette, glancing furtively at Christopher Perrin, as he did so. He saw a man of about his own age, with curiously penetrating eyes and a disarming smile. He liked him at first sight, and found something in the air of the room which swept away his shyness. It was all so different from what he had expected.

"Well, you see, Mr. Perrin, I was advised to come to you by a friend of mine," he said. "He told me that you were awfully clever at getting to the bottom of things. And, though the police have got this affair in hand, I'm quite certain that they're on the wrong tack."

"I shouldn't be too sure of that, if I were you," replied Christopher Perrin. "In my experience the police are a good deal shrewder than people give them credit for. And I would suggest, Mr. Wynter, that Perrins are not in the habit of working in competition with them."

"Oh, but I don't want you to work in competition!" exclaimed Austin Wynter. "You are, I understand, Private Investigators, and I want you to investigate the circumstances to my satisfaction."

"Since you have not told me what the circumstances are, you won't mind my suggesting that they are in some way connected with the murder of your brother?"

Wynter's face lengthened with astonishment.

"Why, how do you know that?" he asked.

"It's very simple. We read the papers in this office, and naturally we saw a report of the murder of Mr. Gilbert Wynter, the senior partner of Wynter & Sons, Electrical Engineers of Yatebury.

You sent me in a card which showed you to be a member of the same firm. That's all. I don't want you to run away with the idea that we are magicians."

"Oh, I see. Well, if you know about it you can probably guess what I have come to you for."

"I only know what has appeared in the papers, and that is very little. I gather that the police have their suspicions as to who committed the crime?"

"Yes, and their suspicions are all wrong, I'm quite sure. Look here, Mr. Perrin. Gilbert was my only brother, and, although we haven't seen as much of one another lately as we used to, I was devoted to him. I don't believe the police will ever find out who killed him, and I want you to try. Expense is no object; I would spend every penny I possess to see whoever it was tried and convicted."

Christopher Perrin made no immediate reply. He lighted a cigarette with great deliberation, and puffed at it slowly, as though to judge of its flavour. "Very well, Mr. Wynter," he said at last, "Perrins will take the job on. But I can't hold out much hope that they will succeed where the police, as you suggest, have failed. The police have far more facilities at their disposal than any firm of Private Investigators could ever have. You understand that, of course?"

"Fully. But, all the same, I shall greatly appreciate your assistance."

"Very well. Now, Mr. Wynter, I shall want you to tell me everything you know about the murder, and I should like my partner to be present, to avoid the necessity for repetition. You have no objection, I suppose."

"None whatever," replied Wynter. Now that he was fairly launched, he felt capable of telling his story to anybody. But he was not prepared for what followed. Christopher Perrin rose from his chair and passed into an adjoining room, whence he reappeared in company with a girl. "This is my sister Vivienne, Mr. Wynter," he said. "Since the death of our uncle, we have run this business between us."

Austin Wynter stammered something, he scarcely knew what. He felt like a man who has suddenly been vouchsafed a vision. He had come, very hesitatingly, to consult a firm of Private Investigators, and had been rewarded by the sight of the most dazzling pretty girl he had ever seen. There was something bizarre about it, like the swiftly changing scenes of a dream.

Christopher Perrin's business-like voice recalled his wandering thoughts. "Now then, Mr. Wynter, would you mind telling us what you know of your brother's murder, in your own words?"

"Certainly. But you will understand that it is only hearsay. I did not reach Fordington until an hour after the event. You see, I live in rooms at Yatebury, where the works are, and that's three miles away. It was Superintendent Swayne who called for me, and drove me out in his car."

"I remember that the papers said that your brother lived at a house called Monk's Barn at Fordington," said Christopher Perrin. "How long had he lived there?"

"Nearly five years; ever since he was married, in fact. Before that, we used to share rooms in Yatebury. He used to come into the office every day. I last saw him alive just after five on Friday, the day that he was murdered, when he left the office to go home."

"You were quite familiar with Monk's Barn, I suppose? You frequently went there to see your brother?"

"Oh yes, quite frequently. But not so often as Gilbert would have liked me to, I'm afraid. To be quite candid. I never got on very well with Anne, my sister-in-law. I always fancied that she made too many claims upon poor Gilbert. And, for another thing, I didn't care about the friends he had made in Fordington. I hadn't anything against them, mind, but I just didn't like them. On this very Friday night Gilbert and Anne were giving a dance, and asked me to make one of the party. I would have gone, but I knew that a lot of Fordington people would be going too. But, look here, I'm talking about myself rather than about the murder, I'm afraid."

"I assure you that what you have told us is very interesting," replied Christopher Perrin politely. "Now, as to that Friday evening. You drove to Fordington with the Superintendent. Who did you find there?"

"Anne had retired, and wasn't to be seen. The first person I met was a man called Cartwright, who lives in the house opposite. The Cartwrights are probably the most intimate friends my brother had. If they were not at Monk's Barn, you might be sure that either Gilbert or Anne were at White Lodge—that's the Cartwrights' place. They called one another by their Christian names, and all that sort of thing.

"Cartwright told me what had happened. He had arranged to go with Gilbert and Anne to their dance, and had looked in shortly before seven to ask what time Gilbert, who was going to drive him there, proposed to start. He came back to White Lodge, and a few minutes later heard something that sounded like a shot. He thought this rather odd, and came to the door to see what it was. There he met the village policeman, whose cottage is next door to White Lodge, and who had heard the sound too. While they were talking, the maid ran out of the door of Monk's Barn, and told them that Gilbert had been shot."

Christopher Perrin nodded. "Did you have a chance of a word with the policeman?" he asked.

"I did. The man's name is Burden, and he seems a pretty intelligent chap. Anyway, he seems to have used his brain on this occasion. He guessed that the shot had been fired from a shrubbery some distance outside Gilbert's dressing-room window, went straight there, and found the gun from which the shot had been fired. Pretty smart, for an ordinary village constable."

"Very smart indeed. Now, about this gun. Has it been traced?"

"I recognized it the moment I saw it. It is an old double-barrelled weapon, which belonged to my father. One barrel is smooth, and takes an ordinary twelve-bore cartridge, the other is rifled, and takes a cartridge holding a bullet. It used to be kept in a sort of cupboard opening off the hall at Monk's Barn."

"When was it last seen there?"

Austin Wynter shrugged his shoulders. "The maid, Phyllis Mintern, swears that she went to the cupboard on the Wednesday previous to the murder for something, and that she saw the gun there. Since then, nobody knows anything about it. It was only occasionally that the cupboard was opened. Now the significant thing about the gun is this. Burden had the sense to wrap it up in sacking, so that it would be examined for finger-prints, it was so examined, finger-marks were certainly found upon it, and they were those of Walter Mintern, Phyllis's father."

"What was Walter Mintern's connection with Monk's Barn?"

"When Gilbert first went there, he engaged Walter Mintern as second gardener, and his daughter Phyllis as parlour-maid. Walter was never satisfactory, and Gilbert often talked of getting rid of him. I think he would have done so long ago, if it hadn't been for Anne. He was afraid that it would mean losing Phyllis as well, and Phyllis is certainly an excellent maid. However, things came to a head recently, and Gilbert had paid off Walter on the Saturday before the murder. Walter took it very badly, and used most offensive language. And what the police consider very significant, he was in the 'Wheatsheaf,' the local public-house, from six to half-past on Friday evening, and threatened that he would get his own back on Gilbert if he got the chance."

"The inference being that Walter Mintern was the murderer," remarked Vivienne Perrin. "It all fits in. I see that. Motive, revenge for his discharge. Opportunity, he knew his way about the place in the dark. He probably knew where the gun was kept, or at all events his daughter did, by her own showing."

"That's just the way the police look at it, Miss Perrin," replied Austin Wynter.

"What has Walter Mintern to say about it? Has he been arrested?" asked Christopher Perrin.

"He has not been arrested yet, but I expect he will be, any minute. Naturally, he flatly denies having anything to do with the matter. He accounts for the finger-prints by saying that Gilbert gave him the gun to clean some weeks ago. So far, nobody has been found to confirm that statement. Personally, I don't think it very likely, for Gilbert always used to clean his guns himself. And yet, I don't believe that Walter Mintern deliberately murdered my brother. He is a rough, uneducated man, with a violent temper, I admit. But he had plenty of native cunning, and I feel sure that he would never have left such an obvious clue as the gun behind him."

"Is that your only reason for believing him to be innocent, Mr. Wynter?" asked Christopher Perrin quietly.

Austin Wynter flushed, and shifted uneasily in his chair. "Well, it is the only tangible reason, I suppose," he replied. "But, somehow I can't bring myself to believe that Mintern did it. It looks too simple, and I can't help thinking that there is a lot more behind it than that."

"Now, Mr. Wynter, you will understand that everything you say is in complete confidence. Have you any suspicions as to the identity of the murderer?"

"Suspicions? I suspect the whole gang at Fordington!" Austin's shyness had entirely left him by now, and it was plain that he was under the stress of a very real emotion. "It was a plot, a damned low-down plot to get Gilbert out of the way, for some reason I don't yet understand. But I'll find out who is responsible, if I have to spend the rest of my life doing so."

CHAPTER III

NEITHER of the Perrins seemed disposed to ask Austin Wynter any further questions, and, very shortly afterwards, he left the office. Christopher Perrin showed him out, and then returned to the inner room, with a smile upon his face. "Well, Vi?" he said questioningly.

"A most interesting young man," replied Vivienne. "Not much experience of life, I should say. But then, one wouldn't expect him to have, living in a provincial town like Yatebury."

"Pretty much my diagnosis," agreed her brother. "What's his game, do you suppose?"

Vivienne lighted a cigarette, and puffed at it thoughtfully before she answered him. "I don't think that he has any particular game, in the sense you mean," she said at last. "I think he is genuinely distressed at his brother's death, and is vindictive enough to be keen that somebody suffers for it. I'm inclined to agree with him about this man Mintern's innocence; as he says, it sounds too simple. You notice that the police seem a bit doubtful themselves, or they would have arrested him long ago."

"Yes, I think Mintern can safely be left to the police. But, if he didn't fire the shot, who did?"

"I'm so glad you didn't ask Mr. Wynter too many questions," replied Vivienne inconsequently. "If you're to take their job on, it will never do for us to allow ourselves to be prejudiced by other people's suspicions. Did you notice that the only time Mr. Wynter allowed himself to be natural, was when he uttered that queer outburst against what he calls 'the Fordington gang'? Interesting, that, I thought."

"It was. I'm still wondering what was in his mind when he said it."

"Don't you see? He's got what one might call a Fordington complex. He said, if you remember, that he was devoted to his brother, but that they hadn't seen much of one another recently. Now, what lies behind that is probably jealousy. He wouldn't admit it, of course; he probably isn't definitely conscious of it. But the two had lived together, probably for some considerable time. Austin no doubt realized that Gilbert's marriage would put an end to their constant companionship, and therefore resented it. He was prepared in advance to dislike the girl that Gilbert might marry, and Mrs. Gilbert—Anne, he called her, didn't he?—seems to have been unable to overcome this dislike. He told us that he never got on with her. All clear so far?"

"My dear Vi, you ought to be a lecturer in psychology, as I've often told you. Go ahead."

"Right. Now Gilbert—we know nothing about him, by the way—may or may not have been as devoted to Austin as Austin was to him. Anyhow, he marries and goes to live at this place Fordington, which I imagine to be a sort of residential village. If Austin had chosen to have seen more of his brother after his marriage, it would probably have been all right. But he didn't, he sat and sulked at Yatebury; wouldn't go to dances with Mr. Gilbert, and that sort of thing. Nursing his resentment, in fact.

"On the other hand, Gilbert and his wife, as a young married couple, naturally made friends in their new environment, people like these Cartwrights, Austin mentioned, for instance. As time went on, they became members of a set from which Austin excluded himself. Austin gradually found his brother drifting further and further away from him, forming new interests, and that sort of thing. For this he blamed, not his brother, but his brother's wife and friends. It is all very natural, and it's not a very long step from blaming people to hating them, as he obviously does."

"But, my dear girl, it is a very long step indeed from hating people to suspecting them of murder."

"Let me finish. I was merely trying to explain how it was possible for Austin to dislike Gilbert's friends without any real cause. Now that we have established that, we can go on. Austin's last astonishingly frank remark reveals the fact that he believes Gilbert to have been murdered to get him out of the way. Now, whose way can he have stood in?"

"Aren't you taking Austin a bit too literally? He probably meant that there is somebody to whom Gilbert's existence was, shall we say, a nuisance."

"Very well, put it like that, if you like. The point seems to be, is there such a person, and, if so, who is it?"

"That question, since, as you say yourself, we know nothing about Gilbert, we can't possibly answer."

"No, but if we're going to undertake the case, we shall have to decide in what direction to look. Now, broadly speaking, the motive for Gilbert's murder is to be found in something connected either with his business or his private life. If it were his business life, Austin would probably have known something about it, and would have told us. But he didn't know anything about his private life, hence his suspicions. And that, I fancy, is what we shall have to explore."

Christopher nodded. "I see what you are getting at," he said. "You suspect the female influence. Well, I don't mind telling you that the same thought struck me while Austin was here. Has it occurred to you that Mintern may be the culprit after all, but that he had a more powerful motive than mere revenge for his dismissal?"

"Meaning that Gilbert had seduced the fair Phyllis, and that he had got to know of it? Too melodramatic, Chris. That sort of thing belongs to the Middle Ages. Nowadays the outraged parent usually compounds for the loss of his daughter's honour with a lump sum."

Christopher laughed. "This business of yours is making a cynic of you, Vi; and I'm not surprised," he replied. "The worst of it is that you're probably right. If that had been the case, Mintern would have been more likely to employ blackmail than powder and shot. By the way, that gun was a queer weapon to use, wasn't it?"

"I'm enormously interested in that gun. I suppose we must assume that it was the weapon from which the shot was fired, at least for the present. The police will have settled that point, you may be sure. But there can't be any doubt why it was chosen, look how easy it was for anyone who knew anything about the internal arrangements of Monk's Barn, to take it! It was kept in a cupboard, accessible to anybody, yet apparently very rarely opened. Phyllis's statement that it was there two days before the murder is very valuable if it's true."

"Why should you doubt the wretched girl? Her story is probably true enough."

"I don't doubt her, but I'll bet the police do. Walter Mintern was discharged on the Saturday, and presumably never came near the place again. If the gun was still in its place on the following Wednesday, then Mintern cannot have taken it. The police will maintain that Phyllis is lying to screen her father, or, alternatively, that the gun was actually in place. But that she took it out and gave it to him."

"That's a possibility, of course. But, failing Mintern, what line would you try next?"

"Can't say, till we find out more about Gilbert's proclivities. And that, I fancy, is just where our client will be no use to us. I expect he knows less about Gilbert's private life since his marriage than anyone else. There's nothing for it but for someone to go down to Fordington, or at least Yatebury."

"I suppose there isn't," replied Christopher thoughtfully. "It ought to be one of us. Any of the staff would be rather too conspicuous in a country place. But I'm afraid I can't go, at least, not yet. The Medhampton case will keep me busy for another fortnight at least."

"Well, I'll go. I daresay that I shall find it easier to discover the local gossip than you would. I bet you that within a couple of days I shall know the complete family history of everybody in Fordington."

"I haven't a doubt you will. But how are you going to manage? It won't do to let people know that you are inquiring into the case."

"Of course it won't. I'm not going to announce myself as the official representative of the firm. I shall be Miss Perrin, an art student studying the picturesque features of out-of-the-way corners of England. There's sure to be something of the sort at Fordington, and I can draw quite well enough for the purpose. If all else fails, I can sketch the church tower as seen from the west, then start again and sketch it as seen from the north-north-east. You leave it to me."

"Well, I should be very glad if you would go and try your luck. What's your idea?"

"Go down to-morrow morning, and find a room in Fordington itself," replied Vivienne decisively. "Now, since that's settled, let's have a look at the report of the inquest, and see if there is any point of importance that our client forgot to tell us."

At Christopher's request, the lady from the outer office brought in a couple of sheets of paper, upon which were pasted half a dozen newspaper cuttings. Vivienne took them from her and looked them over doubtfully. "The case doesn't seem to have attracted as much attention as one might have expected, at least in the London papers. The local rag is full of it, no doubt. The inquest seems to have been held on Saturday, and was adjourned for a week. That was to give the police a chance of getting something definite against Mintern, I suppose. No, there doesn't seem to be much that we don't know already. Hullo! This sounds a bit queer!"

"What have you found now, Vi?" asked Christopher lazily.

"Listen to this report of the policeman's evidence. P.C. Burden, giving evidence, said that about 7.10 p.m. on the night—you don't want to hear all that. This is it. 'He said that on entering the room where the dead man lay, he examined the heavy curtains which were drawn across the window overlooking the lawn, and observed a small hole in them. Upon drawing them aside, he found a corresponding hole in one of the panes of the window.' Well, that's the queerest thing I ever heard of!"

"Why, you didn't expect the bullet to come through the window without making a hole, did you?"

"My dear Chris, I thought your wits were quicker than that. Don't you see the point? The heavy curtains were drawn when Burden entered the room, and since they had a hole in them, it's to be presumed that they were drawn when Gilbert Wynter was killed. Now, I can see as far through a brick wall as most people, but I can't see a man's head through a thick curtain, much less hit it with a rifle bullet."

"By Jove, Vi, there's something in that!" exclaimed Christopher. "Wait a bit, let's see if there isn't some simple explanation. Perhaps the curtains did not quite meet in the middle, and the murderer saw Gilbert's head through the opening."

"Then he would have fired through the opening, and there would be no hole in the curtain. Next!"

"Perhaps the shadow of Gilbert's head fell on the curtain, and was visible from outside. The man may have aimed at that."

Vivienne shook her head. "That won't do either," she replied. "A shadow doesn't show through a *thick* curtain, to begin with. Besides, unless the light was directly behind Gilbert's head, the shadow would have been in the wrong place, and anybody aiming at it would not have hit the actual head. And if it was directly behind him, how could he have shaved by it? That's what he was supposed to be doing at the time, you know."

"I give it up," said Christopher good-humouredly. "What's the right answer, Vi?"

"I don't know, but I'll have a jolly good try to find out when I get down there. Now, look here, since I'm to be in charge of this case, I'll issue my orders. One of the staff can do the necessary routine work. We mustn't forget that some clue to the murder may be found in Gilbert's business life. You had better have the usual inquiries made about Wynter & Son, how they stand, whether they are in financial difficulties, and so forth. You might also find out who they do business with, and to what extent. It probably won't lead to anything, but we can't help that."

"It shall be done. Is there anything else?"

"Yes, you'd better write to our client and tell him not to be surprised if he sees me down there. He'd better pretend that he has never met me before. But put it to him that I don't want his assistance; in fact, that he could help me best by staying away altogether. I have no personal dislike for him, but I mistrust his tact. I don't think it's equal to dealing with a delicate situation. Now then, unless you've anything more to say, I'll go back to my room and clear up ready to start early to-morrow."

She disappeared, but it was not long before she was back again, her eyes lighted up with excitement.

"I say, Chris!" she exclaimed. "About that curtain business!"

"Well, what about it?" he replied, without looking up from the letters he was signing.

"What if Gilbert Wynter was killed before the shot was fired that made the hole in the window?"

CHAPTER IV

EARLY in the afternoon of the following day, Mrs. Marsh, who combined the duties of postmistress and keeper of the general shop in Fordington, woke up with a start from her doze behind the counter as the little bell over the shop door tinkled warningly. Only a dim light struggled into the little shop through the windows obstructed by miscellaneous merchandise, and Mrs. Marsh, even through her spectacles, could make out no more than a slim outline, which she did not recognize.

"Good afternoon," said a clear voice. "Can you tell me if anybody in this village lets rooms?"

Mrs. Marsh made no immediate reply. She could see by now that the stranger was a girl, well but plainly dressed, and carrying sketching equipment with her. Mrs. Marsh classified her at once as a lady, and, at the same time, scented possible profit.

"It all depends what kind of rooms you would be wanting, Miss," she replied cautiously.

"Oh, anything will do. I'm not particular," said the girl. "Just a bedroom. I daresay that I could arrange to have my meals with the family."

"Well, Miss, there isn't much call here for rooms," replied Mrs. Marsh doubtfully. "'Tisn't many as comes to Fordington, except maybe one or two in the summer. There's Mr. Larcom at the 'Wheatsheaf,' he takes in visitors now and then. But perhaps a young lady like you wouldn't care to stop at the public-house?"

"I don't really mind," said the girl. "But I'd rather stay somewhere else if it's possible." Mrs. Marsh assumed an air of deep consideration. "Well, Miss, if so be that it's to oblige you, I daresay I could make shift to take you in myself. There is a nice room you could have, not what you're accustomed to, but there's not a cleaner room in the village, though I say it as shouldn't. There's only me and my daughter in the family, and if you wouldn't mind having your meals with us, why, I daresay we could manage." So it came about that Vivienne Perrin was installed as Mrs. Marsh's temporary lodger. The latter, having suggested extremely remunerative terms, which, rather to her astonishment, were immediately accepted, became the very essence of hospitality.

"You'll like a hot cup of tea, Miss, after your journey," she said. "And I'll take one with you, if you'll pardon the liberty." And very soon the two were sitting together over the fire in the kitchen, Mrs. Marsh chatting as though she had known her visitor all her life.

Vivienne allowed her to lead the conversation, knowing that it would not be long before she got on to the subject of the murder. "Terrible thing it was that happened in this village last Friday," she said, stirring her tea excitedly. "Mr. Wynter, that lived out at Monk's Barn, was shot dead. A nicer gentleman you couldn't have met. But, the things we do hear of nowadays! I tell you, Miss, it shook me up so that I haven't been to bed since without wondering whether I should be alive to get up in the morning."

"I remember seeing something about it in the papers," said Vivienne. "How did it happen?"

"Well, Miss, that's what nobody rightly knows," replied Mrs. Marsh darkly. "I heard all about it next day from Mr. Burden, who's our policeman. He heard the shot fired what killed Mr. Wynter, and he ran across with another gentleman and found poor Mr. Wynter lying dead on his dressing-room floor. He said it was a terrible sight, and no mistake."

"It must have been," agreed Vivienne in a shocked tone. "Did they find the man who fired the shot?"

Mrs. Marsh looked furtively round the room, as though she feared the presence of a possible listener. "No, Miss, they didn't," she replied confidently. "But Mr. Burden himself found the gun as fired it. It's likely he'll get his promotion to sergeant over that, they do say. And there's another thing, Miss. It wouldn't do for you to tell everybody, for there's folks in this village as don't know how to keep a quiet tongue in their heads. But there's no harm in telling you, seeing as you're sensible, like. Mr. Burden told me that they've a pretty good notion who fired that gun."

Mrs. Marsh lowered her voice until it was little more than a hoarse whisper. "They're saying in the village that it was Walter Mintern. But, you take it from me, Miss, 'twern't him, I knows."

Vivienne looked suitably impressed. "Who is Walter Mintern?" she asked.

"Bless you, I've known Walter since he was a lad," replied Mrs. Marsh. "Boys and girls we was together, as you might say. Not but that I won't allow that he was always a wild one. Never seemed to be able to stick to anything long, and always looking out for a fresh job. You could have knocked me down with a feather when I heard that Mary Green, as decent and respectable a girl as you could meet, was going to marry him. But, there, poor soul, she didn't last long. She died when her only child Phyllis was only ten years old. Walter fair broke her heart with his roving ways, I reckon."

"Poor thing!" exclaimed Vivienne sympathetically. "And what became of Walter Mintern after that?"

"I'm just going to tell you, Miss. He drifted from one job to another, picking up what he could. The Vicar let him mow the churchyard, one year, and a fine mess he made of it, I mind. Never seemed to take no pride in his work, Walter didn't. And then, a matter of five years ago now, Mr. Wynter took him on as gardener."

"How did that happen?" asked Vivienne.

"Ah, you may well ask, Miss, seeing that it was due to me, in a manner of speaking. I remember the day as well as though it were yesterday. We'd heard that Monk's Barn had been sold to a gentleman from Yatebury, but we didn't know who it was. Then one day a lady walks into the shop, same as you might have done, Miss. Proper lady she was, too, all dressed up fine. There was a smart car standing outside, with a gentleman sitting in it. 'Good-morning,' she says to me. 'I'm Mrs. Wynter; we've just bought Monk's Barn. Do you know of a young girl in the village who I could train as parlour-maid?'

"Well, there wasn't many girls in Fordington that cared to go into service. They mostly likes to work in the cloth-mills at Yatebury. Then all at once I thinks of Phyllis. She was rising sixteen then, and she'd been out as a daily help since the time she left school. So I says, 'Well, Mum,' I says, 'there's a girl by the name of Mintern as might suit you!" And, to cut a long story short, Miss, Mrs. Wynter saw Phyllis next day, took her on, and she's been there ever since. Gives every satisfaction, as Mr. Wynter told me himself one day when he came in to buy some stamps. 'Twere less than a week before he was killed, poor gentleman."

"I see. And I suppose that Phyllis suggested the employment of her father?"

"That she did, Miss. Phyllis is a smart girl, though you mightn't think it to look at her. Always top of her class at school, she was. Phyllis heard that Mr. Wynter wanted a second gardener, and she persuaded Mr. Wynter to give her father a trial. I said to my daughter at the time that it would never do. You couldn't expect a gentleman like that to put up with Walter's ways. And how it was that he stayed there so long as he did, I can't make out. But, there, poor Mr. Wynter was terrible good natured, and he knew that if he gave Walter the sack he'd never get another job. So I suspect he kept him on for Phyllis's sake. Both he and his lady were very fond of the girl."

"Has he left Mr. Wynter's service now, Mrs. Marsh?"

"Yes, he was sent off on the Saturday before Mr. Wynter died, Miss. I did hear that he cursed something awful, but that's just like him."

"What has he been doing since then?"

"Hanging about and drinking at the 'Wheatsheaf,' Miss. He says he's looking for a job, but it don't seem to me as that's the way to find one. And, betwixt you and me, I shouldn't wonder if he'd been doing a bit of poaching."

"Oh, he is a poacher in his spare time, is he?"

"Well, Miss, I wouldn't go so far as to say that he does it reg'lar, like. But I do know this, that about a month ago he came round to the back door one evening, and asked me if I'd like a couple of nice rabbits. I asked him how he came by them, and he says that Farmer Sprotten had lent him a gun and told him he might shoot over his ground. But I wasn't to say anything, he says, else all the chaps in the village would be wanting to do the same. They was fine rabbits, too. I let him have a quarter of a pound of baccy for them."

"Is that the only time that you've suspected him of poaching?"

"Lor' bless you, no, Miss. I was going to tell you how it was that I know that he didn't kill Mr. Wynter, though I daresay he would have liked to if he'd dared, he was that wild at being sent packing. He came to me the very night that Mr. Wynter was killed, about half-past seven, it might have been, before any of us knew anything about it. 'Mrs. Marsh,' he says, 'what'll you give me for this?' he says. And with that he puts his hand in his pocket and slaps a great hare on this very table. 'Why, Walter, how did you come by him?' I says, 'Why, her just walked into my back kitchen,' he says, 'an' I hit her over the head with a broom-stick.' He always was one for his little joke, was Walter. Howsumever, I looks at the hare, and sees she's been snared, not shot. But I never could abide them things, they be too strong-flavoured for the likes of I. So I wouldn't have her, and he takes her away somewhere else. But what I says is this. If Walter had been out a-looking over his snares, he couldn't have killed Mr. Wynter, could he, now, Miss?"

"No, that he certainly couldn't, Mrs. Marsh. But, if he didn't, who did? There's no doubt that Mr. Wynter was murdered, I suppose?"

"Ah, that's a question I can't answer, Miss. But, you take it from me, there's folks in the village as could answer it if they had a mind to. What was Mrs. Wynter doing in the drawing-room when Mr. Wynter went upstairs to shave? That's what I'd like to know."

Vivienne had seen a brief account of Mrs. Wynter's evidence, at the inquest, where she had stated that she had been sitting in the drawing-room, when she had heard a shock and a crash overhead, whereupon she had immediately rushed upstairs. But Vivienne was anxious not to betray her knowledge. "Doesn't Phyllis know what she was doing?" she asked.

"Phyllis only knows what Mrs. Wynter told her, Miss. Maybe you'll think it a queer thing for me to speak in such a way about gentlefolk, but I wouldn't trust Mrs. Wynter, no, not an inch beyond where I could see her. She's a stranger to these parts, comes from up the country somewhere. I did hear the name of the place, but I can't mind it now. I never liked her, not from the first day she walked into my shop." Mrs. Marsh paused, and then continued, more confidentially than ever. "Now, what I'd like to know, Miss, is this. Phyllis was in here on Sunday, and told me all about it. She and the rest of them was in the servants' hall. They were all talking and laughing and didn't hear the shot. That's likely enough, for the servants' hall is at the far side of the house. First thing she knows is the dressing-room bell ringing like mad, and Mrs. Wynter calling out 'Phyllis, Phyllis!' at the top of her voice. She runs out to see what's up, and Mrs. Wynter calls out to her, 'The master's been shot, get Doctor Palmer at once.' Phyllis didn't stop to think about the telephone, she just rushes out of the door, and, as it happens, ran into Mr. Cartwright, who telephoned for her. But, this is the way I look at it, Miss. How long after that shot was fired was it before Mrs. Wynter started shouting for Phyllis?"

Before Mrs. Marsh could answer her own question, the bell in the shop tinkled once more, announcing the entry of a customer. Muttering something that sounded like "drat the bell!" she bustled out of the kitchen.

Vivienne found time to scribble a note to her brother before the post went out that evening, she addressed it to the flat they shared, and not to the office, feeling sure that Mrs. Marsh, in her capacity of postmistress, kept an inquisitive eye upon the correspondence that passed through her hands.

"DEAR CHRIS,—Here I am, safely installed at Fordington. You can write to me care of Mrs. Marsh, and the letter will probably reach me. Mrs. Marsh is as round as a barrel, avaricious, and a regular mine of gossip. But she has a vein of shrewdness of her own, and I have already gathered from her a few points which may be valuable.

"Walter Mintern seems to be a bit of a bad lad. Disinclined for work, and, according to Mrs. M., a poacher in his spare time. The general opinion in the village seems to be that he committed the crime, but Mrs. M. does not agree. She has reason to believe that he was out poaching when Gilbert was shot. This may explain why he has, apparently, not yet produced an alibi. I can imagine a man of his type, knowing himself innocent of a major crime, disliking the idea of confessing to a minor one.

"If he is actually innocent, I believe that the fact of his finger-marks being found on the gun can be accounted for. I gather that he did not possess a gun of his own. What was to hinder him from borrowing Gilbert's, from time to time, of course, without G.'s knowledge, but with or without Phyllis's connivance?

"Mrs. M. dislikes Mrs. Wynter for no very definite reason, so far as I can make out. Her comments in this direction must therefore be treated with caution. But she astonished me by putting her finger on a point which I hadn't thought of. Did Mrs. Wynter give the alarm immediately she heard the shot, or did some short time elapse between the shot and her calling Phyllis? Mrs. M.'s suggestion is that Mrs. Wynter knows more about the business than she has said. This may or may not be the case. At all events, I shall try to find more about Mrs. Wynter.

"Send me down the results of your inquiries into Wynter & Son as soon as you get them.—Yours, Vi."

CHAPTER V

THE next morning Vivienne was up early, and set out on a tour of exploration in Fordington. She found that the village street ran roughly north and south. Fully three hundred yards of the west side of it was occupied by Monk's Barn, and the gardens attached to the house. The house itself had a frontage of about forty yards, then came a high wall, enclosing the lawn, some seventy yards long. This was then broken by a pair of lofty gates, giving access to the drive leading to the garage. It then continued for nearly two hundred yards, enclosing the kitchen garden.

On the eastern side, a narrow wing of White Lodge reached the street exactly opposite to the northern half of the Monk's Barn frontage. There was only one window in this, on the first floor. White Lodge had no further frontage on the street, since the house faced south, and its garden was separated from the road by a number of small cottages. The first of these was occupied by a policeman, and bore a notice to that effect.

Having thus taken her bearings, Vivienne returned to her room, where she drew a rough plan, for her brother's guidance. Then once more she set out, this time taking her sketching kit with her. She selected a point on the pavement outside Monk's Barn, from which she could see a corner of White Lodge, which was a stone building of the Georgian period, sufficiently pictur-esque to afford a reasonable inducement to sketch it. Here she set up her camp stool and easel, and set to work.

Fordington, she soon discovered, could scarcely be described as a hive of activity. Very few people came near her, and those who did looked at her curiously and passed on. It was not until she had been at work for nearly two hours, and was beginning to wonder whether she was not wasting her time, that a well-dressed woman, some years older than herself, came out of a small side door set in the wing of White Lodge abutting on the street, and crossed over towards her.

"I hope you don't mind my coming to look at your work," she said. "I saw you out of the window just now, and I simply couldn't restrain my curiosity. You see, I live in the house that you are drawing."

Vivienne smiled engagingly. "Oh, not at all!" she replied. "I hope you won't think it cheek on my part to make the sketch without asking permission. But I was so taken with this view of your beautiful house that I simply couldn't resist sitting down and trying to draw it."

"Yes, it does look nice from here, though I must say I never noticed it before," said the other. "But you ought to see it from the garden; it's really very pretty from there. If you like, I'll take you to see it now. You must be perished, sitting out here on a cold morning like this."

"Oh, I couldn't think of troubling you!" exclaimed Vivienne.

"It's no trouble, and I've nothing to do. My husband is at work all day, and I should be grateful for the chance of somebody to talk to. Do come along if you can spare the time."

"Really, it's awfully good of you. I should be grateful for the chance of seeing the house properly."

"I'd love to show it to you." The stranger led the way, Vivienne following her. She opened the side door with a key which she took from her bag, and they passed through a corridor into a hall, where a bright fire was blazing.

"You must stay here for a minute or two, and get warm. I'd better introduce myself. I'm Mrs. Cartwright. My husband owns a cloth-mill at Stourminster, and, as you see, we live here."

"My name is Perrin," replied Vivienne. She paused for a moment. It was just possible that Mrs. Cartwright had heard of Perrins, and might associate the name. But she showed no sign of recognition, and Vivienne continued:

"I've been commissioned to make some sketches of picturesque houses in this part of the country for the book that is shortly to be published. I only came here yesterday, and yours caught my eye at once."

"How very interesting! You ought to see Monk's Barn, on the other side of the road. You can't see much of it from the road, because of the wall, but it's really lovely. Where are you staying, if it isn't a rude question?"

"With Mrs. Marsh, at the Post Office," replied Vivienne.

"Oh, then no doubt you've heard all about the terrible tragedy that happened here last week? Mrs. Marsh, I'm sure, must have told you about it with all sorts of lurid details."

"I have indeed," replied Vivienne gravely. "What a dreadful thing!"

"Dreadful! I can't tell you what a shock it was to everybody, especially to Frank and me. You see, poor Gilbert was one of our dearest friends. I was away on the night it happened, staying with friends. I wanted to get back to a dance there was in Yatebury that night, but I couldn't get away. You know how difficult it is when your hosts have made arrangements for you to do something else. Of course, Frank wired me to come home the very first thing next morning. I went over at once to do what I could for poor Anne."

"It must have been a terrible blow to poor Mrs. Wynter," remarked Vivienne sympathetically.

"When I saw her, she seemed to be still unable to realize what had happened. She couldn't answer any questions, but just shook her head, with a frightened look in her eyes. I realized at once that she couldn't be allowed to stay at Monk's Barn, and I begged her to come here. But, for some reason, nothing would induce her to do that, though she has stayed here often enough when Gilbert has been away. I don't know why she wouldn't come, but I suppose she thought it was too near where it had happened. And then her brother-in-law came out, and persuaded her to go to some relations she has near Ipswich. That's where she lived before she married Gilbert, you know."

"Mr. Wynter had a brother, then?" asked Vivienne, with studied artlessness.

"Oh, yes, a younger brother," replied Mrs. Cartwright carelessly. "We never saw much of him, and, between ourselves, I don't care for him particularly. He never seems to take an interest in things, but spends the time at the works and some poky rooms in Yatebury. He doesn't seem to care about meeting the right sort of people, and getting into the county set. In fact, he's rather difficult, and I'm always rather glad that he keeps away from Fordington. And Anne thinks much the same as I do. She never can get on with him."

"I suppose that Mrs. Wynter will sell Monk's Barn, now that her husband is dead?" suggested Vivienne.

Mrs. Cartwright shrugged her shoulders. "You never can tell what Anne will do," she replied. "She's one of those reserved sort of people that you never seem to get to know properly. Of course, I'm very fond of her, and I suppose she tells me as much as she ever tells anybody. You know, it's a curious thing, but I never thought she was very much in love with Gilbert. They got on very well together, and all that sort of thing. But she always seemed distant, if you know what I mean."

"I think I understand. She seemed to have no really deep affection for him?"

"That's it, exactly. And, do you know, I can't help thinking that her feeling when he was murdered was one of horror rather than grief. She behaved, all the time until she went away, as though she were frightened rather than heartbroken. But then, as I say, you can never tell what Anne's real feelings are. But I'm wasting your time, chattering here. I promised to show you the house, didn't I? Shall we look over the inside first? There's some rather fine panelling in some of the rooms, which I'm sure you'd like to see."

Vivienne followed Mrs. Cartwright through the ground floor of White Lodge, trying to maintain an intelligent conversation with her. But her mind was running upon anything but linenfold panelling and Adams fireplaces. Mrs. Cartwright could hardly be described as an acute observer; she seemed rather an empty-headed person, and had certainly shown herself to be an irresponsible chatterbox. It was easy to understand that, however intimate they might be, Mrs. Wynter would not be likely to confide in her. But, all the same, Vivienne could not help noticing that the scraps of information which she had picked up about Mrs. Wynter tended to fit into one another. Mrs. Marsh's suggestion that she knew more about the murder than she had said, the apparent lack of grief that she had displayed. Could there be any connexion between them?

They completed the tour of the lower rooms, and Mrs. Cartwright suggested that, while they were about it, they might as well go over the rest of the house. So they proceeded from bedroom to bedroom, until at last Mrs. Cartwright opened a door at the end of a dark passage.

"There's nothing to interest you in here," she said. "As you see, it is used as a lumber-room. But it's the only room in the house which looks on to the village street. That's where this house has the advantage over Monk's Barn. Most of their best rooms look straight into the road, and you can't open the windows in summer without filling the place with dust. I really brought you in here because from this window you can see into the garden of Monk's Barn."

Vivienne stood at the window, trying not to betray too great an interest in what she saw. She could see over the wall which bounded the road, and the lawn lay spread out before her. On the right were the greenhouses, and the shrubbery in which Burden had found the gun. But, what interested her most, was the fact that, right opposite to her as she stood, was a corresponding window in Monk's Barn. The curtains of this window were drawn aside, and she could see faintly into the room.

Mrs. Cartwright must have followed the direction of her gaze. "That's poor Gilbert's dressing-room, the very room in which he was killed," she said, in a hushed voice. "It has two windows; the one you can see, and one looking out over the lawn, through which the bullet came. If you look closely, you can see the dressing-table at which he was standing."

Yes, Vivienne could see it; fairly clearly, when her eyes became accustomed to the reflection on the glass. "It must be most inconvenient for the people in Monk's Barn to be overlooked like this," she remarked. "I can see into the room below as well, even through the net curtains."

"That's why we never use this room," replied Mrs. Cartwright. "I should hate the idea of prying upon my neighbours. The room below is the drawing-room. It's full of very beautiful furniture, which I should like you to see. Poor Gilbert was always poking about the antique shops. If Anne decides to have a sale, there are lots of things in the house that I shall try to pick up, if the dealers don't run the prices up too much."

"Does everything go to Mrs. Wynter?" Vivienne asked.

"Everything, including her husband's share in the business. You see, when Gilbert's father died, he left the business equally between Gilbert and Austin. Most unfair, I call it, since Gilbert was the eldest. Now I don't quite know what's going to happen. Anne, of course, knows nothing about business, and she'll have to leave the control of it to Austin. Frank and I were talking about it last night. Frank is going to suggest to her that she appoints someone to look after her interests. Otherwise, you see, Austin would have things all his own way. Shall we go out into the garden now, and you can see the house from outside?"

Vivienne agreed readily enough. But, before she left the lumber-room, she cast a swift glance round it. One end of it was occupied by stacks of trunks and packing cases. At the other end were rows of shelves, upon which were piled all the useless things that collect so mysteriously in every household. A thin layer of dust lay over everything, and it was quite obvious that, as Mrs. Cartwright had said, the room was rarely used.

They went out into the garden, and Mrs. Cartwright displayed the beauties of the house as seen from various points of vantage. But Vivienne found the greatest difficulty in expressing a proper admiration. A question had occurred to her, to which her brain vainly sought the answer.

Where had Mr. Cartwright been that night when the shot was fired? He had heard it so distinctly that he had been moved to go out into the road to see what had happened. Yet, from no room in White Lodge, with the possible exception of the lumber-room, could it have been more than very faintly audible.

CHAPTER VI

IT WAS quite clear to Vivienne that Mrs. Cartwright had taken a fancy to her. Her last words, before she had reluctantly let her visitor go, had been a warm invitation to tea that very afternoon. "My husband always comes home early on Thursdays, and I should so like you to meet him," she had said. "He knows far more about these old houses than I do, and he loves to have somebody to talk to about them. You will come, won't you?"

Vivienne had agreed, readily enough. She had been extraordinarily lucky so far, and this was a heaven-sent chance of meeting one of the principal actors in the strange drama which had taken place on that Friday night. For the sake of appearances she took up her position once more, and set to work to complete her sketch. But, while her fingers worked mechanically, her brain was busy piecing together the scraps of information which she had picked up.

For the present, at least, she was bound to work upon the lines suggested by Austin Wynter's hint that the key of the mystery was to be found among his brother's friends in Fordington. Of these, so far, she had only met Mrs. Cartwright, but that garrulous person's conversation had been, in some respects, very enlightening. How did what she had already learnt bear upon the various possibilities?

To Vivienne it seemed that the solution of the problem depended upon ascertaining two things: the opportunity and the motive. Find a person who might have been hidden in the shrubbery at the moment when the shot was fired, and who at the same time would derive some benefit from Gilbert Wynter's death, and you would probably have found his murderer. Now, of the various people concerned, was there anybody to whom these two conditions applied?

Take Austin Wynter first. The fact that he had called in Perrins to assist in the investigation did not exclude him from the list of possibles. He might have done it as a piece of bluff, feeling certain that his guilt would never be discovered. By his brother's death he had acquired, to some extent, sole control of the business, at least until his sister-in-law appointed someone to represent her interests. Perhaps he had some urgent reason for desiring this, which an investigation into the affairs of the firm would reveal. If so, motive on his part would be revealed.

What about opportunity? By his own account, Austin Wynter had been in Yatebury at the time of the murder. The superintendent had called for him there a short time after the event. Could he have covered the distance, three miles, between Fordington and Yatebury during that time? That had yet to be established. For the present, Austin must be classed among the possibles. Next, Mrs. Wynter. And here Vivienne felt herself at a loss. She had never met her, and all she had to go upon were three points of view. She and Austin had never got on, whatever that might mean exactly. But then, none of the Fordington set seemed to have "got on" with Austin. Mrs. Marsh did not like her, but her dislike seemed to be due mainly to the fact that she was a stranger. Mrs. Cartwright found her an enigma. Vivienne smiled to herself. There must be many people who were enigmas to Mrs. Cartwright.

The point was, could a motive be fastened upon Mrs. Wynter? It might be true that she had not been in love with her husband. She had succeeded to all he possessed. Scarcely sufficient motives in themselves. But there might be something further, some hidden intrigue which had driven her to the deed. Her state of mind after the event, as described by Mrs. Cartwright, would be compatible with this.

But, doubtful though the motive might be, the opportunity was potent. Mrs. Wynter would have had plenty of time to run across the lawn from the shrubbery, enter the house through the drawing-room window, and raise the alarm, between the time when Burden heard the shot and the appearance of Phyllis. It would have been easier for her than for anybody else to take the gun. Yes, undoubtedly Mrs. Wynter was also among the possibles.

And what about Mrs. Cartwright herself? On the face of it, she was excluded from the inquiry. Whoever had committed the murder had done so with considerable skill, and, from what she had seen of her, Vivienne could not credit her with the necessary ability. Nor, apparently, was there any motive. Finally, she had said that she was not in Fordington on the Friday night. That statement could easily be verified, and, if it were proved to be true, Mrs. Cartwright could be absolved from suspicion.

There remained Mr. Cartwright. Vivienne realized that at present she could attribute no motive to him. But it was a very remarkable thing that he, with the exception of Mrs. Wynter and Burden, had been, apparently, the only person in Fordington who had heard the shot. That Burden should have heard it was natural. His cottage was within a few yards of the shrubbery. Once more the question presented itself to Vivienne's brain: Where had Mr. Cartwright been when the shot was fired?

Not in the shrubbery, that was obvious. Burden had run out into the street immediately he heard the shot fired, and, a few seconds later, Mr. Cartwright had joined him from the side door of White Lodge. There was no possibility that in those few seconds Mr. Cartwright could have covered the distance from the shrubbery to White Lodge, even neglecting the fact that in order to do so he would have had to pass the spot where Burden was standing.

Vivienne frowned as she considered the matter. She could have produced such a delightfully convincing theory had the facts been only slightly different from what they were. If the bullet-hole had only been in the window of the dressing-room overlooking the street, instead of in the one overlooking the lawn, as, by all the rules of logic, it ought to have been, Vivienne could picture the scene, almost as though she had witnessed it. Mr. Cartwright coming back from Monk's Barn, knowing that Gilbert Wynter had gone upstairs to dress. Then his entering the lumber-room at White Lodge, gun in hand, and creeping to the window. From here he could see, through a gap in the curtains of the opposite window, the brightly-lit interior of the dressing-room, and Gilbert Wynter shaving before the dressing-table. An easy target, impossible to miss.

A beautiful theory, perfect in every detail. But, unfortunately, the unreasonable stubbornness of facts rendered it impossible. No man could make a bullet travel in a semicircle and enter by the other window. And what about the gun? Could Mr. Cartwright, having fired the shot, have hurled it into the shrubbery from the lumber-room window? Most certainly he could not, such a feat would be impossible. But, all the same, it was a very pretty fancy. Reluctantly Vivienne had to confess that, facts being what they were, Mr. Cartwright must join his wife among those who must be excluded.

By this time she had finished the sketch. She packed up her traps, and returned to the Post Office, to join Mrs. Marsh in her midday meal.

Mrs. Marsh was very interested to hear of her having met Mrs. Cartwright. "A nice lady she is, to be sure," she said. "Always so kind and ready for a chat. Why, many's the time that she's come into the shop after some trifle and stood there talking to me nigh on half an hour. Very different from Mrs. Wynter, she is. Mrs. Wynter, she walks in as if the place belonged to her, asks haughty-like for what she wants, and goes out again with her nose in the air."

"Mrs. Cartwright has asked me to go to tea with her this afternoon, to meet her husband," Vivienne observed.

"That's just like her, Miss," said Mrs. Marsh. "'Tis because she thought you might be lonely like, you may be sure. A very quiet gentleman is Mr. Cartwright, it isn't often that we see much of him. He and Mr. Wynter was very good friends. They seemed to take to one another as soon as Mr. Wynter came to live here."

The meal being over, Vivienne decided that she had done enough sketching for one day. She had learnt that a bus ran from Yatebury to Stourminster every couple of hours or so, passing within a short distance of Fordington. She determined to walk to Yatebury, and come back by a bus which would bring her back to Fordington about four o'clock.

Yatebury proved to be the usual small provincial town, with a market-place, a row of shops, and some fine old houses in the High Street. It was, however, saved from the prevailing sleepy appearance of such places by the presence of two or three factories scattered about the town. And of these the largest and most important bore the legend "Wynter & Son, Ltd., Electrical Engineers," painted upon the gate.

It seemed, even to Vivienne's inexperienced eyes, that the works were pretty busy. The whir of machinery was clearly audible, and, from what she could see through the half-open gate, a large number of men were actively employed. She walked past hurriedly, and, having made a few purchases in the town, picked up the bus and returned to Fordington. Having put on the prettiest frock that she had brought with her, she proceeded to White Lodge.

She was shown into the drawing-room, where Mrs. Cartwright rose eagerly to greet her. "I'm so glad you've been able to come!" she exclaimed. "Frank, this is Miss Perrin, whom I was telling you about."

Frank Cartwright rose from his chair and shook hands with her gravely. "I am very glad to meet you, Miss Perrin," he said. "Ursula tells me that you are interested in the old houses of this part of the country. I shall certainly buy a copy of the book when it is ready. Perhaps you will tell me the title and the name of the publishers, and I will order it in advance?"

"I don't think that has been settled yet," replied Vivienne, readily enough. "My only connexion with the book is that the author, who is a personal friend of mine, has commissioned me to do a few sketches for it. The book is only in its early stages as yet."

"Well, I must keep a look out for it when it appears," said Frank Cartwright pleasantly. "The author is familiar with this district, no doubt?"

"Oh, yes, she knows it very well," Vivienne replied. "She suggested Fordington, among other picturesque villages, for me to visit." Vivienne was profoundly grateful when Mrs. Cartwright came to her assistance. There was something about this tall, dark man, with his deep-set and piercing eyes, that made her feel vaguely uncomfortable. She blamed herself for not having rehearsed more thoroughly the part she had determined to play. As it was, she felt that she had not been very convincing.

"Do come and make yourself comfortable over here by the fire, Miss Perrin," Mrs. Cartwright interrupted. "It has been bitterly cold all the afternoon, and you must have been perished, sitting about sketching."

"I'm afraid that I have been neglecting my work since I saw you last," replied Vivienne. "I took a walk into Yatebury, and came back by bus."

"You must have been disappointed in Yatebury, if you had not seen it before," remarked Mr. Cartwright. "There is very little to interest you there. The towns in this part of the country were never very picturesque, and such features of interest as they possessed have mostly been spoilt by rebuilding."

"I was telling Miss Perrin this morning that she ought to see Monk's Barn," said Mrs. Cartwright. "The old part of the house is really lovely."

"Perhaps, under the circumstances, Miss Perrin would not care to see it," replied Mr. Cartwright. "I feel sure that she does not share the vulgar curiosity which drives people to gaze at the scene of a tragedy. You have, of course, heard of the terrible affair which took place there last week, Miss Perrin?"

"Nonsense, Frank!" put in Mrs. Cartwright, before Vivienne could reply. "It isn't a matter of vulgar curiosity at all. I told Miss Perrin all about it this morning. And I don't see that it's any reason why she shouldn't look at the house if she cares to. I promised Anne that I would look in occasionally while she was away, and, if Miss Perrin likes, I will take her with me tomorrow morning."

"That settles the matter, then," said Mr. Cartwright with a smile. "By the way, I saw Burden for a few moments as I came back this evening, and I gathered from him that the police are pretty well satisfied that Mintern is the man. It seemed to me pretty obvious from the first. There's nobody else who could have done it."

"I said so as soon as I heard about it," replied Mrs. Cartwright. "Mintern is a thoroughly bad character, and Anne always hated having him about the place. She told me, often enough, that she'd like to get rid of him, even if it meant Phyllis going too. But Gilbert wouldn't listen to her."

"Gilbert was inclined to be obstinate sometimes," remarked Mr. Cartwright. And then, suddenly, he looked inquiringly at Vivienne. "We're neglecting our visitor," he said. "This subject can't be very interesting to her, is it, Miss Perrin?"

"Well, you see, I don't know the people concerned," replied Vivienne apologetically. But Mr. Cartwright certainly had the power of making her feel uncomfortable. There was something about his manner which puzzled and at the same time disturbed her. Hitherto her inquiries in Fordington had been ridiculously easy. But here, she felt instinctively, was a man from whom it would be very difficult to derive any information whatever.

CHAPTER VII

ON THE following morning, Vivienne met Mrs. Cartwright, as she had arranged with her. They rang the bell beside the front door of Monk's Barn, and were admitted by Phyllis.

Vivienne was prompted by the opportunity to have a good look at the girl. She decided at once that she was more than ordinarily pretty, with a refined prettiness that was rather unexpected in a country-bred girl. But she looked utterly miserable and woebegone, and there were traces of recent tears in her eyes. Vivienne's sympathy went out to her at once. The knowledge that her father was suspected of the murder was obviously preying upon her mind, as well it might. Dearly Vivienne longed for the chance of a word alone with Phyllis, but of this there appeared to be no prospect. Mrs. Cartwright was clearly far too anxious to display the beauties of the place to let Vivienne out of her sight for a moment.

"This is the hall, you see, Miss Perrin," she said, as soon as they were inside the door. "Some people say that the panelling is by Grinling Gibbons, but Frank doesn't believe it. It isn't quite in his style, or something. But I expect that you know more about that than I do. We'd better go round the rooms first, before I take you outside."

Mrs. Cartwright's energy seemed to be tiresome. A second perambulation began, similar to the one that had taken place at White Lodge on the previous day. Vivienne, although heartily sick of being treated like a visitor to a series of museums, realized that she was being given a wonderful opportunity of examining the house. Whether this would prove of any use in discovering how the crime was committed seemed doubtful.

However this might be, Vivienne exercised her powers of observation to the utmost. In the drawing-room, while Mrs. Cartwright was expatiating upon the beauties of the ceiling, her attention was concentrated upon the french window leading out on to the lawn. She noticed that it exactly faced the shrubbery, and that it was secured by a lock and by two bolts, top and bottom. It would take no more than a few seconds for anyone to run from the shrubbery, across the lawn, and into the drawing-room. Further, they would be completely hidden from the road by the high wall.

The other rooms on the ground floor failed to interest her, and it was not until Mrs. Cartwright led the way upstairs that her inward eagerness revived. It was quite obvious that Mrs. Cartwright herself was secretly thrilled by the tragedy, and that she thoroughly enjoyed displaying the scene of it to somebody else. Having reached the first floor, she went straight to the door of the dressing-room, and turned the handle softly.

"This is the room in which poor Gilbert was murdered," she whispered. "We may just as well take a peep in, since we are here. Police locked it up as soon as they got here, and I haven't been in myself. But I see it's open now. I think I ought to look in, just to see that every—"

She opened the door, and crept in on tiptoe, followed by Vivienne, who could scarcely conceal her curiosity. The room was exactly as it had been described at the inquest. The curtains over the window facing the street were drawn back, so as to afford light, but those over the other window were tightly closed. In front of this window was a dressing-table, upon which stood a small shaving mirror. Above this hung an electric light pendant. On the opposite wall, directly in line with the window, was a jagged hole in the plaster. Vivienne guessed that the bullet had lodged here, and that the hole had been enlarged in order that the bullet might be extracted.

Her observations were interrupted by a sudden convulsive clutch upon her arm. "Oh, my dear, look!" exclaimed Mrs. Cartwright, pointing to the floor in front of the dressing-table.

Vivienne followed the direction of her horrified gaze. There, on the dark carpet, was a still darker stain, which told its own story.

"How dreadful!" replied Vivienne absently. Her mind was not on the stain, which was only significant in her eyes as marking the spot where Gilbert Wynter had fallen. There was one thing which she must ascertain before she left the room, and her eager eyes examined every inch of the drawn curtains. For a few seconds Mrs. Cartwright, still clutching her arm, stared at the ominous stain, as though fascinated. Then, as though with an effort, she averted her eyes.

"Let's leave this horrible room!" she whispered urgently. "I can't stand it any longer. I feel quite faint."

She walked unsteadily to the door, followed, willingly enough, by Vivienne, to whom those few seconds had told all she wished to know. She had seen the bullet-hole, which was in the left-hand curtain. But she had also seen that the extreme edge of the right-hand curtain was slightly frayed, on exactly the same level as the hole.

Mrs. Cartwright shuddered as she closed the door behind her. "I wish we had never gone in," she said. "I shall dream of that room for weeks. Do you mind if we go out into the garden now? I don't feel as if I could stand the atmosphere of the house much longer. And, if you don't mind, I think we'd better not say anything to Frank about having looked in there. He would say it was morbid, I'm sure."

They went downstairs again, and through the drawing-room on to the lawn. Once in the open air, Mrs. Cartwright's spirits revived. "Ah, that's better!" she exclaimed. "I'm so sorry, Miss Perrin, I should never have taken you in there. You will forgive me, won't you?"

"Of course," replied Vivienne soothingly. "We'll forget about it. It was rather terrible, wasn't it? Is this the only way from the house into the garden?"

Mrs. Cartwright was obviously grateful for the abrupt change of subject. "Yes, it is," she said, much more brightly. "I've always said that it was one of the drawbacks of the place. The only other way to get into the garden from the house is through the back premises and out at a side door, and that's most inconvenient. You have to walk right through the scullery, and past the door of the kitchen and the servants' hall. Otherwise, if this window happens to be locked, you have to go through the stable yard, down the drive that leads from it into the street, and so into the house by the front door."

The significance of Mrs. Cartwright's words was not lost upon Vivienne. "I suppose that there is another way of getting into the garden from outside?" she asked casually.

Mrs. Cartwright shook her head. "Only through the drive," she replied. "The whole place is surrounded by a high wall, like the one you see between the lawn and the street. The end of the drive on the street is closed by a pair of high gates, which are locked at night, as soon as the gardeners leave."

"That must have been very inconvenient, if Mr. Wynter wanted to take the car out after the gate was locked."

"It was, very. Gilbert had to unlock the gates, and lock them again behind him. Then, when he came back, he had to do it all over again. Up to a year or so ago he used to leave the gates open, but he used to find that things disappeared from the garden. I always suspected Mintern of pilfering them, but Gilbert declared that it must be people from Yatebury or Stourminster. You see, if the gates were open, there was nothing to prevent anybody from walking up the drive, through the stable yard, and into the garden." During this conversation they had been walking slowly across the lawn, Vivienne, apparently unintentionally, trying to lead the way towards the shrubbery. They were within a few yards of it when Vivienne turned round, and gazed admiringly at the side of the house, as now revealed.

"Oh, isn't that lovely!" she exclaimed. "I should love to make a sketch of it. Do you think there would be any objection, Mrs. Cartwright?"

"Not at all," replied Mrs. Cartwright. "The only person who could possibly object is Anne, and I'm sure she wouldn't mind. Would it take you long?"

"Oh, dear me, no. I could get in the outlines in half an hour or so. I have a sketching-block with me, and if I could find something to sit on?"

"That's easily arranged. I see Croyle, the gardener, in the greenhouses. He'll find us a garden chair."

Croyle proved to be an old man, with a stoop acquired from much bending over the soil and inclined to be hard of hearing. He went off to get a chair, and meanwhile Vivienne moved thoughtfully about, as though seeking the best spot from which to make the sketch. She finally planted herself about a yard from the shrubbery. "This is the very spot!" she exclaimed.

The chair was brought, and Vivienne settled herself in it, her sketching-block on her knees. Mrs. Cartwright watched her for a few moments in silence, and then shivered. "Don't you find it terribly cold, Miss Perrin?" she asked. "I think, if you don't mind, I'll go indoors for a little. I want to see Phyllis for a moment."

"Don't you worry about me, Mrs. Cartwright," replied Vivienne brightly. "I shall be all right here."

Left alone, Vivienne looked about her furtively. Her position was extremely tantalizing. Aided very largely by luck, she had contrived to gain access to the scene of the crime. She was sitting within a yard or two of the spot from which the shot had been fired. Dearly she longed to explore the shrubbery itself. But this she dared not do. She was in full view of the windows of the house, and Croyle had returned to his work in the greenhouse, from which he could see her every movement.

She sketched away eagerly, hoping against hope for some chance of slipping into the shrubbery, if only for a moment. Nobody appeared at the windows, and she was prepared to risk being seen from that direction. If only Croyle could be lured away from his work for a few minutes! And then, just as she was beginning to despair, Croyle came out.

Vivienne's hopes soared, only to fall with a crash as Croyle, after glancing at her work curiously, passed into the shrubbery behind her. She could hear him fumbling about among the flowerpots, and muttering under his breath as he did so. In a minute or two he emerged, carrying a load of pots. But his curiosity overcame him. He paused, and glanced over Vivienne's shoulder. "My, Miss, that's fine!" he exclaimed, in undisguised admiration.

"I'm glad you like it," replied Vivienne, turning round. "I think the house looks lovely from here, don't you?"

"Aye, that it does Miss," said Croyle slowly. "You'll be drawing it for the papers, no doubt, Miss?"

"For the papers!" exclaimed Vivienne, with studied innocence. "No, why?"

"I hope there's no offence in my asking, Miss. I thought, perhaps, seeing what happened here last week—"

"Oh, you mean that terrible murder. Wasn't it a dreadful thing? I'm quite a stranger here you know."

"You be the young lady as is staying with Mrs. Marsh, I reckon. Aye, terrible's the word, Miss. And you mark my word, we haven't heard the rights of it yet. There'll be some pretty revolutions when that chap Mintern's arrested."

Revolution? For an instant Vivienne was puzzled. Then Croyle's meaning dawned upon her. "You mean that he'll confess when he did it?" she asked artlessly.

Croyle shook his head. "Mintern didn't never do it," he replied darkly. "'Cos why? 'Cos he couldn't have got into the shrubbery that night. I knows that, sure enough. Mintern's a rotten lot, I allow that. Look at these here pots. I told him to stack them away tidy like behind them shrubs, so's they'll be handy for the greenhouse. And he just chucks 'em down anyhow, so's half of them gets broken. And he seems to have used this one to clean a paint-brush on."

He held up a fragment of a large pot as he spoke, upon which was a thick patch of whitish-grey paint. Vivienne could hardly restrain a gasp of amazement as she saw it. "What a pity!" she remarked, as casually as she could. "I suppose you'll have to throw away all those broken pots?"

"Well, they won't be wasted, in a manner of speaking," replied Croyle reluctantly. "They'll go into the potting-shed, and come in for crocks later on. But, as I was saying, Miss, you'll find, when the time comes, that Mintern has a thing or two to say. There've been goings on in this house as no one wouldn't hardly believe. And Mintern knew more about it than he ever let on. Else why did the master keep him all these years? He wasn't no good about the place, and no one knew that better than the master did. We'll be hearing strange things in a day or two, you mark my words, Miss."

Croyle walked away, carrying his load of pots, and shaking his head sagely. As he disappeared, Vivienne resumed her work. But her mind was full of what she had just seen. She had recognized the whitish-grey patch on the flower-pot as luminous paint. And who would smear a flowerpot with luminous paint except for the purpose of seeing it on a dark night?

CHAPTER VIII

VIVIENNE finished her sketch, and, as she did so, Mrs. Cartwright came out of the house. "I can't think what's the matter with that girl Phyllis," she said. "She is quick and bright usually, but, since this has happened, she doesn't seem to understand what one says to her. I suppose it's the shock, or something. Have you done all you want to do?"

"Yes, thank you very much," replied Vivienne. They left the house together, and Vivienne, after refusing Mrs. Cartwright's invitation to come and lunch with her at White Lodge, returned to the privacy of her own room.

It was becoming clear to her that the various scraps of information she had picked up required piecing together. The firm of Perrins had had enough experience of inquiry work for Vivienne to know that the solution of any problem lay not so much in gaining information as in understanding its significance. Up to the present, information, more or less reliable, had flowed in upon her almost without an effort on her part. But she was bound to confess that, in many respects, it seemed curiously contradictory.

She decided that the best thing she could do was to go back to London and consult her brother. In any case she would not stay at Fordington indefinitely. Somebody, sooner or later, was bound to suspect her motives. Vivienne already had an uneasy feeling that Mr. Cartwright disbelieved her rather lame pretext about the book. It might avert his suspicions if she were to disappear, at least for a while. The only real inducement for her to stay would be the hope of meeting Anne Wynter. But, so far as she could learn, it was quite likely that she would not return to Monk's Barn for some considerable time, if, indeed, she ever did.

But, before she left the neighbourhood, she determined that she would seek an interview with Austin Wynter. An excuse for this would easily be found, since she was investigating the case by his instructions. But it was not as a client that she wished to see him. Her review of the people concerned had shown that he was to some extent under suspicion. In her heart, Vivienne did not believe in the likelihood of his guilt. But, nevertheless, it was her duty to believe in the possibility until it was disproved.

That afternoon, she took a bus into Yatebury, where she entered the Post Office and put a call through to the office of Wynter & Son. A female voice answered her, and Vivienne, assuming her most business-like tone, asked if she might speak to Mr. Austin Wynter.

"What name, please?" came the curt reply. Vivienne hesitated. Austin Wynter might not like his staff to know that apparently irresponsible women rang him up at his office. "Will you tell him that it is a message from Mr. Christopher Perrin," she said.

She heard a click as the instrument was switched over, and then a voice she recognized. "This is Austin Wynter speaking."

"I am Miss Perrin. Can you arrange to see me for a few minutes this afternoon?"

"Why, of course!" Vivienne could not restrain a smile at the sudden change in Austin Wynter's voice. "Where are you? I'll come at once."

"No, don't do that," she replied. "I think it will be better for us not to be seen together. I am in Yatebury at present. I shall start now to walk back towards Fordington. Will you drive out in that direction in a quarter of an hour's time, and overtake me?"

"Rather!" exclaimed Austin eagerly. "That's a jolly good idea. Anything else I can do?"

"No. I'll explain when we meet." Vivienne replaced the receiver, and left the Post Office.

Twenty minutes later she was walking along the lonely road that led towards Fordington. A car came up behind her, and she could hear it slowing down as the driver caught sight of her. There was nobody else about, and Vivienne drew to the side of the road, as though to let it pass. It stopped as it reached her, and in a moment she was sitting in a saloon beside Austin Wynter.

"I say Miss Perrin, I'm awfully glad to see you again," he began rather awkwardly. "It's really very good of you to take all this trouble. I've been longing to come and look you up, but I didn't like to after what your brother said in his letter."

"Quite right," replied Vivienne. "It would spoil the plans Christopher and I have made if it were to become known that you and I were acquainted. I have let it be understood in Fordington that I am a complete stranger, with no friends in the district. I should like you to turn off the road before we get there, in case I am recognized in your company."

"That's easily done. There's a turning half a mile ahead. Where would you like to go to?"

"It doesn't matter. I think it will be best if you just drive about the country for half an hour or so, avoiding any place where we might be recognized. I can talk to you as you drive. The first thing I want you to tell me is what you know about Mr. Cartwright?"

Austin frowned. "Cartwright?" he replied. "I don't know much about him personally. I've met him once or twice when I've been over at Monk's Barn, but I've never cultivated his acquaintance. I never liked the man, from the first moment I saw him. He's got a patronizing way about him that irritates me profoundly. Why, you don't think he did it, do you? It always struck me that he and Gilbert were very fond of one another."

"No, I don't think he did it. In fact, of all the people I have met or heard of in Fordington, he seems to be most positively ruled out. He had no relations with your brother other than those of friendship, I suppose?"

"Not that I know of. He certainly had no connexion with the business. The only business dealings we have had with him were when we supplied him with some machinery for his mill at Stourminster a year or two ago. He has a very flourishing business of his own there. I believe that Gilbert was helping him to perfect some device or other. They had a model in one of the empty looseboxes at Monk's Barn, which they kept up and used to work at in the evenings, together."

Vivienne nodded. Her questions about Mr. Cartwright had been merely preliminary. It would not have done to approach the vital subject too abruptly. "There's another small point, Mr. Wynter," she said casually. "How did you first hear of the news of your brother's death?"

She could see a faint reflection of Austin's face in the glass screen in front of them, and upon this she kept her eyes fixed. But, beyond a slight contraction of the brows, Austin's expression underwent no change.

"Superintendent Swayne came round in the car and broke the news to me," he replied. "I couldn't believe it at first, as I'd seen Gilbert only an hour or two previously, which was rather unusual, for, as a rule, we didn't see much of one another in the afternoon. You see, Miss Perrin, we each had our own department. Gilbert supervised the office, and I looked after the works. We met in the morning to exchange notes, but, after that, we very often never saw one another again all day.

"However, last Friday I spent nearly the whole afternoon in Gilbert's room. A matter of policy had arisen, which required a good deal of discussion. In fact, we had not come to a definite decision when Gilbert left, at half-past five. The works close at six, unless we are working overtime, which we are not, just now. But I stayed on a little longer, as I had some routine work to do. I was alone in the place till about a quarter to seven, I suppose. Then I came out, and locked the door behind me."

"The Superintendent picked you up at your rooms, I suppose?" asked Vivienne idly.

"Yes. I hadn't been in many minutes when he came. If I go the direct way, I can walk to my rooms from the works in ten minutes. But, that evening, I didn't take the direct route, I walked right round by the Park, which is rather more than two miles, and I didn't hurry. My mind was full of what Gilbert and I had been talking about that afternoon. It was an extremely important matter, which affected the whole future of the business, and I had been unable to make Gilbert see it from my point of view. I was rather worried, and I wanted to think the whole matter out by myself. I didn't want to get back to my rooms at once in case anybody came in. People do drop in about seven sometimes, as they know I'm to be found then.

"It was after half-past when I did actually get home, and the Superintendent came in a few minutes later. All he said then was that he had had a telephone message from Burden, saying that Gilbert was dead. He told me the rest on the way out to Fordington."

"It was quicker for you to drive out with the Superintendent than to take out your own car, I suppose?"

"Oh, yes, much quicker. You see, I don't keep the car at my rooms, there's no accommodation for it there. I keep it at the works. That's how I was able to come so quickly after you telephoned just now."

"That must be rather awkward," remarked Vivienne. "How do you manage at night, or during the week-ends, when the works are closed?"

"There's no difficulty about that. The garage at the works has a separate entrance, into a side road behind the main building. I have a key, and I can get in and out when I like."

Vivienne said nothing. A sudden feeling of depression had taken possession of her, and she was powerless to shake it off. She had hoped that Austin would have given some account of his movements on that fatal evening which could easily be checked. She liked him, felt instinctively that he could not be his brother's murderer. Her instinct told her that he was telling the truth. And yet . . .

It was Austin who broke the silence. "I'll give you a penny for your thoughts, Miss Perrin," he said gaily. "I might even run to sixpence, for I'm sure they're worth that."

"I was thinking of what you have just told me," she replied slowly. And then, with an abrupt change of tone, she added, "Did you meet anybody as you were walking from the works to your rooms, Mr. Wynter?"

"Meet anybody?" he exclaimed, in some surprise. "No, I don't think so. What makes you ask?"

"I just wondered, that's all. You didn't see anybody you knew?"

"No, I certainly didn't. I didn't speak to a soul from the time my secretary left at six o'clock until my landlady came in and told me that the Superintendent wanted to speak to me, and I suppose that was about twenty minutes to eight. I didn't walk through the town, as I told you, and I didn't notice anybody all the way. It was pitch dark, and I was engrossed in my own thoughts. Somebody may have seen me, but I don't think it's likely. What's the idea, Miss Perrin?"

A car approached them, blinding them in the glare of its headlights. Austin drew into the side of the road to allow it to pass. He was about to accelerate again when Vivienne stopped him.

"No, wait a moment, Mr. Wynter. I want you to give me all your attention for a moment. Don't you understand what the fact that you were alone during that particular time means?"

Austin looked at her, a puzzled smile on his face. "No, I can't say that I do," he replied.

"It means that you cannot bring any evidence to confirm your statements as to what you were doing," she replied, slowly and distinctly.

Then at last he understood. He uttered a sharp exclamation, then sat very still, staring straight in front of him. Vivienne watched him with an anxiety she made no attempt to conceal. This was the crucial moment. Upon it, she knew, depended far more than the mere solution of an impersonal problem.

But, as she watched him, she saw that his face bore no sign of fear, only of horror and repugnance. The hand which rested on the wheel tightened its grip, until the muscles became rigid as steel and the knuckles stood out white and glistening. And when he spoke, his words came to Vivienne's ears as though from a great distance.

"In other words, people might believe that I drove out to Fordington and murdered my brother," he said, in a curiously detached tone.

Somehow she could not bring herself to answer him. She could only bend her head in assent.

Suddenly his attitude relaxed, and he laid his hand lightly upon her knee. "Do you believe that, Miss Perrin?" he asked, looking her straight in the eyes.

Her eyes were as steady as his as she replied, "No, I do not, Mr. Wynter."

He uttered a strange little laugh. "Then I don't very much care who else does," he said.

CHAPTER IX

AUSTIN said no more. The shyness he had displayed at his first meeting with Vivienne seemed suddenly to return. He put the car in motion once more, and Vivienne, conscious of a certain vague feeling of awkwardness, decided to put an end to the interview.

"I must be getting back now, Mr. Wynter," she said. "You had better not drive me into Fordington. If you will put me down a little distance from the village, I can walk the rest of the way."

"Yes, I suppose that will be best," agreed Austin. He relapsed into silence, and for some minutes they drove through the gathering darkness without exchanging a word. At last Austin pulled up at a place where the road forked. "If you go up there to the left, you'll be in Fordington in five minutes," he said.

"Thank you very much," replied Vivienne quietly. She opened the door and prepared to get out, but before she could move she felt his hand upon her arm, detaining her.

"When shall I see you again?" he asked, almost fiercely.

Gently she disengaged herself. "I really don't know, Mr. Wynter," she said lightly. "I am going back to London to morrow."

"You're not!" he exclaimed. "Surely you haven't finished your work here yet, have you?"

"I've done all that I can for the present," she replied. "Perhaps, later on, I shall find it necessary to come down again. It all depends upon what my brother says. I expect he'll send you a report in due course."

"Oh, confound the report!" exclaimed Austin impatiently. "I'd much rather, if there is anything to tell me, that you came and told me yourself. Couldn't you do that?"

"I can't promise, Mr. Wynter, it depends upon so many things," she replied. "Good night, and thank you again."

She set off down the road which he had pointed out, without looking back. But it was not until she had turned the corner and was out of sight that she heard the car start upon its homeward journey.

As she walked towards the village, Vivienne asked herself whether she had acted wisely. She had, in effect, warned one of the people who might possibly be the criminal that he might be suspected. But, argue with herself as she might, she refused to believe that Austin had murdered his brother. She had been perfectly sincere when she had told him so, and she felt strangely elated at the reply which he had made to her. If anybody else expressed any suspicion of Austin, she would be the first to ridicule them.

But, upon what grounds? Austin's story, however implicitly she might believe it, was not of the slightest value until it was supported by evidence. It would be quite a possible thing that he had taken out his car, soon after the works had closed, and driven out in the direction of Fordington. He would have had plenty of time to fire the shot, regain the car, drive it back to the works, and walk to his rooms, before the Superintendent had arrived to call for him. And, since he had seen nobody during that period, he could not disprove the theory.

With something of a shock Vivienne realized that it was only because the police had concentrated their attentions upon Mintern that they had, apparently, not pushed their inquiries further. But, if Mintern were able to prove his innocence, as both Mrs. Marsh and Croyle believed he could, the police would immediately seek the culprit in other directions. And, if they could attribute the slightest motive to Austin, his movements that night were bound to come into question. It was a distinctly unpleasant prospect. Vivienne had reached this conclusion, when she became aware that somebody was coming towards her. She could not make out at first whether it was a man or woman. Vivienne was not a nervous girl, but she shared the usual dislike of the town-dweller to meeting a stranger in a lonely road at night. She therefore stepped quietly under the shadow of the hedge, hoping that whoever it was would pass without seeing her.

The figure advanced uncertainly, swaying from side to side. It came close enough for Vivienne to see that it was a woman, and, at the same moment, she became aware that the unknown was sobbing violently. She made a slight movement, and the woman stopped and looked up, uttering a stifled cry of terror. As she did so Vivienne recognized, to her amazement, Phyllis Mintern.

"Why, Phyllis!" she exclaimed. "What on earth's the matter?"

The girl shrank away from her. "It's nothing, Miss," she said between her sobs. "I—I'm in rather a hurry."

She made as though to pass, but Vivienne laid a hand upon her shoulder. "What is it, child?" she insisted. "It's no business of mine, I know, but perhaps I can help. Where are you going?"

Vivienne could feel the girl trembling beneath her touch, but she made no further attempt to move. She had evidently reached the point where she was incapable of any reasoned action. And it was some seconds before she could find words with which to answer Vivienne's question. And then the reply was scarcely audible. "I —I don't know, Miss."

"Then there's no particular hurry about getting there," said Vivienne cheerfully. "Why not tell me all about it, Phyllis?"

The girl shuddered, as though chilled to the bone. "No, no, I can't, Miss," she muttered. "Please let me go on. I must get away. I can't stay in Fordington, any more."

It was obviously useless to question the girl in her present state. But that she had some urgent reason for flight was clear enough, and that reason, Vivienne guessed, must be connected with the murder. She hesitated for a moment, and then spoke again. "Will you tell me this, Phyllis. Do you want to get away from Fordington because you're afraid of the police?"

She felt the girl start. "The police?" she replied. "The police, Miss? No, I'm not afraid of them; they can't touch me for what I've done."

"Very well, then," said Vivienne decisively. "If you're not trying to run away from the police, perhaps I can help you. You can't just leave the village like this, without any idea where you are going to. Now, I live in London, as I daresay you know already. Would you like to go up there?"

"I'd go anywhere where people don't know me, Miss," replied Phyllis eagerly.

"Very well, then. Will you wait here for a few minutes, until I have time to go into the village and back?"

Phyllis hesitated. "You—you won't tell anybody that you've seen me, Miss?" she asked anxiously.

"I won't tell anybody in the village. I only want to write a note for you to take to my brother, who will look after you till I get back to London myself. You'll promise to wait here for me."

Phyllis gave the necessary promise, and Vivienne started to walk rapidly in the direction of the village. She reached the Post Office in a very few minutes, to find Mrs. Marsh bustling about in a fever of excitement. "There, Miss, what do you think?" she exclaimed, as soon as she set eyes on Vivienne. "They've arrested Walter Mintern for the murder of Mr. Wynter!"

"Have they?" replied Vivienne. "When did that happen?"

"This very afternoon, round about three o'clock the Super came out from Yatebury himself in a car, with another man with him. They called for Mr. Burden, and then they drove to Walter's cottage. They must have known he was there, for they just walked in and took him. Went off quietly enough he did, so they say. And he'll have to spend the night in the cells, for they can't bring him before the magistrates till the morning."

"Does Phyllis know of this?" asked Vivienne.

"Oh, yes, she knows, Miss. I couldn't let the poor girl be in ignorance of such a thing, so I just runs over to Monk's Barn and breaks it to her gentle like. I don't know what's come over that girl, she seems all flummoxed-like ever since poor Mr. Wynter was killed. She didn't hardly listen to me, and when at last I ask her if she understood, she sort of smiles. 'Dad'll be all right, don't you worry, Mrs. Marsh.' There, I did my best to comfort her, but she doesn't seem to take no sort of notice."

"How long ago was this, Mrs. Marsh?"

"Directly I see the car drive away from the village, Miss. 'Twasn't no more than half-past three, of that I'm sure. I didn't want the poor girl to hear about it sudden like, so I thinks I'll tell her myself afore any busybody gets round with their gossip. It's terrible how quick things get about this village, Miss. I've never been able to understand it, myself."

Vivienne smiled. One reason, at least, for things getting about was fairly apparent. She escaped from Mrs. Marsh, went up to her own room, and scribbled a hasty letter to her brother.

"DEAR CHRIS,—The bearer of this is Phyllis Mintern. I want you to take care of her for the present. Put her up in the flat for a night or two. Tell Mrs. Clutterby any yarn you like. She'll probably think your morals are in a pretty bad way, but that can't be helped. Above all, don't ask the girl herself any questions; she's not in a fit state to be cross-examined just now.

"I am coming up to-morrow. For one thing, I can't face the prospect of a week-end in Fordington, and, for another, I want to talk things over with you. I'll explain exactly why I sent this girl up to you when I see you. But you'd better know the position, in case you're called upon at any moment to produce her to the police.

"Her father, Walter Mintern, has been arrested this afternoon on the charge of murdering Gilbert Wynter. This was generally expected by those who only knew him by reputation. But, as I told you before, there is considerable doubt as to his guilt, and, from what I have heard, I personally believe him to be innocent. In that case, he will eventually be released, and the police inquiries will be directed elsewhere.

"There is a very strong suspicion that somebody in, or closely connected with, Monk's Barn know more about the matter than has yet transpired. That is why I have kidnapped Phyllis. Under proper treatment, she may be induced to tell us what she knows. I came across her this evening, obviously in a state of acute distress. Her trouble was not due to her father's arrest, of that I am pretty certain. She had already known of it two hours before I met her, and when the news was broken to her, she took it quite quietly and seemed certain that her father would be all right.

"I believe that if we can find out what is on her mind we shall be in a fair way to solving the mystery. I have been hampered here by the fact that one of the principal persons is missing, Anne Wynter, I mean. I have hoped that Phyllis may help to fill in the gap. But I don't want you to try your wiles on the girl. She will want very careful handling, and she will probably tell me more than she would you. In any case, she'll be easier to deal with when she has had a day or two away from Fordington.

"That's all till I see you, which I shall some time to-morrow. Warn Mrs. Clutterby that I shall be home to-morrow night, will you?—Yours, Vi."

She put the letter in an envelope and sealed it. Then, taking advantage of Mrs. Marsh being momentarily occupied in the shop, she slipped out and made her way down the lane towards the spot where she had left Phyllis. Vivienne was a little doubtful whether the girl would still be waiting for her. She might have thought better of her promise, and decided to escape on her own account. It was with a distinct feeling of relief that she saw the girl walking towards her.

She seemed far more collected, and listened to Vivienne's instructions with respectful attention.

"Here you are, Phyllis, here's the letter. Now, how are you going to get to Yatebury station?"

"There's a 'bus passes close by here in a few minutes, Miss."

"That's all right, then. You will be able to catch the last train to London. Have you any money?"

"Yes, Miss, I've got what I've saved from my wages."

"Very well. Take a ticket to Paddington. Do you know London?"

"No, Miss, I've never been there."

"Get a taxi, then, and tell the man to drive to Shillingstone Mansions, South Kensington. When you get there, ask for Mr. Perrin's flat. Mr. Perrin is my brother, and this letter is addressed to him. Give it to him, and he'll see that you are looked after until I arrive to-morrow. Is that quite clear?"

"Yes, Miss, quite. I'm sure I don't know how to thank you—"

"Oh, that's all right. Now then, off you go, Phyllis, and take care of yourself."

Vivienne turned away abruptly and walked back towards the village. She felt a strange elation at the thought that the action she had taken might help to avert the danger which she saw hanging like a thunder-cloud over Austin Wynter.

CHAPTER X

ON THE next day, which was Saturday, Vivienne bade farewell to Mrs. Marsh, after assuring her that if she found it necessary to return to Fordington she would again avail herself of her hospitality. No mention was made of Phyllis, from which it was clear that the news of her disappearance had not yet spread. A few hours later Vivienne was sitting over the fire at the flat in Shillingstone Mansions.

Her brother leant against the mantelpiece, regarding her with a twinkle of amusement in his eyes. "Well, Vi, I'm glad to have you back again," he said. "Do you want to see this girl of yours? She's in the kitchen, I believe."

"No, she can wait," replied Vivienne. "I've got a lot to talk to you about first. How does she seem?"

"I've scarcely seen her. I handed her over to Mrs. Clutterby as soon as she arrived. It's lucky for you, by the way, that it's Mrs. Clutterby's afternoon out. She's dying with impatience to know who Phyllis is and what she's doing here. She says the girl's very quiet and moody, but admits, rather grudgingly, that she makes herself useful in the kitchen."

"We'll talk about her later. First of all, I want to tell you exactly what I've been doing. As it happens, my idea of posing as an artist has come in very useful. I've been able to make some sketches which will help you to understand what I'm going to tell you. Here they are."

Vivienne proceeded to give a clear and concise account of her experiences at Fordington. Christopher listened attentively, putting in a question here and there. When she had come to an end, he nodded approvingly. "That's splendid, Vi, old girl," he remarked. "You haven't wasted your time, that's certain. I've got hold of the facts all right. Any deductions?"

"That's just what I want to talk to you about. There are one or two things which strike me very forcibly. You see this rough plan of Monk's Barn and the gardens surrounding it. The whole place is enclosed in a high stone wall. On one side the wall runs along the road, on the other sides it is surrounded by other people's gardens. It would be impossible to climb it without a ladder. You get that?"

Christopher nodded, and Vivienne, thus reassured, continued.

"There are three ways of getting into the garden. One is through the drive and the stable yard. The drive is closed by wooden gates, as high as the wall, which are locked at six o'clock in the evening. The second way is through the french window in the drawing-room. The third way is through a side door leading into the kitchen premises. So that in order to reach the garden except by the drive, it is necessary to pass through the house. There are two ways of entering the house from the street, the front door, which opens on the street itself, and the back door, which opens on a narrow side alley."

"Yes, that's clear enough. I think I see what you're getting at."

"I expect you do. What I want to know is this. It is, to my mind, absolutely certain that the shot was fired from the shrubbery. The gun was found there, and if you were to draw a line through the hole in the window of the dressing-room and the bullet mark on the opposite wall, it would lead straight to the shrubbery. How did the person who fired the shot get to the shrubbery, and, again, how did he or she leave it?"

Christopher looked up from the plan which he had been studying. "I'll try to answer the first half of your question to begin with," he replied. "Unless the criminal possessed a key to the drive gates—that's a point to remember—he must either have entered the gates before they were locked at six, and concealed himself somewhere about the place, or he must have passed through the house."

"Exactly, but how did he get out?" Vivienne demanded. "Burden was standing in the village street within a few seconds of the shot being fired. Admittedly, it was very dark, but he could scarcely have failed to see or at least hear the drive gates being opened. The front door of Monk's Barn is also ruled out, for Burden was standing nearly opposite to it. The back door is possible, but to reach that from the garden you have to go through the servants' hall, where, at the time, all the servants were sitting."

"Yes, that does seem a bit of a teaser," agreed Christopher meditatively. "It doesn't seem likely that the criminal concealed himself somewhere in the garden and escaped later. He wouldn't have had much of a chance of slipping out before, I suppose, the place was pretty thoroughly searched. What's the answer, Vi?"

"Isn't it just possible that the criminal never escaped at all?" said Vivienne intently.

Christopher frowned. "Umm. Mrs. Wynter? Or, I suppose, possibly Phyllis?"

"I leave that to you for the moment. Now, let's glance round the others. Mintern first. I don't think he could have had a key to the yard gates, though, as you say, it's a point to be investigated. If he hadn't, he must have entered the gates before six, which he didn't, as he was seen at the 'Wheatsheaf' at half-past. Alternatively, he entered the garden through the house, which involves the connivance of somebody within the house. That same person might have found an opportunity of letting him out again through the back door, but I don't quite see how. In any case, if Mintern is guilty, he must have had an accomplice inside the house."

"Which brings us back to Mrs. Wynter or Phyllis. This is getting interesting, Vi. Carry on."

"Next, the Cartwrights. Mrs. Cartwright is out of it, since she was away from Fordington at the time. I haven't verified that, but there seems no doubt about it. And I'm afraid that Mr. Cartwright is out of it too, since, beyond any possibility of doubt, he was outside Monk's Barn when the shot was fired. He joined Burden from the side door of White Lodge, which is in the opposite direction."

"That's that, pretty definitely. Any other possible starters?"

Vivienne turned to a table that stood beside her chair, so that her face was hidden from her brother. She busied herself in selecting a cigarette and lighting it as she replied.

"I had a talk with Austin Wynter while I was down there," she said, in a tone of rather forced negligence. "It happens that there are no witnesses to his actions between six and a quarter to eight that evening."

Christopher whistled softly. "By Jove, our rather diffident client," he exclaimed. "That's a most extraordinary thing, especially—but I'll tell you about that later. You don't think he's the man, do you, Vi?"

"No, I don't!" replied Vivienne, with a suggestion of defiance in her voice. "I only mentioned it in case some over-astute policeman hits upon the same fact. Of course, he didn't do it, the idea's absurd. Putting everything else aside, how could he have got out of the shrubbery in time to get back to Yatebury before the Superintendent called for him? But we've spent enough time on that point. There's another thing I want to talk to you about."

Christopher glanced curiously at his sister. It struck him that her examination of the possibilities of Austin's guilt had not been nearly as logical as in the case of the others concerned. And it was also quite clear that she wished to avoid the subject. But he said nothing, and Vivienne continued hurriedly.

"You remember, when we first heard about this business, I was struck by the difficulty of whoever fired the shot seeing Gilbert Wynter as he was shaving. Now that I've seen the place, the thing seems more puzzling than ever. There is a pair of heavy lined curtains over the window, through which the shot was fired, and, that evening, they were so closely drawn that they overlapped by some inches. Nobody could possibly have seen through them from the shrubbery."

Christopher shook his head. "They must have seen through them in order to take aim," he objected. "Who told you that the curtains were drawn that evening? How do you know they weren't drawn after the shot was fired?"

"Nobody told me, I saw it for myself," replied Vivienne triumphantly. "There was a bullet-hole in one of the curtains, and the bullet had caught the hem of the other. How could it have done that unless the curtains had been overlapping?"

"That's one to you, Vi," conceded her brother. "As you say, it introduces a bit of a puzzle. Any suggestions?"

"Well, I don't know. If you were going to shoot at anybody you couldn't see, would some sort of illuminated aiming-point help you at all?"

"Yes, I suppose so. But why these problems in gunnery?"

"Because, quite by accident, I came across a very curious thing. I'm not a gardener, but I can't imagine that flowers would grow any better if you painted their pots with luminous paint."

"No, it doesn't sound likely. Unless, of course, any particularly tender seedlings are afraid of the dark. What on earth are you talking about, Vi?"

"Simply this, that while I was sketching Monk's Barn the gardener found a bit of a flower pot in the shrubbery with a patch of luminous paint on it. It struck me at once that it must have something to do with the mystery of the drawn curtains. Couldn't the pot have been put on the window-ledge, as something to guide the aim? It could have been thrown into the shrubbery afterwards."

"I suppose it could," said Christopher doubtfully. "But when, and by whom? Certainly before Burden got on the spot, or he would have noticed it, one would suppose. Another pointer towards someone in the house being concerned."

"I know, and I fancy that's the line we've got to work on. Well, that's about all I've got to say for the moment. Of course, there are plenty of minor points, but we can discuss them later. Have you got anything to report?"

"Well, yes, I have," replied Christopher slowly. "I don't quite know what you'll make of it, though. I began to make inquiries through the usual channels about Wynter & Son, as you asked me to. The replies were most satisfactory, as to financial status, and so forth. The firm seems to have a very good reputation, and is believed to be thoroughly prosperous. And in the course of these inquiries I happened to find out that Wynters are manufacturing, under licence, of course, several of the patents of our friend Sir Stephen Peacock."

"The man we carried out that investigation for, last year?" asked Vivienne.

"The very same. You remember how grateful he was, and how he kept on assuring us that if he could ever help us in any way, he would be very glad to do so. I thought I'd see if he meant it, and went to see him. When I asked him if he knew anything of Wynters, he told me that he knew both brothers personally, and would be only too glad to tell me all he could."

"He had heard of the murder of Gilbert, I suppose?"

"Yes, of course. I told him that we had been instructed to look into the matter, but I didn't say by whom. He has seen quite a lot of both of them lately, for he has been trying to induce the firm to take up the manufacture of a new device of some kind. I couldn't quite follow the technicalities, but it seems that it's got something to do with this new grid system of electrical supply that is to spread all over England. Anyhow, hundreds of thousands of this thing, whatever it is, will be required, and Sir Stephen says that there will be a fortune for the firm that takes up the manufacture.

"Well, the two brothers Wynter couldn't agree as to whether they should do it or not. Austin, who, according to Sir Stephen, knows far more about the technical side of the business than his brother ever did, was enthusiastically in favour. But Gilbert wouldn't agree. He pointed out that it would mean a great expense, since the whole of the works would have to be remodelled. He was afraid, Sir Stephen says, that, for a year or two at least, his share of the profits would decrease. I gather, from what you tell me, that his expenses were considerably greater than Austin's."

"Yes, he was married, and had a biggish place to keep up," said Vivienne impatiently. "Go on."

"Well, Sir Stephen gave me to understand that the two of them had some pretty heated arguments on the subject. Austin was in despair at his brother's obstinacy. He told Sir Stephen that he would stop at nothing to have his scheme adopted. And then, of course, Gilbert was murdered. A few days later Sir Stephen got a letter from Austin saying that the decision had been made, and that the necessary remodelling of the works had immediately been put in hand."

Vivienne shrugged her shoulders. "Well, there's not much to help us in all that," she said, with a forced smile. "Anything else?"

"No, that's about all," replied Christopher. "But, my dear girl, don't you see—?"

"Oh, we can talk about all that later, if it's worth it," interrupted Vivienne. "As it is, we're wasting time. We'd better hear what Phyllis has to say before Mrs. Clutterby comes in, or she'll wonder what it is all about. And I think, if you don't mind, Chris, that I'd better see her alone."

CHAPTER XI

"All right, I'll go out and send her in," said Christopher. He walked to the door, then hesitated, as though to make some remark. But he thought better of it, and left the room. Vivienne's expression changed as soon as she was left alone. Although she had feigned to treat it as being of no importance, her brother's account of the differences between the two brothers had affected her deeply. Hitherto she had seen in the lack of motive a card to play against any assumption of Austin's guilt. The motive was now supplied, and, in conjunction with the opportunity, could be worked up into the beginnings of a case against the man to whom, in spite of herself, she felt genuinely attracted. A thrill, almost of fear, ran through her at the thought of what this might mean.

A tap on the door interrupted her train of thought. "Come in," she replied, and Phyllis appeared.

"That's right, Phyllis, come along," she said encouragingly. "Sit down. So you found your way here all right? Are you quite comfortable?"

"Very comfortable indeed, thank you, Miss," Phyllis replied. Vivienne waited, in the hope that she would say something more, but the girl relapsed into silence, her eyes fixed upon the floor at her feet.

Vivienne profited by the opportunity to study her more closely than she had yet done. There was no doubt that Phyllis was a most attractive girl; to her natural prettiness was added a grace of movement and a daintiness beyond the common. By the look of her, she should have been of a lively and cheerful nature. But of this there was no trace. She sat there with the air of one utterly dispirited and worn out, for whom the future held nothing but bitterness.

Vivienne's brows puckered as she looked at her. It was going to be a difficult matter to learn this girl's secret; far more difficult even than she had expected. There was a hunted expression in her eyes, as though she stood in instant dread of discovery. And yet, at the same time, her attitude irresistibly suggested that she was the prey to some bitter sorrow, so potent that it almost drowned her fear.

"Well, Phyllis, I hope you're feeling better than you were yesterday evening," said Vivienne suddenly. "You aren't sorry that I sent you up here, are you? I've been talking to Mr. Perrin and we've agreed to ask you if you'd care to stay for the present and help Mrs. Clutterby?"

Phyllis looked up for an instant, and Vivienne saw that her eyes were filled with tears. But she shook her head feebly. "It's very kind of you, Miss, but I couldn't," she murmured. "There's nothing left for me, Miss, but just to run away."

There was something infinitely pathetic in her tone, which went straight to Vivienne's heart. She rose swiftly, crossed the room, and settled herself on the arm of the chair upon which the girl was sitting.

"Nonsense, my dear," she said softly. "You mustn't talk like that. I sent you up here so that I could look after you. Perhaps some day you'll tell me all about it, and then I can help you."

She passed a strong and comforting arm round the girl's shoulders. At her caressing touch Phyllis broke into a passion of tears, the reserve which she had imposed upon herself utterly destroyed. So, for many long minutes the two girls remained; the one wise beyond her years, the other hardened with a load of misery almost too great to be borne.

Vivienne made no effort to check the storm which possessed her companion. She knew that this outburst was a symptom of relief from the repression which she had forced upon her mind. Her sobbing grew less violent, and after a while she raised a haggard and tear-stained face, to glance timidly at Vivienne.

"I don't know what you must think of me, Miss," she said. "But you're the first who has had a kind word for me since—since it happened. If you hadn't stopped and spoken to me yesterday evening I don't know what I should have done. There seemed to be nothing for it but just to throw myself into the river."

"Well, we aren't going to let you do that now," replied Vivienne cheerfully. "Won't you tell me what it's all about? It's something to do with the death of Mr. Wynter, isn't it? Are you anxious about your father?"

The girl's head dropped once more, and Vivienne could scarcely hear her whispered reply. "It—it isn't altogether that, Miss. Not what you think, I mean. And Dad had nothing to do with that. It isn't him I'm afraid for. Oh, Miss, I don't know whatever will become of me!"

She showed signs of relapsing into another fit of weeping, but Vivienne's voice seemed to steady her. "Now, look here, Phyllis, you really must pull yourself together," she said severely. "If you know anything about Mr. Wynter's death, it is your duty to say so. You're beginning to make me think that you know who murdered him."

Phyllis shook her head violently. "No, no!" she cried. "I don't know anything about it. I'd have spoken long ago, if I had. Oh, Miss, how could anyone be so cruel as that?"

Like a flash of lightning it dawned upon Vivienne that Phyllis's grief was due to the death of Gilbert Wynter. Curiously enough, it had never occurred to her that this could be the case. She had, during her visit to Fordington, met with so little expression of grief at Gilbert's death, that it came as a real shock to her to find it in this girl, who was, after all, only a servant in his household. Could it be that a suggestion she had herself made so lightly contained within it the elements of truth?

Vivienne determined to try another means of approach. "You have been at Monk's Barn for a long time, haven't you, Phyllis?" she asked.

"Nearly five years, Miss. I wasn't much more than a kid when I first went there. It was my first place, except that I had done odd jobs about the village before. And I was very happy there, until—until—"

Vivienne waited, but the girl seemed unable to find words with which to express her thought. So once again she tried a new opening.

"You understand, Phyllis, that we are all very anxious to find out who murdered Mr. Wynter," she said. "It would help us a lot if we knew more about the life he and Mrs. Wynter led at Monk's Barn. And I expect you know more about that than anybody else."

Phyllis shuddered violently. "Yes, Miss, I know," she replied in a low tone. "I don't believe anybody else suspected how it was between them, except perhaps Mr. Cartwright. You never can tell what Mr. Cartwright is thinking, Miss. It wasn't as if they ever quarrelled, or anything like that. But they were just tired of one another, if you understand what I mean."

"Yes, I think I understand. But they had only just been married when you went to Monk's Barn first."

"Yes, Miss. Everything was all right for the first year or two. Though, even then, they were not like what I'd seen of other newly married couples. But, as time went on, I began to see that Mr. Wynter was much more interested in his friends, his house, his garden, and all that, than he was in Mrs. Wynter. I wasn't altogether surprised, if I may say so, Miss. Mrs. Wynter never seemed to show that she was fond of him in any way."

"Perhaps she was undemonstrative by nature. But, after all, you never saw them when they were alone together, you know."

"No, Miss," replied Phyllis hesitatingly. "But it wasn't only what I saw. Mr. Wynter was always very kind to me from the first, and latterly he used to tell me things. I used to look after him when Mrs. Wynter was away, and he would often chat to me then. He said once that he felt much freer when Mrs. Wynter wasn't there."

So this was the beginning of it! Gilbert's boredom with his wife, and the temptation of his attractive parlour-maid. Vivienne felt that she knew the rest of the story already.

"And, as a result of these chats, an affection grew up between you?" she suggested.

"Yes, Miss," replied Phyllis in a low voice. "I didn't see any harm in it at first, until Mr. Wynter began to make suggestions. And then, for a long time, I wouldn't have anything to do with him. I thought of leaving the place, but I knew that Dad wouldn't let me. It was only because I was there that Mr. Wynter kept him on in his job. And I daren't tell Dad what the real reason for my wanting to go was. Not that he'd have minded, but he might have tried to get money out of Mr. Wynter if he'd known.

"And then, besides, Miss, I loved Mr. Wynter, I just couldn't bring myself to go away. A lady like you wouldn't understand, but to a poor girl like me Mr. Wynter was the most wonderful gentleman that ever was. I used to look forward to waiting at table, even if there was company there, for I could watch him and listen to his voice. I can't believe, even now, that I shall never see him again!"

She hid her face in her hands, and rocked silently to and fro. Vivienne made no attempt to intrude upon her grief, and suddenly she began to speak again, in a tone so low that Vivienne could scarcely hear her words.

"And so I just stayed on, Miss. And then, there came one summer night. Mrs. Wynter was away, and Mr. Wynter was dining with Mr. and Mrs. Cartwright. I took my evening out, and spent it with some friends in the village. I came back at eleven o'clock, and let myself in at the back door. I always was allowed to take the key with me when I went out. All the other servants were in bed. I just looked round the house to see that everything was all right, and I went into the drawing-room to see that the windows were shut. And—and Mr. Wynter was there—

"Nothing was the same after that. It was as if I was a different girl altogether. I didn't feel any shame, and I didn't trouble about what was going to happen. My Wynter had told me that he loved me, and that I could trust him to find some way of putting everything right. We were to go away and live abroad somewhere, until he could marry me. But I must give him time to arrange things so that the business wouldn't suffer. I would have waited for ever, Miss, so long as I knew he cared for me. And then he was killed, and I don't know what'll become of me and the baby that's to be born! There, now I've told you, Miss, and you'll turn me out, as I deserve!"

"I shall do nothing of the kind," replied Vivienne. "Now, look here, Phyllis, you're not to worry any more. We'll look after you, and there's no reason why anybody in Fordington should know anything about it. You are quite certain, I suppose, that nobody so much as guesses what has happened? Your father, or Mrs. Wynter, for instance?"

"Quite certain, Miss. I never breathed a word, and I know Mr. Wynter didn't either. He never even knew about the baby, Miss. I couldn't bring myself to tell him, I thought it might worry him. And now it's too late."

"That's all right, then," said Vivienne cheerfully. "You shall stay here for the present, and well see what's best to be done later. You can leave it all to us." She scarcely heard the girl's muttered thanks, so busily was her mind occupied with the story she had just heard. She was deeply sorry for Phyllis, her simplicity and obvious frankness touched her deeply. That she had allowed herself to be persuaded by an unreasoning and hopeless love for Gilbert Wynter was clear enough. Perhaps it was far better for her that he had died before her illusion was shattered. For Vivienne guessed that he would never have sacrificed the life he loved so well for Phyllis's sake. Vivienne's sympathetic heart conceived a violent loathing for this man, whom she had never seen.

But, however deep her sympathy might be, her immediate problem was whether the episode had any bearing upon the murder. Phyllis's assurance that nobody knew of it but the parties concerned seemed to suggest that it had not. There was one possibility, remote indeed, but still to be considered. Had Gilbert Wynter realized what the consequences of his conduct must be? Had he contemplated the scandal, the devastating effect upon his life? And, contemplating it, had the horror of it so wrought upon him that he had preferred to take his own life rather than face it?

From all appearances, suicide was utterly ruled out. Such a possibility had never for a moment been raised. It was impossible that Gilbert Wynter could have shot himself with a gun which was subsequently found in a shrubbery seventy yards away. And what about the bullet-hole in the window? And yet, on the other hand, the theory of murder was equally difficult to suggest. It was impossible that anybody should have been concealed in the shrubbery.

Vivienne gazed reflectively at the lowered head of the girl beside her. Was her tragedy the key to the mystery? Had she, in some way entirely hidden from herself, been the indirect and unconscious cause of Gilbert Wynter's death? Or was she merely an unconsidered pawn in some mysterious game of which the mover was still hidden?

One thing alone was certain, that there were many secrets yet to be revealed.

CHAPTER XII

PHYLLIS seemed much calmer now that she had been persuaded to unburden her soul to Vivienne. It seemed to the latter that she was in a fit state to be questioned about the actual details of the fatal night. It was very possible that she would be able to throw light upon many things which were yet obscure.

"We want you to help us," said Vivienne quietly. "You tell me that you have no idea who killed Mr. Wynter, but perhaps, if you tell us everything you know, we may be able to form some idea. There is no need to mention anything about what you have just told me, but Mr. Perrin and I are very anxious to ask you some questions. Will you answer them for us?"

Phyllis raised her head, and Vivienne noticed with satisfaction that the look of terror had almost vanished from her eyes, leaving nothing but a profound sorrow. "Oh, Miss, you've been so kind to me that I'll do anything you ask me to," she replied.

"Very well, you stay where you are, and I'll ask Mr. Perrin to come in."

Vivienne left the room, and found Christopher busy with some papers next door. He looked up as his sister came in. "Any developments?" he asked shortly.

"I don't know yet. You remember my suggesting, rather flippantly, I'm afraid, that there might have been something between Gilbert and this girl? Well, I was right. It's a pretty sordid story; I'll tell you the details later. All you need know for the moment is that they were pretty intimate, and that she genuinely loved him. Now then, come along. Her mind is much more at rest now that she's got her troubles off her chest, and she's ready for us to talk to her."

The two returned to the room in which they had left Phyllis, and settled themselves down comfortably. "Now, Phyllis," began Vivienne briskly. "You say that you're quite sure that your father had nothing to do with this business. I'm not going to ask you why you are sure of this, for I think I know already. But the police have discovered that his finger-marks were on the gun when it was found. He accounts for this by saying that Mr. Wynter had given it to him to clean. Do you think that is true?"

Phyllis shook her head. "No, Miss, I don't," she replied. "So far as I know, Mr. Wynter had not used a gun this year, and, when he did, he always cleaned them himself."

"Can you suggest any way in which the fingermarks could have got there?"

"Well, Miss, I shouldn't like to get Dad into any trouble," replied Phyllis hesitatingly. "But he, and several of the men in the village did a lot of poaching when they got the chance. He used snares mostly, for he hadn't a gun of his own. But I know that sometimes he used to bring back rabbits that had been shot."

"Now, you needn't mind being perfectly frank with us. The police are bound to find out about these poaching adventures, anyhow. Is it possible that your father, while he was in Mr. Wynter's service, used to take this gun from the cupboard sometimes?"

"He may have done, Miss, though he never said anything to me about it. You see, Miss, he used to go to the cupboard every morning. There is an anthracite stove in the hall, which it was his duty to fill up. It has a special scuttle, which is kept just inside the door of the cupboard where the gun was."

"It wouldn't have been difficult for him to take it one morning and bring it back the next," remarked Christopher. "You said at the inquest that you saw it in its place on the Wednesday before the murder, didn't you, Phyllis?"

"That's right, sir. I didn't often go to the cupboard, but Mr. Wynter had asked me to look for some old fishing-boots of his, that morning before he left for the office. I couldn't find them in his dressing-room, and then I thought that they might have been put away in the cupboard. That's how I came to see the gun, sir."

"You saw the gun itself, and not merely the case, it was in, I suppose?"

"It hadn't got a case, sir, at least I never saw one. It just lay on a shelf."

"Were there any visitors to Monk's Barn between Wednesday and Friday?"

"Only a couple of ladies who came to tea on Thursday, sir. There was nobody else came to the house at all, except of course, Mr. Cartwright. He and Mrs. Cartwright, when she was at home, were always in and out, sir, the same as Mr. and Mrs. Wynter were always in and out of White Lodge."

"Mr. Austin Wynter didn't happen to come to the house, I suppose?" asked Vivienne carelessly.

"No, Miss. He hadn't been to the house for some time. The last time I saw him was when he came to dinner, some time about the end of October."

"I should like you to try to remember exactly what happened on the Friday evening," said Christopher. "When did you last see Mr. Wynter alive, for instance?"

"At lunch-time, sir. He always came back from the office to lunch, unless he had to meet anyone in Yatebury. Mrs. Hewitt, the vicar's wife, had been at Monk's Barn all the morning, helping Mrs. Wynter with some things which she was making for a bazaar. And she stayed to lunch with Mr. and Mrs. Wynter."

"After lunch, Mr. Wynter went back to the office, I suppose? What did the ladies do?"

"They sat in the drawing-room most of the afternoon, sir. Mrs. Hewitt left about four o'clock, as she was expecting some people to tea at the Vicarage. Mrs. Wynter had tea by herself."

"What time did Mr. Wynter come back from the office that evening?"

"I don't know, sir. But it must have been before six o'clock."

"What makes you so sure of that, Phyllis?"

"Well, sir, I'll tell you. Mr. Croyle, the gardener, always locked the drive gates sharp at six, and hung the key up on a nail inside the garage. Then he came to the side door, through the house, and out of the back door. He couldn't get out of the garden any other way, you see, sir. I saw him that evening as he came through, and asked him if Mr. Wynter's car was in, and he said it was. That's how I know, sir."

"I see. Were you in the habit of asking Croyle whether the car was in or not?"

"I usually asked him, if I happened to see him pass through, sir, so that I should know whether Mr. Wynter would want me or not."

Vivienne looked puzzled. "I don't quite understand, Phyllis," she said. "Why should Mr. Wynter want you?"

Phyllis lowered her head, but not before Vivienne had seen a sudden flush in her cheeks. "Well, you see, Miss, if Mr. Wynter came home after six, he couldn't open the drive gates, as the key was in the garage. He would stay outside the front door, and ring the bell three times. I knew what that meant, and I used to go through the garden, take the key from the nail, and open the gates, so that Mr. Wynter could drive in."

Vivienne nodded. She could perfectly well picture the other side of this little subterfuge. The meeting in the garage, the few words of endearment, the lingering kiss, before these two returned to the house to resume their respective roles of master and servant.

"Well, we can take it that Mr. Wynter was in before six," remarked Christopher. "I understand that he and Mrs. Wynter were going to a dance that night, and that Mr. Cartwright was going with them. What time were they going to start?"

"They were going to dine at eight, as usual, sir, and start after dinner. Some time between half-past six and a quarter to seven, the doorbell rang, and Mr. Cartwright came in. I showed him into the drawing-room, where Mr. and Mrs. Wynter were."

"You said just now that Mr. and Mrs. Cartwright were always in and out of the house," put in Vivienne. "Did they always come to the front door?"

"Not always, Miss, except when the drive gates were shut. If they were open, they often went in through the garden. The two families were very friendly, especially Mr. Wynter and Mr. Cartwright. They spent a lot of time together, especially during the week-ends. In fact, they had arranged to go away together on the very next day. Mr. Wynter kept a yacht at Stourmouth, about fifty miles from Fordington. He and Mr. Cartwright often used to go down there together, even during the winter."

"Do you happen to know what time Mr. Cartwright left Monk's Barn that Friday evening?" asked Christopher.

"No, sir, I don't. After I had let him in, I took some hot water up to Mr. Wynter's dressing-room, as I knew he liked to dress in plenty of time, if he was going out anywhere. After that, I went back to the servants' hall."

"Thank you, Phyllis, that's quite clear so far. Now, you know, of course, that Wynter was shot at from the shrubbery at the end of the lawn. Nobody could have reached that shrubbery after Croyle had locked the gates without passing through the house, could they? Do you think that it's possible that anybody did pass through the house between six and the time Mr. Wynter was killed?"

"They couldn't have, sir," replied Phyllis positively. "That is, unless either Mr. or Mrs. Wynter let them in by the front door. The back door opens into the servants' hall, and either I or one of the others was in there all the time."

"How did you first hear that anything had happened?"

"The bell in Mr. Wynter's dressing-room rang, sir. I thought that Mr. Wynter wanted some more hot water or something, and ran out to see what it was. Then I heard Mrs. Wynter's voice calling, and telling me to get Doctor Palmer at once, as the master was shot. I was too dazed to know properly what I was doing. I forgot that there was a telephone in the hall, and rushed out of the front door to go to Doctor Palmer's house, which is only a short distance away. Then Mr. Cartwright called me, and I found him and Mr. Burden standing in the road."

Christopher glanced at his sister, who shook her head. "I think that's about all we want to ask you now, Phyllis," he said. "I'm very much obliged to you for what you've told us."

When the girl had left the room, the two sat silent for a few moments, absorbed in their own thoughts. Vivienne spoke first. "You come to this comparatively fresh, Chris," she said, "What do you make of it all?"

"I don't know," replied Christopher slowly. "What strikes me most forcibly is the impossibility of any outsider having fired the shot from the shrubbery. Of course, somebody may have climbed the wall with a ladder, but it strikes me as being highly improbable. The risk of being seen, even on a dark night, was too great. You see, I suppose, that there is one vital gap in our knowledge?"

"You mean what happened between the firing of the shot and the ringing of the dressing-room bell? Yes, I've thought of that."

"And there is only one person who can fill that gap," remarked Christopher significantly.

"Yes, I've thought of that, too. I've been wondering all along if she told the whole truth in her evidence at the inquest."

"So have I. Was she actually sitting in the drawing-room when the shot was fired? Did she run upstairs directly she heard it, or did a few seconds elapse? Nobody but Mrs. Wynter herself can tell us. And there's another thing which may not have struck you. Why was the gun left in the place where it had been fired?"

"Owing to the difficulty of disposing of it elsewhere, I suppose."

"If the gun reached the shrubbery from outside the house, would there be any greater difficulty about taking it away than there had been in bringing it there? I think not. At all events, the natural instinct on the part of the murderer would have been to conceal it. But it appears to have dropped directly it had been fired. Doesn't that, combined with the difficulty of accounting for the presence of any outsider in the shrubbery, suggest anything to you?"

"I see what you mean!" exclaimed Vivienne eagerly. "You mean that if Mrs. Wynter fired the shot, she would not dare carry the gun into the house with her, in case she met Phyllis or one of the other servants. Nor would she have time to hide it anywhere else; she had to be back in the house before anyone who might have heard the shot could come and investigate."

"Exactly. But we mustn't rush to conclusions. I think we are agreed that of all the people concerned, Mrs. Wynter had the most favourable opportunity of committing the murder. But, on the other hand, I don't see as yet how we can establish an adequate motive on her part. She may have greatly desired his death. She knew, one supposes, that she would inherit his money, and she may in some way have learnt of his affair with Phyllis. But would that be sufficient to drive her to deliberate murder? I'm inclined to think not."

"I could give you a better opinion about that if I'd had any opportunity of studying the woman," replied Vivienne. "I don't see that we shall get very much further until we've had a chance of meeting her."

Christopher shook his head. "We haven't got unlimited time before us," he said. "You seem to forget, Vi, that we're not the only people with a hand in this game. There's the police to be thought of. If, as you believe will happen, Mintern manages to clear himself, they'll start other inquiries. We've got to make the next move, my dear. I think you'll be the first to see that."

CHAPTER XIII

VIVIENNE sighed with an air of discouragement. "It's easy enough to say that, Chris, but what do you suggest we should do?" she asked.

"I suggest that we come out into the open and beard the police in their den," replied Christopher calmly. "Private investigators are all very well in their way, and I think we can flatter ourselves that Perrins are as efficient as any of them. You've certainly done wonders, anyhow. But they are at a hopeless disadvantage as compared with the police. They haven't got their powers, or the vast organization at their disposal. My idea is that we should make a bargain with the police. You've picked up a lot of information that they'll be glad to have. We'll offer to put it at their disposal, if, in return, they will keep us informed of the progress of their inquiries."

"We shall have to be pretty careful what we say. For instance, you have certain information about—about our client. You wouldn't hand that on to them, I suppose?"

"Most certainly I should. You must remember that we have found out nothing that the police could not find out just as easily, if they tried. It would be the worst possible tactics on our part to appear to be trying to shield Austin Wynter by withholding what we know about him. Let's be perfectly frank about this, Vi. You immediately spotted him as being on the list of possibles, and the police are bound to do the same. If they once suspect us of trying to shield him, they will, quite rightly, refuse to take us into their confidence. And, after all, since you are convinced of his innocence, there can be no harm in telling all we know about him."

"I am convinced of his innocence," said Vivienne steadily. "But are you sure that the police will agree to your scheme? They may listen to all you have to say, and tell you nothing in exchange."

"It all depends on the local man at Yatebury, Superintendent Swayne. I propose to go down to-morrow and size him up. If he's a decent sort of chap there won't be any difficulty. But, naturally, I shan't tell him much till I've got some sort of undertaking out of him."

Thus it happened that Christopher presented himself at the Yatebury police station on the following afternoon. He was agreeably surprised to learn that, although it was Sunday, the Superintendent was in his office. Christopher produced a card, which bore his name and, in the corner, "Perrins, Private Investigators."

He held that it was frequently a wise policy to make no show of mystery, and he had scribbled across the card "With reference to the Monk's Barn affair." He gave this to an attendant constable, and prepared to await the Superintendent's pleasure.

He was not kept waiting long. The constable returned immediately, with the message that the Superintendent would be pleased to see him. Christopher followed the man, and was shown into an office, in which sat a large and benign-looking individual, who rose to greet him.

"Glad to meet you, Mr. Perrin," he said. "I've heard of Perrins often enough, and I met your father once, years ago. Sit down, and smoke if you want to. I can't offer you a cigarette, I'm a pipe smoker myself."

Christopher sat down and lighted a cigarette. He liked the look of Superintendent Swayne. There was something essentially human about him, but he could detect a native shrewdness behind his careless manner. A man one could trust, thought Christopher. Also it was significant that he had asked no questions, but had left it to Christopher to state his business.

"I've come here to make a confession," said Christopher, breaking the silence.

Swayne glanced at the card which lay on his desk. "About the Monk's Barn business? Good, we're badly in need of a confession in that affair. Is it necessary to warn you that anything you may say may be used in evidence against you? You didn't do Gilbert Wynter in yourself, by any chance, did you?"

"No, it's not so bad as that. What I've got to confess is that I've kidnapped one of your principal witnesses."

Swayne lay back in his chair and laughed heartily. "The devil you have!" he exclaimed. "I think I can guess who it is. We've been wondering where Phyllis Mintern had got to. Yet one might have guessed, for, after all, it was a bit suspicious that she and Miss Perrin left Fordington within a few hours of one another."

It was Christopher's turn to smile. "So you knew of my sister's visit to Fordington?" he said.

"My dear man, of course we knew. You can't go wandering about the country bearing the name of Perrin without somebody smelling a rat. As a matter of fact, Frank Cartwright rang me up and told me about it, and I admit we kept a benevolent eye upon her, from a distance, of course. But I confess I don't know who you are acting for, or what your game was in spiriting Phyllis away."

"There is no harm in my telling you that we are instructed by Mr. Austin Wynter."

The Superintendent's eyes narrowed a trifle. "Is that so?" he replied. "I rather thought it might be Mrs. Wynter. Still, that's not my business. What about Phyllis?"

"That's what I've come to tell you about, among other things, Superintendent. But, first of all, I want to make our position quite clear. Our only aim is to find out, if possible, who murdered Gilbert Wynter. In this we are no respectors of persons, and we certainly have no intention of becoming accessories after the fact! Now, we have collected a few scraps of information which may be useful to you. I won't say that you couldn't obtain them for yourself, but if I tell you, it may save you some time and trouble. I'm quite ready to do so, if you will agree to let us work side by side with you for the future, both of us pooling our knowledge."

"That's a very fair offer, Mr. Perrin. I'll agree to that readily enough. I don't mind telling you, in confidence, that I'm pretty sure we haven't got the right point of view in this case, by a long way. We've arrested Mintern, of course. We couldn't very well do anything else, under the circumstances."

"Evidence against him too strong for you to be able to neglect it?" suggested Christopher.

"Not exactly that, though there is that little matter of the finger-marks to clear up. But you know what it is in a little place like this, or perhaps you don't. Unless the police do something sensational, people think that they are doing nothing. Very soon we get an outcry against the inefficiency of the local police, and we are asked why we didn't call in Scotland Yard in the first place.

There are plenty of people who believe that Scotland Yard spends its whole time in working miracles."

"Yes, I know. I come across that particular outlook, often enough. My own opinion is that, where a crime has been committed in a rural area, and there is no question of any stranger being involved, the local police are far more likely to detect the criminal than any outsider, even though he may belong to the C.I.D."

"Well, I think the same, and so, I am glad to say, does the Chief Constable. We both felt it would be a good thing to arrest somebody, so we chose Mintern. It wasn't only eye-wash. Mintern may be induced to say something which will put us on the track. He was employed at Monk's Barn for five years, and ought to know something about what went on there. Besides, his arrest will very likely throw the real criminal off his or her guard. And that is always something gained."

Christopher nodded. It had not escaped his notice that Superintendent Swayne had used the expression "his or her." He too, then, had a suspicion that a woman might be involved. "You don't really believe that Mintern is the criminal, then?" he remarked.

"No, I don't. But it won't do him any harm to spend a day or two in gaol. He's a notorious poacher, for one thing, though we have never been able to get sufficient evidence to secure a conviction."

"Did he make any statement when he was arrested?"

"Not he. He just grinned at us, and came along quietly enough. We took him before the magistrates, gave formal evidence of arrest, and applied for a remand till next Wednesday."

"I see. But I'm not sticking to my bargain, Superintendent. If you have the patience to listen, I'll tell you what the firm of Perrins have learnt about the various people concerned."

Christopher told Swayne everything that he and Vivienne had heard. The Superintendent listened carefully, occasionally making a note.

"All this is very valuable," he said, when Christopher had come to an end. "I can't tell you how grateful I am. I'm not above confessing that I don't move in the same social circles as these people, and that it would be very difficult for me to ferret out the situation as you have done. Now, in return, I'll answer any questions that you may care to ask."

"Well, there are one or two points which have struck me. That gun that Burden found in the shrubbery, for instance. I suppose that there isn't any possibility of doubt that it was the weapon with which the shot was fired?"

Swayne rose ponderously from his chair and unlocked a cupboard at the far side of the room. From it he produced a bundle which he laid upon the table. "There you are," he said, "that's the gun, in the original wrappings that Burden put round it."

The wrappings consisted of some old sacking, secured with a piece of tarred twine. "Burden carries a good mark for that," continued the Superintendent. "A lot of chaps would have handled the gun without a thought of finger-marks. Of course, he was lucky to find sacking and string ready to his hand in the shrubbery. We have to thank Mintern's untidy habits for that."

Something about the piece of tarred twine attracted Christopher's attention. He picked it up and passed it through his fingers. It was about eight feet long, and had a loop at each end, one large, one small.

"Anything peculiar strike you about that?" he asked, showing it to the Superintendent.

"No, I don't think so. It looks to me a very ordinary bit of garden twine."

"So it is. But look at the knots with which those loops are tied. They're what are known as bowlines, and are essentially a seaman's knot. I'll bet you won't find one gardener in a hundred who could tie one."

"Well, then, they must have been tied by Gilbert Wynter. He was a keen yachtsman, as I daresay you've heard. I suppose he made these loops for some purpose, and then threw the twine away when he had finished with it. Mintern picked it up, and chucked it out of sight behind the shrubbery, with the rest of his rubbish."

"Quite likely," agreed Christopher. "The sacking, I suppose, was used to cover garden frames. What about the gun?"

Swayne unwrapped it, and laid it on the table for inspection. "We sent it and the bullet, which we dug out of the dressing-room wall, up to London for an expert's opinion. It had previously been identified by Mr. Cartwright as the property of Gilbert Wynter. There are his initials engraved on a plate let into the stock as you can see for yourself. Phyllis Mintern recognized it as the one which was always kept in the cupboard in the hall. So there's not much doubt about the identification."

"Apparently not. What had the expert to say about it?"

"He said it was an old-fashioned weapon, such as you don't often see nowadays, with one barrel smooth and the other rifled. The idea is, I suppose, that one can take it out for a day's sport, and be prepared to shoot anything from rats to elephants. The rifled barrel had very recently been fired, and had not been cleaned after use. The smooth barrel had also been used, but not so recently, and had been fairly carefully cleaned. The bullet found in the wall fits the gun, and was undoubtédly fired from it."

"That's pretty conclusive. Now, about these finger-marks. Whereabouts on the gun were they?"

The Superintendent winked. "So that point has occurred to you too, has it?" he said. "Well, I don't mind telling you that they were on the stock only, and near the heel of it at that. Pick up the gun and aim it at the clock."

Christopher obeyed, and smiled as he did so.

"There you are!" exclaimed the Superintendent.

"You hold it with your right hand on the small of the stock, and your left on the barrel. That's just where I looked for finger-marks, and there wasn't a trace of them."

"The inference being that whoever fired it that night wore gloves," remarked Christopher, as he laid the gun down. "And yet Mintern, when he last handled it, certainly didn't, since he left his finger-marks elsewhere."

Swayne grinned. "I know," he said. "But, mind you, this is in the strictest confidence. I haven't pointed it out to anybody but you. I have merely stated that Mintern's finger-marks were found on the gun. It's for him to explain how they got there."

"I don't think, from what Phyllis told us, that he'll have any difficulty about that, if he cares to."

"Probably not. But then, as I said just now, I don't expect to see Mintern swing for this particular crime, anyhow."

"Then, if it wasn't Mintern, who was it?" asked Christopher.

Superintendent Swayne was engaged in putting the gun back into the cupboard. He turned and looked keenly at his questioner. "That's just what I'm expecting you to tell me, Mr. Perrin," he replied.

CHAPTER XIV

THE Superintendent resumed his chair, and leant across the desk towards Christopher. "Now, look here, Mr. Perrin," he said. "I've laid my cards upon the table, and it's only fair to ask you to do the same. I quite understand your position. You've been instructed by your client, and, naturally, you've got to look after his interests. But this isn't like an ordinary civil dispute. It's a criminal matter, and I need not tell a man of your experience that if you obtain any evidence and do not reveal it to the police, you are on very dangerous ground. And, there's another thing. Tampering with witnesses is not a very safe game, I may tell you."

Christopher met the Superintendent's gaze without faltering. "I am quite well aware of the truth of what you say," he replied steadily. "Will you believe me when I tell you that I have no intention of withholding the smallest detail from you, and that neither my sister nor myself have made the slightest attempt to influence Phyllis Mintern in any way?"

"I will believe you if you will give me a true answer to two questions. The first is, what reasons did Austin Wynter give for employing Perrins in this matter?"

"He told me that his affection for his brother impelled him to bring his murderer to justice. He was convinced that he was to be found among his brother's friends at Fordington, and that you were on the wrong track in suspecting Mintern."

"Very well. Now, what was the real reason why Miss Perrin removed Phyllis Mintern from Fordington, and sent her up to your flat in London?"

"My sister met Phyllis entirely by accident, when she was already running away from Fordington. She saw that she was in a state of acute mental distress, and that she would probably do something desperate unless steps were taken to put her in a place of safety. My sister did not then know the cause of her distress, but Phyllis told her later that she was expecting a child by Gilbert Wynter, and that, in her distress at her condition and at Wynter's death, she was actually contemplating suicide when my sister met her."

The Superintendent stared at Christopher in amazement. "Oh, so that's the way the land lies, is it!" he exclaimed. "Are you quite sure that girl's telling the truth? We've sifted the Fordington gossip pretty thoroughly, and we haven't come across a whisper of anything of the kind."

"Well, naturally, we've only got her word for it. But she told a most circumstantial story, and I see no reason to disbelieve her. That sort of thing isn't uncommon, as you must know well enough."

"No, and Gilbert Wynter was a bit of a gay spark before he was married. Well, you've answered my questions, Mr. Perrin, and I'm prepared to believe in your good faith. But you must have formed some opinion as to the murderer, and I should be very glad to hear it."

"That's rather a leading question, isn't it?" laughed Christopher. "I haven't so much as seen the place myself, you know, but from what my sister tells me the chief difficulty in spotting the criminal is how to account for *he* or *she* getting into the garden and out of it again."

"I know. I've looked at that all ways. But I'll tell you, in confidence, something that perhaps you don't know. You've heard, I suppose, that it was the duty of that chap Croyle, the gardener, to lock the drive gates at six, and hang the key in the garage?"

"Yes, I've heard that from Phyllis."

"Well, Burden knew all about that, too. He'd been asked to keep an eye on the place, as some vegetables or something had been missing from time to time. Burden's an intelligent chap, and when he had rung me up that evening, he went to the garage to see if the key was hanging on its usual nail. Well, it wasn't."

Christopher almost started out of his chair with excitement. He saw in a flash the significance of the missing key. "You don't mean it!" he exclaimed. "Where was the key, then?"

"That's what Burden wanted to know. He waited till I arrived and took charge, then ran over to Croyle's cottage and asked him about it. This must have been about eight o'clock. Croyle produced the key from his pocket, and said that he'd taken it home, because he wanted to get back into the garden about half-past eight. When Burden asked him why, he said that he was afraid the greenhouse furnace would not stay in all night if he stoked it up as early as six o'clock. He knew that Mr. Wynter was going to take the car out about nine, and would want the key in order to do so, but he would have put it back on the nail by then."

"Very plausible. Did this explanation satisfy Burden?"

"I fancy so," replied the Superintendent, with a rather sly smile. "Doesn't it satisfy you?"

"Most emphatically it doesn't. There seems to me to be a hole in it that you could drive a motor-'bus through. Croyle was in, locks the gates behind him, and hangs the key on the nail. How is he going to get out again?"

"Through the house, in the same way that he went out at six o'clock."

"Then why shouldn't he have come in the same way? What did he want the key at all for?"

"Croyle would probably say that he didn't want to disturb the servants, and that he meant to wait till Mr. Wynter took the car out at nine o'clock, and then come out with him. But that's a detail. The fact remains that the key was not on its nail from six o'clock to eight."

"That upsets some of my theories a bit, I'm afraid," said Christopher thoughtfully. "What has Croyle to say about it?"

"He swears that the key was in his pocket all the time, that he went straight home at six, and that he didn't see or speak to anybody until Burden came to him at eight. Now Croyle is a widower with no children, and lives quite alone. Does all his own cooking and that. So he can't produce any evidence in support of his statement."

"Then it is quite possible that Croyle is the man who fired the shot?"

"Possible, but extremely unlikely. For one thing, Croyle, besides being a bit deaf, is also very blind. He can see things well enough if they are close to him, but Doctor Palmer assures me that he could hardly make out the side of a house fifty yards off. And I think you'll agree that whoever shot Mr. Wynter from the shrubbery was a pretty useful shot. And, for another thing, what was his motive?"

"Your theory being, then, that Croyle passed on the key to somebody else, who gave it back to him before eight?"

"I won't say that I've formed very definite theories. But we've got to consider the possibility."

"Well, who can that person have been? Mintern? I rather fancy that he was otherwise engaged at that particular time. Besides, I gather that there's no love lost between Mintern and Croyle. The people at Monk's Barn wouldn't have wanted to borrow a key, since they were inside the place already. The Cartwrights aren't in the picture either. Mr. Cartwright was not in the garden when the shot was fired, as Burden can testify, and Mrs. Cartwright, I believe, was away that night."

Swayne nodded. "I'm with you, so far, Mr. Perrin," he said. "But I'd like to tell you something of Croyle's history. He worked at Wynter & Son's factory once, as a fitter. He was always a very keen gardener in his spare time, used to take prizes at the local flower-shows, and that sort of thing. Then, one day, he met with an accident, got very badly burned with some molten metal, I believe. It wasn't very long before Gilbert Wynter was married.

"He was getting on in years, and the firm wanted to pension him off. But the old chap didn't like the idea of doing nothing, although he didn't want to go back into the works. Lost his nerve a bit, I expect. Austin Wynter had a chat with him, and found out that his height of ambition was to become a gardener in some place where there was plenty of scope for him to display his talents. Austin promised to do what he could for him, and managed to persuade his brother to take him on at Monk's Barn. He's been extraordinarily grateful to Austin ever since, has often been heard to say that he'd do anything to oblige Mr. Austin, in fact."

The Superintendent looked significantly at Christopher, who, however, refused to be drawn. After a pause, the Superintendent continued.

"As you might suppose, we know a good deal about the affairs of Wynter & Son, here in Yatebury. Things get about, and one can't very well avoid hearing them. I don't suppose that you are particularly interested in that side of your client's affairs, though, are you?"

Christopher smiled. "Perrins are in the habit of making inquiries about everybody concerned in a case upon which they are engaged," he replied. "The fact that this may include their clients makes no difference. Only, as you will understand, they do not always find it necessary to inform their clients of the results of their inquiries concerning them."

"Following your usual rule, I suppose you have made inquiries about Wynter & Son?"

"Yes, we have," replied Christopher carelessly. "From what we can learn, they are sound and flourishing enough. There seems to have been some slight divergence of opinion between the two brothers on matters of policy, but it does not seem to have affected the position of the firm to any extent."

"Oh, so you know that, do you? But perhaps you don't know that it's pretty generally believed in Yatebury that if Gilbert Wynter had been allowed to have things his own way the place would have been closed down by now?"

"No, I certainly did not know that," admitted Christopher. "What's the reason for thinking so?"

"Well, you see, it's been a perpetual struggle between the two brothers, ever since Gilbert got married. He always had rather expensive tastes, and as soon as he found himself at Monk's Barn he launched out pretty extensively. He kept a yacht, and hunters, and goodness knows what. He always gave me the impression that he wanted to live in the style of one of the big county families. You know what I mean?"

Christopher nodded. "I understand perfectly," he replied.

"Well, naturally, this took money. Gilbert always wanted to take as much as possible out of the business, so that he could have it to spend. Now Austin was quite the reverse. He's a shy, reserved sort of chap, and to look at him you wouldn't think there was much in him. But he's one of the longest-headed people in this part of the country. He knew that things weren't any too easy nowadays for these smaller engineering firms, and he was all for taking as little as possible out of the business and piling up reserves. He knew that, sooner or later, they'd have to spend a dickens of a lot on new machinery, and so forth."

"I rather guessed that Austin wasn't such a fool as he looked, when I first saw him," remarked Christopher.

"You were about right there. The two brothers used to get on very well together while they lived in the same rooms in Yatebury. Where one was, you could be pretty sure of finding the other, and that sort of thing. But, all the same, I fancy that Gilbert must have resented the fact that their father hadn't left him, as the eldest son, a controlling interest in the business. They were on exactly equal terms, and that, though it didn't matter before Gilbert took to living like a lord at Fordington, made things pretty awkward later.

"Austin didn't blame his brother so much as the set he'd got into. But all the same, he's had his work cut out to keep his brother within bounds. Gilbert wouldn't, hear of anything being done that in any way threatened his share of the profits, even temporarily, and he always had a hard struggle if he wanted to spend anything on the works. I fancy that he'll find things very much easier now that Gilbert's dead."

This time there was no possibility of ignoring the significance in the Superintendent's tone. "But that's no reason to suppose that he had any hand in killing him," Christopher replied. "There's nothing to connect him with the crime, is there?"

"No more and no less than there is to connect anybody else with it. But there are one or two things I've made a mental note of. There's that matter of Croyle and the key, for one. Then, it's common knowledge that Austin was a very fine shot. Finally, it's a curious coincidence that I can't find anybody who saw Austin between six and a quarter to eight that evening."

"I don't know," said Christopher reflectively. "I don't somehow see Austin in the rôle of a murderer, myself." He paused, and then said suddenly, "You haven't forgotten Mrs. Wynter, I suppose?"

Superintendent Swayne smiled grimly. "You take it from me, Mr. Perrin, that we have not lost sight of Mrs. Wynter," he replied.

CHAPTER XV

CHRISTOPHER spent his time during the tedious journey back to London in the corner of a first-class carriage, pondering over his interview with Superintendent Swayne, and wondering how he should describe it to Vivienne. As a result, he arrived at Shillingstone Mansions in a rather despondent frame of mind, which his sister was quick to detect.

She said nothing, however, until he was seated in his favourite chair by the fire, a whisky and soda at his side. Then, in as casual a voice as she could command: "How did you get on?" she asked.

"Very well," he replied. "At all events, my scheme succeeded. Swayne and I agreed to exchange notes in future, and I think he is the sort of chap who'll stick to his word."

"Well, that's satisfactory, anyhow. Did you learn anything fresh from him?"

"I learnt a good many things," replied Christopher with a smile. "Among others, that your friend Mr. Cartwright spotted that you were a member of the famous firm of Perrins."

"Did he? I was afraid he might. He didn't seem particularly impressed by the reasons I gave for my presence in Fordington. I suppose there is no great harm done?"

"No, I don't think there is. I had to assure him most positively that we had no ulterior motive in carrying off Phyllis. He was inclined to be a bit nasty about that, till I explained things. However, I managed to put that right. Now, there's one thing I want to ask you. You had a chat with Croyle, the gardener at Monk's Barn, you said. What did you make of him?"

"I thought he was a very decent chap. A little bit inclined to grouse, like most gardeners. Why?"

"Because, although we didn't suspect it, he's likely to become an important factor in the case. Do you know, Vi, Swayne told me one extraordinary thing. The key of the drive gates was not in its usual place between six and eight on the evening of the murder!"

Vivienne opened her eyes wide as the full significance of this statement dawned upon her. "Not in its usual place!" she exclaimed. "Then whoever had it could get in and out of the garden without any trouble. I say, that puts an entirely different complexion on things, doesn't it? Does Swayne know who had it?"

"He does," replied Christopher sombrely. "It was, or it is supposed to have been, in Croyle's pocket. Listen, and I'll tell you the story."

He recounted, as nearly as possible in the Superintendent's own words, Burden's actions and the reason given by Croyle for the key being in his possession. But he was careful to say nothing of the relations existing between the old gardener and Austin Wynter. He had guessed already that Vivienne's interest in the latter was greater than that which she might be expected to feel in an ordinary client. It was clear that a bond of sympathy had been established between them, and Christopher was anxious that this sympathy should not obscure the clarity of her judgment.

"But, my dear Chris, that's a most extraordinary thing!" she exclaimed. "I'm inclined to believe that Croyle's story is true. But, if it isn't, if he's shielding somebody else! It means that we've got to start all over again looking for the murderer."

"Swayne doesn't seem to think so," replied Christopher. "He is of the opinion that the murder was committed by someone closely connected with Monk's Barn or its inmates. He doesn't think any outsider was concerned, I mean."

"Did he tell you whom he suspected?" asked Vivienne steadily.

The question had come, as Christopher had known all along that it must. "He didn't tell me in so many words," he replied. "But, all the same, he gave me a pretty clear hint. But I don't think that you and I need be greatly influenced by Swayne's suspicions, all the same. He has, at present, no more real evidence against anybody than we have."

"Who is it that he suspects?" persisted Vivienne, in a curiously dry tone.

"Well, I gather that he has come to the conclusion that it lies between two people. He didn't actually tell me so, mind, and, for all I know, he may have another card up his sleeve that he did not reveal. But it struck me that his attention is divided between Mrs. Wynter and our client."

Vivienne laughed, but her merriment struck Christopher as sounding strangely unreal. "It took you a long time to tell me that," she said. "I'm not surprised, it's ridiculous to think that Aust—that our client could have done it. There's one pretty obvious reason, that your super-intelligent policeman seems to have overlooked. I suppose his theory is that Croyle borrowed the key and complacently handed it over to our client. I'm prepared to admit that that, by itself, is remotely possible. But how could our client have got hold of the gun? He hadn't been near the house for weeks."

"I don't know, my dear," replied Christopher, without any great enthusiasm. "I don't believe that Austin Wynter did it, any more than you do. But we shan't help him by averting the issue. I suppose Swayne would argue that when Croyle gave him the key, he also gave him the gun. After Mintern left, Croyle probably took over his job of stoking the hall stove, and he would have had the same opportunity of taking the gun as Mintern had."

"That's all pure conjecture," said Vivienne, almost petulantly. "From what I can see, the police haven't any more evidence than we have, and we're in quite as good a position as they are. The point seems to me to be to decide what we are going to do next?"

"I'm afraid that there's only one thing for it, Vi, and that is to wait and see. There's Mrs. Wynter, for instance. I suppose that she's bound to return to Fordington sooner or later. And we have to see what happens to Mintern. Swayne doesn't pretend to think that he did it, but he may know something about it. Anyhow, you can't very well go back to Fordington now that it's known there who you are. You wouldn't do any good if you did."

It was not easy for Vivienne to resign herself to sitting down and doing nothing. She spent the next day at the office, reading and re-reading the notes that she and her brother had made upon the case, recalled every incident and every conversation during her stay at Fordington. She saw that, failing any evidence for or against, the only way to disperse the cloud of suspicion that was gathering round Austin's head was to form an alternative theory, which should be at least equally convincing.

On the Tuesday afternoon she was sitting in her room at the office, still engaged upon her task, Christopher was out, engaged upon one of the other cases which Perrins were investigating at the time. Her door opened and the secretary appeared. "Mr. Austin Wynter is here," she said. "I told him that Mr. Perrin was out, and he asked me if he might see you."

"Mr. Wynter?" replied Vivienne, with elaborate carelessness. "I wonder what he wants. Yes, I'd better see him, I suppose."

Austin came in, an eager smile upon his face. "I say, Miss Perrin, it's awfully good of you to see me like this, without an appointment," he said. "Are you terribly busy? There are a lot of things I want to talk to you about."

"Not too busy to hear what you have to say," replied Vivienne. "Wait a moment, I'll just tell them that I don't want to be interrupted."

She took up the telephone, and gave the necessary instructions. "Now then, Mr. Wynter," she said. "I'm ready."

"Well, the first thing I want to tell you doesn't really bear on Gilbert's murder at all, but, as it's connected with it in a way, I think you had better hear about it. I was busy in the works this morning, when I was told that a gentleman had called to see me. I went to the office, and there was that fellow Cartwright. I was very much surprised to see him, as you can imagine. I was still more surprised when he produced a letter, and asked me to read it. It was from Anne, and was addressed to me. The gist of it was that she wished me to regard Cartwright as the representative of her interest in the business, pending his formal appointment as such."

Vivienne, remembering a casual remark made by Mrs. Cartwright, was not so astonished as she might have been. Mr. Cartwright was, from her point of view, a natural choice. He had been a close friend of her husband, and was a business man himself, she could not regard it as such an enormity as Austin, judging by the tone of his voice, obviously did. She was far more greatly interested in another aspect of the matter.

"Has Mrs. Wynter returned to Monk's Barn, then?" she asked.

"No, the letter was written from the place near Ipswich where she is staying. But she is coming back to-night, I believe. I'm told that Mintern is to appear before the magistrates to-morrow, and she has been warned to attend in case her evidence is required.

Cartwright told me that; it seems that he'll have to be there too. But I can't think what possessed Anne to appoint a chap like Cartwright. She must know well enough that he and I don't get on together. And he hadn't been in the place very long before I was ready to chuck him out, neck and crop. I don't mind being criticized by anybody who knows anything about the business, but when it comes to an utter stranger like Cartwright raising objections!"

Vivienne could hardly restrain a smile at Austin's indignation. He was obviously bursting with the desire to tell somebody all about it, and she saw no harm in encouraging him. "What happened?" she asked.

"Why, you remember my telling you, when we last met, that Gilbert and I had a long dissension that Friday afternoon. I needn't worry you with the details of what it was all about. I hate to think of it, now that poor Gilbert's dead. He would have seen in time that I was right, I know that well enough.

"Well, the decision had to be made, it was the sort of thing you can't put off, and I made it off my own bat. There can be no question that I was right, everybody in the works, with the exception of Gilbert, had seen the necessity for the step I proposed to take, long ago. Well, if you please, this fellow Cartwright told me that I had exceeded my powers by acting as I had done without consulting Anne! As though a woman like Anne, who has never, to my knowledge, been inside the gates, could be expected to understand anything about the matter!"

"Sometimes even women have rudimentary powers of intelligence, Mr. Wynter," murmured Vivienne mischievously.

"Oh, I beg your pardon, Miss Perrin, I didn't mean that!" exclaimed Austin. "Besides, you're different. And this was a highly technical matter, which nobody who hadn't been brought up in the business could be expected to understand. How Cartwright knew anything about the matter at all, I don't know. I suppose Gilbert must have talked to him about it. Anyway, I told him that the decision had been made, and that it was too late to reconsider it. And I think I showed him pretty clearly that I wasn't going to stand any interference in technical matters."

"I can quite understand your feelings in the matter, Mr. Wynter," said Vivienne. "But, after all, perhaps it will be easier for you to deal with Mr. Cartwright than directly with your sister-in-law. Men usually understand one another better. Have you any idea what Mrs. Wynter proposes to do in the future?"

"Really, I know so little about Anne that I have no idea what she's likely to do. I don't suppose she'll stay on at Monk's Barn. For one thing, the place can't have very pleasant associations for her, and, for another, I don't know what she'll do with herself alone in a place that size. She'll probably sell it, and settle down in a smaller house in Fordington, if she can get one."

"Yes, I suppose she will. She would be able to take the servants and gardeners with her then."

"I don't know much about the indoor servants, and she's only got one gardener now, old Croyle. If she doesn't take him with her, I shall have to do something for him myself. He's an old employee of the firm, and he took a job as gardener rather than accept a pension. I'm afraid he'll never get another job, though. He's too deaf and blind."

Vivienne inwardly congratulated herself upon the skill with which she had induced Austin to mention Croyle. Her ruse had been entirely successful. Austin had exhibited no reluctance to mention his name, nor had his tone been anything but quite natural when he spoke of him. Vivienne felt more than ever convinced that the idea of collusion between them was fantastic.

Austin was clearly about to say something else, when the door opened and Christopher came in. He greeted Austin courteously, and the three sat talking for several minutes longer. But Vivienne noticed that Austin did not refer again to his brother's murder, and that Christopher made no attempt to lead him to the subject. After a while Austin rose and took his departure.

"Had your visitor anything important to say?" asked Christopher, as soon as the door had closed behind him.

"He might have, if you hadn't butted in like that," replied Vivienne. "Really, Chris, you're extraordinarily tactless sometimes. You know how shy Mr. Wynter is."

"Sorry. Did you get anything out of him at all?"

"I learnt that Mrs. Wynter is going back to Monk's Barn to-day. I'm going down there, on some excuse or other. I'm convinced that that woman holds the key of the mystery."

"Very well, I'll come down with you. Oh, it's all right, I'm not going to interfere with you. But I'm particularly anxious to be in Court when Mintern comes up before the magistrates. I'd recommend you to be there, too."

So it was arranged. But, for the rest of the evening Vivienne wondered, with a pleasurable feeling of curiosity, what was the true reason which had induced Austin to come and see her.

CHAPTER XVI

VIVIENNE and Christopher travelled to Yatebury by an early morning train on Wednesday, and went straight to the Magistrates' Court. It was lucky that they were early, for the courtroom was nearly full when they arrived, and they secured almost the last of the available seats.

They had some time to wait before Superintendent Swayne appeared, leading a procession to a group of chairs at the front of the Court. "Here they come!" whispered Vivienne. "That tall man is Mr. Cartwright, and the woman in black with him must be Mrs. Wynter. I wish I could see her better!"

"It's rather odd that they should bring the witnesses into Court like this," replied Christopher. "And it's been puzzling me for the last day or two why Swayne hasn't called on Phyllis to attend. It looks to me as though all he meant to do was to apply for a further remand, and has merely summoned the essential witnesses, in case his application is refused. Ah, there goes our client!"

Austin appeared, and was shepherded into a chair next to Frank Cartwright. The two men nodded curtly, and Austin moved towards his sister-in-law. After that, he rather pointedly edged away a trifle, and appeared to become absorbed in his own thoughts.

Christopher frowned. "It's a pity for that young man to advertise the fact that he doesn't get on with his brother's wife or friends," he whispered to Vivienne. "In a place like this everybody is full of curiosity, and on the look out for the slightest thing to gossip about. To say nothing of the reporters, to whom that sort of thing is a godsend. It all creates a bad impression, and makes people talk."

Vivienne's reply was interrupted by the entry of the magistrates. A full bench had assembled, and the members of it filed in slowly, wearing expressions of portentous gravity. The effect produced was not unlike the opening chorus of *Iolanthe*. The chairman, a much respected local landowner, led the way. He conveyed the impression that one might expect from him a rough-and-ready justice, tempered with a rather contemptuous leniency towards any prisoner who might be brought before him.

Most of those who followed him looked common-place and inclined to be aware of their own importance. Among them one only picked out a figure here and there. A short, saturnine figure with a limp, a tall and angular middle-aged woman, with a hard face which showed no traces of the milk of human kindness. They all took their seats, under the concentrated gaze of the public in the body of the court. In the hush which ensued after the scraping of their chairs had subsided, a single nervous cough of the packed throng echoed and re-echoed with startling persistency.

The Magistrates' clerk rose and gabbled something in a hard, metallic voice. He subsided as suddenly as he had risen, and a sudden stir of expectancy thrilled the whole hall. There was a shuffling of feet, men and women half rose from their seats, craning over one another's shoulders. And suddenly, as though he had been transported there by some mysterious agency. Mintern appeared in the dock, a stolid constable by his side.

He was a shambling, clumsily built man, with a coarse and rather malevolent face. But his expression could not be described as stupid. It was compounded rather of cunning and self-satisfaction, as though he felt that he had done something clever and was proud of the fact. You expected him to break into a grin every moment, while the charge was being read. Then, in obedience to a glance from the clerk, Superintendent Swayne rose.

Again a faint murmur of excitement, quickly suppressed by a stern cry of "Silence!" And then the Superintendent spoke, in a clear and distinct voice: "The police do not propose to bring any further evidence against this man."

For a second or two the silence was so intense that the whistling of an errand-boy passing outside the Court dominated the hall. Then the murmuring recommenced, penetrated by loud voices here and there. The renewed cries of "Silence!" seemed to have no power to subdue it, and Vivienne and Christopher, from their seats at the back of the Court, could not hear the remarks that ensued between the chairman and Swayne. They saw the members of the bench lean towards the chairman, who glanced quickly at each in turn. Then they caught one word only, "Discharged!" Mintern, now grinning openly, walked out of the dock and left the Court, to be followed by a crowd of reporters, like a queen bee drawing her swarm with her.

"Oh, for heaven's sake let's get out of this!" exclaimed Vivienne. "I'm nearly suffocated already."

Christopher nodded, and led the way into the street. "There's a place a few yards away where one can get a cup of coffee," he said. "I noticed it when I was here on Sunday. Shall we go and sit there for a bit?"

Vivienne nodded, and in a few minutes they were seated at a table, from which they could see the crowd emerging from the Court.

"What a yarn!" exclaimed Vivienne. "We all knew pretty well that Mintern wasn't guilty, but what on earth was the good of making all that fuss, calling witnesses, and all that? Why couldn't they just let the man go?"

"Well, for one thing he had to be formally discharged by the magistrates," replied Christopher with a smile. "If a man has been remanded in custody, you can't just open the door of his cell, and say, 'Sorry you've been troubled,' or anything like that. And, for another, the whole scene was a very clever bit of staging on Swayne's part. I always thought he was pretty shrewd, and, after this morning, my opinion of him has gone up several degrees. I'm only waiting until the Court is over to go and congratulate him."

"You're getting too subtle for me, Chris," said Vivienne. "I can't see anything particularly clever in it."

"Can't you? Don't you see Swayne's game? He says nothing whatever about his intentions, but brings everybody together in the hope that there will be dramatic revelations. Then he puts the people in whom he is most interested in such a position that they are within a few yards of him when he proclaims Mintern's evidence. You bet he was watching them like a cat watches a mouse! I only wish that we had been in such a position that we could have watched them too."

"Well, if you're right, it certainly was rather a clever move," admitted Vivienne grudgingly. "However, I should prefer to trust my own observations rather than Swayne's. I don't know what your plans are, Chris, but I'm going to stay here until I've managed somehow to have a talk to Mrs. Wynter."

Christopher nodded. "I think you're right," he said. "I don't quite know how you'll manage it, but that can safely be left to you. Ah, here comes our client!"

From the window of the tea-shop in which they were sitting they could see Austin come out of the Court, and walk rapidly along the street towards them. Christopher slipped out and intercepted him. "Good morning, Mr. Wynter," he said. "My sister and I are in here, having a cup of coffee. Perhaps you will join us, if you're not too busy?"

Austin looked at him in amazement. "Why, I never expected to see you here, Mr. Perrin!" he exclaimed. "Were you in Court just now? I didn't see you. Of course, I shall be only too glad to join you."

Christopher watched with interest the meeting between his sister and his client. Austin made no attempt to disguise his delight at seeing her again. Vivienne, more self-possessed, confined herself to a polite smile, which betrayed nothing.

There was, naturally, only one possible topic of conversation. "As I told you, the first time we met, I knew that the police were on the wrong track when they suspected Mintern," remarked Austin. "I'm only sorry, for Swayne's sake, that he made the mistake of arresting him. He is a very decent chap, and I'm afraid this little episode won't do his reputation any good."

"Even the police make mistakes at times," replied Christopher. "But you must not suppose that this marks the end of their activities. They will be more anxious than ever to lay their hands on the real culprit."

"I wonder what they'll do next?" asked Vivienne. "Call in Scotland Yard, I suppose."

Christopher shook his head. "I should hardly think so. It all depends on the Chief Constable. But no police force likes to call in the Yard so long after the crime, especially when they have made an arrest and been forced to release their man. It looks far too like a confession of failure on their part. I think, on the whole, that you will find that Swayne remains in charge of the case."

"Well, let's hope he makes a better shot next time," said Austin. "Look here, what time are you going back to London? Won't you both lunch with me at the 'King's Head' before you go?

Vivienne and Christopher exchanged a quick glance. "It's very good of you, Mr. Wynter," replied Christopher. "We shall be very pleased. Hullo! there is Superintendent Swayne just coming out. I want to see him, if you'll excuse me. Where shall I meet you?"

"At the 'King's Head' at one o'clock," said Austin.

Christopher left the shop, and hurried after the retreating figure of the Superintendent. The latter, hearing footsteps behind, turned round. When he recognized his pursuer, he waited, with a rather sardonic smile upon his face. "Hullo! Mr. Perrin, so you thought it worth while to come down and see the fun, did you?" he said.

"I did, indeed," replied Christopher. "And, if I may say so, I very much admired the way you handled the situation."

Swayne smiled, with evident pleasure. "That's more than Sir Henry did," he said. "That's the chairman of the bench. Sir Henry Hepworth owns most of Yatebury. He seemed to think that I'd been trying to make a fool of him or something. But I can't help that. It was worth it. Where were you sitting?"

"Right at the back, where I couldn't see the effect."

"Pity. If you'd come to me before the Court opened I'd have found you a seat up in front. Never mind, come along to my office. I've got a few minutes to spare, and I'll tell you about it."

They reached the Superintendent's office, where Swayne broke into his explanation without unnecessary delay. "It was like this, you see. As I told you on Sunday, I was pretty sure that Mintern hadn't done it. However, I thought that a day or two in gaol might make him disposed to open his mouth a bit, so yesterday I went and had a little quiet talk with him. You'll understand, of course, that what I'm telling you isn't for publication.

"He was a lot more reasonable than I'd seen him before, and I talked to him pretty straight. I told him that if he'd tell me where he was between half-past six and half-past seven on that Friday evening I'd get him out of the mess he was in. And I also told him that if he could give me any information bearing on the case, I wouldn't raise the question of poaching, either against him or anybody who might have been concerned with him.

"He very soon came out with it, after that. It seems that he and a crony of his left the 'Wheatsheaf' about half-past six, and went straight to some snares they'd set the night before. They didn't get back to the village till nearly eight. It sounded true enough at the time, and we verified it later. Then I asked him about the finger-marks, and he admitted that it was likely enough his were on the gun, as he'd often borrowed it, knowing that Mr. Wynter wouldn't want it, and put it back again before it was missed."

"Yes, that's very much what we expected," remarked Christopher. "Did you get anything else out of him?"

"Now we come to it, I'll give it to you in return for what you gave me on Sunday. I got him talking about the people at Monk's Barn, and I saw at once that he was very bitter against Mrs. Wynter. He murmured something about his being sent away being due to her. I pricked up my ears at that, and he told me something that may or may not be significant. It seems that, some weeks back, he came upon Mrs. Wynter and Frank Cartwright in the garden. As he put it, "'is arm was round 'er waist, and 'er 'ead was on 'is shoulder.'"

Christopher laughed. "Quite a pastoral idyll," he remarked. "You wouldn't draw any very damaging inferences from a little incident like that, even if it happens to be true, would you?"

"Well, I don't know. Mintern says that they seemed very much annoyed at having been seen. He also says that he told Croyle, who advised him to forget about it. He gathered from Croyle's manner that it didn't surprise him. Anyhow, he is convinced that from that moment Mrs. Wynter used her influence with her husband to get rid of him."

"It certainly looks rather as if Mrs. Wynter and Mr. Cartwright were on rather more affectionate terms than they cared to display in public," commented Christopher thoughtfully. "But does it affect the case much?"

Swayne laughed. "Deep, aren't you, Mr. Perrin," he exclaimed. "You know as well as I do what I'm thinking about. Perhaps they found Gilbert Wynter a bit in their way."

He paused and looked significantly at Christopher. "And we know that Frank Cartwright didn't shoot him," he added quietly.

CHAPTER XVII

A SUDDEN silence fell upon Vivienne and Austin after Christopher had gone out. It was broken at length by Vivienne. "I'm sure you must be wanting to get back to the works, Mr. Wynter," she said.

"Don't let me keep you. I'm quite capable of looking after myself till one o'clock."

"I'm quite sure you are, Miss Perrin," replied Austin. "But, as it happens, I'm not expected back at the works this morning. I imagined that the case would last a good deal longer than it did, and made my arrangements accordingly. So, unless you want to get rid of me, I will stay with you."

Vivienne smiled. Now that Austin seemed to have got over his shyness, he had a direct way of expressing himself which pleased her. "No, I've nothing to do," she replied. "Yatebury isn't a very amusing place to be alone in, you must admit. I'm just wondering how I'm going to manage something that I particularly want to do."

"What's that?" inquired Austin eagerly. "Is it anything that I can help you with?"

"I'm afraid, as it happens, that you are the very last person in the world who can help me. I want to get to know your sister-in-law, and I'm afraid that, under the circumstances, an introduction from you would not be the best beginning."

"No, perhaps you're right," said Austin. "I never was very popular in that quarter, and I fancy that I'm even less so now. I feel quite sure that Anne, or rather Cartwright on her behalf, means to kick up the deuce of a fuss about that matter I mentioned to you yesterday. It's really very irritating. I've got quite enough to think of just now without having a family quarrel thrust upon me. I wish Anne would be content to draw her share of the profits and leave me to run the business."

"It must be a nuisance," replied Vivienne sympathetically. "But, after all, it is only natural that she should take some interest in the firm. She's part owner of it, now that your brother is dead. I don't want to seem inquisitive, Mr. Wynter, but what happens to her share eventually?"

"That is provided for by my father's will. If either Gilbert or I died childless, our share was to go to the other, or his descendants, after the death of the widow. That is to say that Gilbert's share comes to me if I survive Anne. But, as we're both almost the same age, that doesn't seem to be a likely solution of the difficulty. Now, I'm going to be inquisitive. Why are you so anxious to make Anne's acquaintance?"

"Because I've had an opportunity of studying everybody in your brother's circle, with the exception of her," replied Vivienne lightly. "That's enough reason in itself isn't it?"

"Well, I suppose it is, but I fancy that you've got a better reason still, haven't you, Miss Perrin?"

"Perhaps I have. I should very much like to know whether she told everything she knew at the inquest."

For a moment Austin made no reply. He stared absently out of the window, a frown upon his handsome face. "I've wondered, myself," he said abruptly. "Look here, Miss Perrin, you know by this time that I don't like Anne, that I have never liked her, in fact. I don't know why, for, really, I know very little about her. It's instinctive, I suppose. But I don't want you to think that I'm prejudiced by my dislike. I have no reason whatever for supposing that Anne knows more about Gilbert's death than she has said. But I can't help remembering that she was sitting in the drawing-room at the time, directly under the spot where he was killed, and facing the shrubbery from which the shot was fired."

Vivienne nodded. "I know," she replied. "That point struck me as soon as I saw Monk's Barn. And that's why I'm terribly anxious to make the acquaintance of Mrs. Wynter, if it can be managed."

"I thought it must be something like that!" exclaimed Austin triumphantly. "But, even then, I don't see that you'll be much forrader. Anne's a reserved sort of person, you know, and she isn't likely to say anything if she thinks it better to keep quiet about it."

Vivienne lay back in her chair and laughed heartily. "I'm afraid that you'd never do for our profession, Mr. Wynter!" she exclaimed. "Your methods are far too honest and direct. Of course, Mrs. Wynter wouldn't say anything. Why should she, to a total stranger? But there are ways of getting an inkling of the truth that you have never dreamed of, I expect. People's expression, their way of putting things, their avoidance or otherwise of certain subjects, and a thousand little things like that. Haven't you ever noticed?"

"No, honestly, I can't say that I have," replied Austin simply. "And, if I had, I'm afraid that I should never have the courage to trust to my own judgment. I find things much more easy to understand than people, if you see what I mean. Take a piece of steel, for instance. You can do almost anything you want to with it, it's only a matter of treating it the right way."

"Well, isn't it the same with people? You've only got to treat them the right way to make them do what you want."

"Have you?" asked Austin eagerly. For a moment Vivienne felt a strange tension in the air, as though some cord, tightly stretched, were about to break. She could not bring herself to face Austin's burning eyes, which she felt fixed upon her. And then suddenly the tension relaxed, and he spoke again, in a curiously deadened voice.

"Yes, I daresay you have, Miss Perrin. But, you see, in the case of steel there are certain hard-and-fast laws, which have been determined by experiment. But it seems to me that you can't lay down laws for the proper treatment of human beings. No two of them are alike."

"Oh, that's a matter of experiment, too," replied Vivienne carelessly. "But this isn't helping me to decide how I am to get to know your sister-in-law."

"Couldn't you get to know her through Mrs. Cartwright? You made her acquaintance easily enough, it seemed to me."

Vivienne made a grimace. "Yes, but that stunt won't work again. Mr. Cartwright spotted who I was, and he is certain to have told his wife by this time. I don't like going near her again; she probably wouldn't speak to me. From her point of view, I made her acquaintance under false pretences."

"Yes, there's something in that. However, I'm quite sure that if you want to meet Anne, you'll manage it somehow."

"Thank you, Mr. Wynter. It is comforting to feel that you have so much faith in the efficiency of the firm of Perrins. But isn't it about time we went to the 'King's Head' to meet my brother? It is ten to one already."

They found Christopher sitting in the lounge of the hotel, watching the passers-by with a sort of quiet interest which was typical of him. Austin left his guest for a few minutes to see about a table for lunch, and Christopher glanced inquiringly at his sister.

"Nothing much," said Vivienne. "I'm still more settled in my original conviction, that's all. And you?"

"Swayne has started a new hare, but I'm not sure yet that it isn't a rabbit. Tell you later."

Austin returned and escorted them to the dining-room. The "King's Head," though quite unpretentious, made a speciality of its cooking, and, Austin being well known there, the lunch was of the best. He had selected a table in an alcove, where the three could talk without being overheard.

It was Christopher who was the first to refer to the subject that was uttermost in their minds. "I had a few words with Swayne," he said. "He made no mention of calling in Scotland Yard, and I gathered that he was still in charge of the case. He did not suggest that he contemplated any immediate action. By the way, Mr. Wynter, has your sister-in-law returned permanently to Monk's Barn?"

"I really can't say," replied Austin. "I haven't so much as spoken to her since she came back. The only time I have seen her was in Court just now. I have no idea what she means to do."

"Mrs. Wynter was, I take it, a stranger to this part of the world until she married your brother?"

"Well, not entirely a stranger. She used to come and stay in Yatebury sometimes, and that's how Gilbert met her. There were some people living here called Rawlings—they've left the district now—and she was a friend of theirs. They would ask her down for dances, and so forth. I never noticed that Gilbert paid her any particular attention, and I was immensely surprised when he told me one day that he had proposed to her and been accepted."

"You were more surprised at the proposal than at its acceptance, I take it?"

Austin smiled. "I see what you mean," he replied. "Yes, to be quite accurate, I was. Gilbert was always looked upon as the most eligible bachelor in Yatebury. He knew this as well as anybody else, and it used to amuse him to watch the attempts made to snare him. 'Purely in vain is the net spread in the sight of any bird!' That's where Anne was so clever. She never seemed to make any attempt to captivate him."

"Surely, Mr. Wynter, you are being unnecessarily cynical, aren't you?" said Vivienne with a mocking smile. "I don't believe that the girls of Yatebury are half so predatory as you try to make out. In fact, they can't possibly be. Your brother wasn't the only bachelor in the town worth angling for. He only owned half the business, after all."

Austin blushed furiously. "Well, you see, Miss Perrin, for one thing I was a year or two younger than Gilbert. And somehow I was never so attractive to women as he was. I suppose I never knew how to treat them. I've always been shy and awkward when they're about, and I always have an uncomfortable sort of feeling that they're laughing at me. It's very difficult to explain exactly what I mean."

"Your brother was different, no doubt," remarked Christopher, anxious to keep the conversation to the point. "Was he engaged to your sister-in-law for long?"

"No, Gilbert was always impetuous. Once he had made up his mind to do a thing, he went ahead with it regardless of everything else. I hardly saw him during those weeks. He was busy with a thousand things; finding a house and all manner of details like that. I fancied that he would live in Yatebury, as our parents had done. But he wouldn't hear of it. He was fully determined to live outside the town, and cultivate an entirely new society. He seemed suddenly to have got the idea that there was something disgraceful in being a mere manufacturer, and living close to the works. He seemed to see some subtle difference in being a director, and living at Fordington."

There was a bitterness in Austin's tone which neither of his hearers could fail to recognize. Nor was it difficult to perceive the cause of it. Austin had been, and to some extent was still, jealous of the new influence which had been brought to bear upon his brother's life and outlook. It was clear that he attributed all their later disagreements to these influences, and hated them accordingly.

"It's perfectly true that, before the wedding, I hadn't seen Anne more than two or three times," he continued. "They were married from Anne's home at Ipswich. She had a mother alive then, who's died since. The two of them lived on some sort of pension, her father had been an official of some kind in the Far East. Anne hadn't a penny of her own to bless herself with. That's why it annoyed me that they set up in such style at Monk's Barn."

"There was, I suppose, no question that your brother lived in recent years beyond his means?" asked Christopher.

"Well, it depends how you look at it. He lived within his income, but that income was larger than it should have been. He always insisted upon drawing more from the profits of the business than I considered advisable. My policy was always to build up a strong reserve, which could be used to reorganize the business when it became necessary. That time has now arrived, and I am faced with a very difficult task, since our reserves are not so strong as they should be. I am very much afraid that I shall have to persuade Anne that it is necessary for her to curtail her expenses considerably, at all events for a year or two."

Austin paused, and glanced at the clock. Christopher hastened to his aid. "Don't let us keep you, Mr. Wynter," he said. "I know how busy a man you must be, just now."

"Well, I am rather anxious to get back to the works, if you don't mind. What are you and Miss Perrin going to do?"

"I'm going back to London this afternoon," replied Christopher. "I don't know what Vi's plans are."

"I'm going to take a room here, and stay in Yatebury for a day or two," said Vivienne. "I haven't finished my job yet."

Austin's eyes lighted up with pleasure. "Then I shall see you again?" he asked.

"Possibly," Vivienne replied carelessly. "At all events, you will know where to find me."

It was not for some minutes after Austin's departure that Christopher spoke. "It's an interesting situation altogether apart from Gilbert Wynter's murder," he said. "On the one hand, you have Austin, enthusiastically keen on the business, and wrapped up in its future. On the other, you have Anne Wynter, owning half of it, but apparently regarding it merely as a means of keeping her in luxury. There's trouble to come yet, I'm afraid."

"Yes, especially as Anne Wynter has appointed Frank Cartwright as her representative," said Vivienne. "You mustn't forget that."

"I don't forget it, especially in the light of what Swayne told me just now. Do you know, he's got reason to believe that those two are in love with one another?"

A sudden look of comprehension flashed into Vivienne's eyes. "So that's what Croyle was hinting at so darkly, was it!" she exclaimed cryptically.

CHAPTER XVIII

"There's one thing that becomes startlingly clear, with every fresh bit of information we pick up," said Vivienne with decision. "I've got to have a chat with Anne Wynter at all costs. How I'm going to set about it, I don't quite know yet. You'd better leave that to me. What exactly did Swayne tell you?"

Christopher repeated the Superintendent's account of Mintern's adventure, to which his sister listened with a doubtful expression. "Precious little to go upon," she commented. "I shouldn't be inclined to attach much weight to it, if it hadn't been that Croyle had hinted at queer goings on."

"I don't think that Swayne thought it of any great importance," replied Christopher. "He's bound, as we are ourselves, to

examine every trifle, and add it to the scale. In this case, if Anne
Wynter is really in love with Cartwright, the fact provides her with
an additional motive for wishing Gilbert out of the way. Beyond
that, one can't go for the present."

"I wonder. Domestic affairs at Monk's Barn seem to have been
in a bit of a tangle, don't they? How did they become so? Let's try
to trace it out. We have Gilbert, impetuous in everything he did,
according to his brother. He feels a sudden attraction for Anne,
decided that he wants to marry her, and apparently carries out
his decision without taking any further thought. Anne—I don't
like to judge her without knowing her, but this is what it looks
like—jumps at the chance of marrying a rich husband. Agreed?"

"Yes, with possible minor reservations. Carry on."

"Now, which got tired of the other first? Did Gilbert begin his
intrigue with Phyllis because he knew that his wife didn't care
for him? Or did Anne know of this intrigue and turn to Frank
Cartwright for consolation? That's what I should like to know."

Christopher smiled. "Is this mere psychological inquisitive-
ness?" he asked. "I can't see that the point is of much importance."

"Can't you? I can. These matrimonial differences usually end,
sooner or later, in the divorce court, don't they? In this case,
which would have divorced the other? Unless they arrived at
some mutual arrangement, Anne would not dare to give Gilbert
grounds for divorcing her. She would have been left penniless,
and she couldn't marry Cartwright. Even if she divorced Gilbert,
she wouldn't have been half so well off as she was as his wife, or
is now as his widow."

"Suggesting, of course, that she found murder a more suitable
weapon than divorce? It's possible, I'll admit, but I must confess
that the motive scarcely seems adequate."

"It's as adequate as any other you can suggest. After all, we
are faced with the fact that Gilbert was murdered, since I take it
that nobody could seriously imagine that he committed suicide,
or that the shot was fired by accident. I tried out those alterna-
tives pretty thoroughly when I was at Fordington, and abandoned

them. They don't seem even to have occurred to the police, and they were on the spot almost at once."

"I'm quite ready to accept as a postulate the fact that Gilbert was murdered," replied Christopher. "In fact, after all this time, that seems to be the only thing we know with any certainty."

"Don't be so discouraging. What I was going to say is that, if Gilbert was murdered, it follows that somebody had a motive for murdering him. It's no good saying that any particular person couldn't have murdered him, because their motive wasn't adequate. No motive for murder ever is adequate, except to the mind of the murderer. If it was, the deed wouldn't be murder. That's logic, isn't it?"

"It's common sense, anyhow," agreed Christopher.

"That's better still. Put it this way, then. Anne had a motive, adequate in her eyes, for murdering Gilbert. But then, it seems to me, we come to the aspect of the case which would puzzle the criminologist. A woman in her circumstances would never tackle the job herself. I don't mean that she wouldn't have the courage, but she'd feel a natural repugnance at the idea, and she probably wouldn't know how to set about it. She would naturally confide in her lover, and get him to do the dirty work for her. You would have expected, in this case, that if Anne had wanted Gilbert killed, she would have employed Cartwright as her agent. And that's where this particular theory becomes unstuck. The shot was fired from the shrubbery. Cartwright, unless he possesses the power of being in two places at once, could not possibly have been in the shrubbery at the time. Therefore he didn't kill Gilbert, though he may know who did so."

"Yes, we're all agreed upon that, including Swayne," said Christopher. "Unless something else turns up, the issue narrows down to two people only, Mrs. Wynter or—our client."

"Then there isn't a shadow of doubt that Anne Wynter is the criminal," replied Vivienne confidently. "And it seems to be my job to find the elusive clue that will bring the crime home to her.

It sounds horrible, put like that. But, after all, our duty to our client must come first, mustn't it?"

There was a queer note of appeal in Vivienne's voice, which went straight to her brother's heart. In spite of the fact that they were devoted to one another, their affection was singularly undemonstrative. But on this occasion he took her hand in his and patted it comfortingly. "You needn't worry, old girl," he said. "You know very well that I'll work as hard in our client's interests as you do yourself. Now, unless you want me to stay here and help you, I'll get back to the station and catch my train."

Vivienne, having seen her brother off, took a 'bus out to Fordington. She had made up her mind that the direct method would probably be the best, if she were to achieve her object without waste of time. If that failed it would be time enough to think out some new line of approach. She went straight to White Lodge and rang the bell.

The servant who answered it evidently recognized her, for at her inquiry as to whether Mrs. Cartwright was at home, she smiled and led the way to the drawing-room. Vivienne followed her rather diffidently uncertain of the reception she would meet with. But all her fears were set at rest as soon as she saw the expression of welcome on Mrs. Cartwright's face.

"I am glad to see you, Miss Perrin!" she exclaimed. "I have been hoping ever since you left that you would come back to Fordington. Are you staying with Mrs. Marsh again?"

"No, I'm not," replied Vivienne. "I'm staying in Yatebury. I came out to see you this afternoon, because I have a confession to make."

"A confession! Well, I'm sure it can't be anything very serious. Are you quite sure you want to tell me?"

"Quite sure. I want to apologize and ask you to forgive me. I let you think, when I was here last, that my business in Fordington was to sketch old buildings. It wasn't anything of the kind, really."

Mrs. Cartwright opened her eyes to their fullest extent. "Really, this sounds most mysterious!" she said.

"The mystery is soon solved," Vivienne replied, feeling in her bag. "You'll understand, if I show you my card."

She handed a card to Mrs. Cartwright, who uttered an exclamation of astonishment as she caught sight of the words "Perrins, Private Investigators" engraved in the corner. "But, my dear, how frightfully thrilling!" she said. "You don't mean to say that you're really a—a sort of detective?" A sudden look of comprehension came into her eyes. "Then you must have come here to investigate poor Gilbert's death!" she continued in an awed whisper.

"That's it, exactly," replied Vivienne. "Now, can you possibly forgive me for deceiving you?"

"Of course I can. I quite understand that detectives have to pretend to be other people, what I can't get over is how frightfully clever you must be. Just fancy! I've read such a lot about detectives, but I never thought that a lady detective would be as young and pretty as you."

Vivienne made no reply. Indeed, Mrs. Cartwright's conversation was habitually of a type that does not call for a reply. To Vivienne the curious thing was that Mr. Cartwright had not told his wife who the pseudo-artist really was. She would only suppose that he had not thought it worth while.

Meanwhile Mrs. Cartwright was rattling on. "I'm so glad you have come in this afternoon. I'm all alone, as it happens. Frank had to spend his morning in Yatebury, attending the trial of that man Mintern, and he'll be late back from the mill in consequence. I do so wonder what happened to Mintern. I haven't seen Burden, or I should have asked him. Oh, but I forgot, for the moment, I expect you know?"

"Yes, he was discharged. The police offered no evidence against him."

"You mean to say that the magistrates let him off?" inquired Mrs. Cartwright with a horrified expression.

"Well, yes. You see, the police had come to the conclusion that he did not do it."

"Oh, but that's ridiculous. If he didn't do it, who did? I'm sure there's no one else in Fordington who'd think of such a thing. But I suppose, as you're engaged upon the case, I must be discreet, and not ask questions. As I was saying, I am alone to-day. Frank will be late, and though Anne came back to Monk's Barn last night, she naturally doesn't see very many people just now. She promised to look in here for a few minutes after tea, so you'll meet her. You'll stop to tea, of course. They'll be bringing it in in a minute. Poor Anne, I'm afraid she has her troubles to face. First of all there was Gilbert's murder, and then, just before she came back, her parlour-maid, Phyllis, you may remember her, she's the girl who opened the door to us that day, ran away and nobody knows what's become of her."

Vivienne listened to this rigmarole with what patience she could. Her efforts had been rewarded, and she was to meet Anne Wynter! Her luck had not yet deserted her, it seemed.

Yet, when Anne Wynter entered the room, Vivienne felt a sudden thrill of despondency. At first glance she saw that here was a woman armed in every way to defend her secrets. She was about thirty, Vivienne supposed, tall and slight, with a face which would have been beautiful but for a certain hardness and lack of sympathy. The features were perhaps too perfect, too finely cut, the hazel eyes a trifle too penetrating.

Curiously enough, she did not seem to resent the presence of a stranger. Indeed, after her first introduction to Vivienne, she seemed almost anxious to include her in the conversation. Naturally no mention was made of the tragedy which had taken place at Monk's Barn, and no one would have guessed from Anne's manner that she had so recently become a widow. She talked easily enough upon general subjects, was, in fact, quite a brilliant conversationalist. But Vivienne had an irritating feeling that all this was on the surface, that she was gazing on a mirror which merely reflected, without allowing her to penetrate the depths.

Vivienne stayed as long as she decently could, then, making the excuse of having to catch a 'bus back to Yatebury, left the house.

But not until she had had a last word with Anne. "I'm very glad to have met you, Miss Perrin," she had said. "I'm going to ask Ursula to bring you in to see me, next time you come over here."

This was something, certainly. But, during the whole of her journey back, Vivienne found herself wondering how much it would really be worth. The invitation had been worded so curiously, as though Anne had deliberately ruled that a third person should be present at their interview. It was in keeping with what Vivienne had already remarked in her, a curious reserve, an impersonal way of speaking and of acting. Acting, yes, that was it. That was the secret of Anne's impenetrability. She was acting a part, had probably been doing so, in public at least, longer than she cared to remember.

When she reached the "King's Head," she found Austin sitting in the lounge, watching the door eagerly. He rose as she came in, and came swiftly towards her. "I say, Miss Perrin, I wonder if you'd dine with me and go to the pictures afterwards? I'm sorry I can't suggest anything more thrilling, but that's about all the entertainment Yatebury provides."

Vivienne accepted the invitation gratefully enough. They dined together, perforce at the "King's Head," since Austin declared that it was the only place in the town where one could count on getting a decent meal.

"I've met your sister-in-law," Vivienne remarked casually as the coffee was served. "I went to see Mrs. Cartwright this afternoon, and she came in."

"You did? I told you that if you wanted to make her acquaintance you'd do so. Well, what do you think of her?"

"I hardly know," replied Vivienne, frowning slightly. "I should think she was a very difficult person to get really intimate with. She was very nice to me, and asked me to go and see her the next time I was in Fordington."

"Did she? Did she know who you were?"

"I'm not sure. Certainly Mrs. Cartwright didn't know till I told her. It's curious, I don't quite understand it. I have a fancy that your sister-in-law and Mr. Cartwright tell one another most things."

"I shouldn't wonder. I've thought so myself, since Cartwright has been acting as her representative. The more I see of that man, the less I like him. You don't think there was anything between him and Anne, do you?"

"I don't know," replied Vivienne hurriedly, looking at the clock. "Isn't it time we made a move?"

They left the hotel and walked a few yards up the street to the cinema. Austin stopped in the entrance and bought a box of chocolates which he shyly presented to Vivienne.

"That's very sweet of you," said Vivienne graciously. "But you mustn't be offended if I don't eat them. It's a shocking thing to have to admit, but I never eat chocolates. My taste has become blunted by too many cigarettes and cocktails, I suppose?"

A look of acute disappointment came into Austin's face. "You don't like chocolates?" he said. "I'm so sorry. Well, it can't be helped. Shall we go in?"

CHAPTER XIX

VIVIENNE was not in the habit of cross-examining herself on the subject of her own feelings. Indeed, her tendency was to put these into the background, and to regard life as a spectator, purely objectively. Not that she was in any sense unimpressionable, but simply because it seemed obvious to her that any problem was bound to become enormously complicated if one approached its solution with any personal bias.

Yet, in spite of this, she found it increasingly difficult to regard Austin Wynter merely in the light of a client. She had, probably, more experience of men than most girls of her age. As a rule, she was more attracted to them than to members of her own sex. She enjoyed their admiration, and was happy in their company. But, hitherto, she had never felt more than a mild interest in any of them. Flirtation, mild or otherwise, had never appealed to her. There were so many other interests in life which seemed far more worth while.

But now she knew, rather to her own secret annoyance, that she was more interested in Austin than she had ever been in any man, always excepting her brother. But his attitude towards her puzzled her. It was plain enough, to use the common phrase, that he was in love with her. But that phrase covered such a large range. Was his love for her merely a passing attraction for a pretty girl, or was it something infinitely deeper? Vivienne would have given a good deal to know.

All the time-honoured symptoms were visible, of that there could be no doubt. His whole face lighted up at the sight of her; he had overcome his natural shyness sufficiently to talk freely to her when they were alone, though he still showed his old restraint in the presence of others. There could be no doubt that he looked upon her as somebody far more individual than a mere member of the firm of Perrins, to put his sentiments on no higher plane than that.

Yet never, by word or deed, had he allowed any trace of his feelings towards her to escape him. His looks he could not so successfully control. He treated her with the strictest courtesy, which might have been the cloak of indifference, while all the time his eyes sought hers, as though seeking the answer to an unspoken question. Twice, at least, he had seemed to be on the verge of expression, once in Perrin's office, when Christopher had interrupted their tête-à-tête, and once that very morning in the tea-shop, when he had suddenly pulled himself up. Was it because he was not yet sure of her, or of himself?

These were the thoughts that filled Vivienne's mind as she sat by his side in the darkened picture-hall. Austin made no attempt to interrupt her; he seemed quite content to be sitting by her side, to feel her presence near him. She knew well enough that his attention was no more fixed on the screen than was hers.

The real drama was not there. It was being played silently, almost blindly, in their own hearts.

So acute did the invisible strain become that Vivienne, when the performance came to an end and they joined the crowd filing slowly from the building, felt as though an intolerable weight had been removed from her. The sensation was so vivid as to be actually physical; she drew a long breath as she felt the cold night air strike her.

Austin turned swiftly towards her. "You don't feel cold after that stuffy hall, do you?" he asked solicitously.

"Not a bit," she replied. "It's nice to be in the fresh air once more."

"I'll see you back to the hotel." He paused suddenly, and glanced at a man by his side, who was also making his way out of the building. "Good evening, Superintendent. I didn't know you were a movie fan."

"I'm not, as a rule," replied Superintendent Swayne, taking off his hat, "but sometimes I go to the pictures by way of diversion. They're so very different from anything one has ever seen in real life."

He glanced inquiringly at Vivienne, in such a way that Austin could hardly ignore the hint. "Let me introduce you," he said. "Miss Perrin. This is Superintendent Swayne."

"I am very glad to meet you, Miss Perrin," said Swayne politely. "I have heard a good deal about you, and I know your brother, of course. Are you staying in Yatebury?"

"Yes, as an alternative to staying with Mrs. Marsh in Fordington," replied Vivienne, with a slightly malicious smile. "My brother pointed you out to me this morning, in Court."

"Oh, so you were there too? I am afraid the proceedings must have disappointed you."

"They certainly were rather in the nature of an anti-climax. But I don't think anybody can be really disappointed when an innocent man is released. You must have been relieved yourself,

Superintendent. I don't share the popular belief that the police must have a victim, innocent or guilty."

Swayne laughed pleasantly. "I'm glad to hear you say that, Miss Perrin. Unfortunately, it's the public rather than the police who clamour for a victim. But, as you say, it's always satisfactory when a suspected person manages to prove his innocence. Mintern found it considerably easier than many others. Not that there are very many who will rejoice at his character being cleared, except, of course, his daughter."

Vivienne was quick to parry the stroke. "Phyllis? Oh, I don't think that she ever had the slightest doubt of her father's innocence of this particular crime. She'll be glad to know that he's been cleared, of course. But I don't expect that she'll be anxious to join him again at Fordington."

"Well, you're in a position to know more about that than I do, Miss Perrin. But, of course, we may yet want her as a witness. We have by no means given up hope of laying our hands upon the real culprit."

"I hope your second attempt will be more successful than the first, Superintendent. I expect you'll be rather more careful to verify your evidence, next time, before you take action?"

Again Swayne laughed, this time not quite so pleasantly. "I expect we shall," he replied. "But you must remember that the police have means of obtaining evidence that aren't available to other folk. And very often they know more than comes out, even in Court. Well, I mustn't keep you and Mr. Wynter hanging about out here in the cold. Good night, Miss Perrin, and don't hesitate to let me know if I can be of any use to you."

He lifted his hat once more, and walked swiftly away. Austin, who had listened to this conversation in silence, turned to Vivienne. "He's a clever chap, is Swayne, in spite of his blunder over Mintern," he said. "It sounds to me very much as if he'd already got some suspicions in another direction."

"So it does to me," replied Vivienne, rather dryly. "The field is getting a bit limited, you know."

"Yes, I suppose it is. By Jove, you don't think—"

Vivienne interrupted him swiftly. "I don't trouble to think of the possible direction in which the Superintendent's reasoning may lead him. Perrins have a way of pursuing their investigations independently. And I should advise you not to trouble about it either."

They had reached the door of the hotel by now. It was closed, and Austin pressed the bell. Then, with a sudden movement he took Vivienne's hand, and held it for an instant. "I have perfect faith in you, you know," he whispered. Then, as the door opened, he was gone.

Vivienne went straight up to her room, but she felt not the slightest inclination for sleep. As much to occupy herself as anything, she sat down and wrote a note to her brother.

"DEAR CHRIS,—I saw Anne Wynter this afternoon. I claim no credit for this; it was really a piece of sheer luck. But things were much easier than I expected, since Mr. Cartwright had not told his wife of the little deception I had played upon her. I'm rather puzzled to know why.

"Anne Wynter, for the present, remains a greater enigma than ever. I feel somehow that she knows who I am, and what my business is. But she went out of her way to be nice to me, and to ask me to go and see her at Monk's Barn, not alone, but with Mrs. Cartwright. She doesn't strike me as particularly subtle, only intensely reserved. Naturally, I shall accept her invitation, if ever it becomes definite. But, for the present, I am at a loss. She doesn't fit in with any theory I can form.

"Rather a curious thing happened just now. Our client took me to the pictures. I fancy that he considers it his duty to entertain me while I'm here. Coming out, we found ourselves next to Swayne, and he introduced us. I'm pretty certain, myself, that Swayne is keeping an eye on our client, but, of course, I said nothing of this to him. Swayne and I indulged in a little badinage, which was quite lost on our client. But Swayne's hints were so broad that even he smelt a rat. I'm very much afraid that there is trouble brewing in that direction. If anything happens, I shall send for you at once.—Yours, Vi."

The writing of this letter brought a slight sense of relief to Vivienne. She went to bed, and, after an hour or two of wakefulness, fell off to sleep.

She was awakened next morning by the entry of the chambermaid, bringing her a cup of tea. At the same time, she laid on the table by the bed a parcel and a letter. Vivienne glanced at these with some surprise. She had not expected correspondence so early in her stay. Her curiosity impelled her to open the parcel first. It bore no stamps, and had evidently been delivered by hand. On the label was printed "Birdley & Sour, Confectioners, Yatebury."

It proved to be a large box of chocolates. Vivienne smiled, rather wistfully. Austin, of course. It was very sweet of him; he must have ordered them the day before. She wished she had not been so outspoken the previous evening. Of course he was disappointed when she had said she did not like chocolates. Well, for his sake she would conquer her dislike and try just one.

She opened the box and found that the chocolates were of two kinds, round and square. She took one at random and tasted it. They were certainly beautiful chocolates. But, it was no good, she simply didn't like them. She put the lid on the box, wondering idly as she did so how she could dispose of them. Then she picked up the letter and opened it.

It was from Mrs. Cartwright, written in a large sprawling hand.

"DEAR MISS PERRIN,—I did enjoy seeing you again so much this afternoon. I told my husband that you had been to see me, and he was very sorry to have missed you. I know he would love to meet you again. Could you come to tea to-morrow, or Thursday is the day he comes back early from the office? I know you will if you can. Yours very sincerely, URSULA CARTWRIGHT."

Vivienne's brows puckered as she read this letter. It seemed curious that, after Mr. Cartwright's exposure of her to Superintendent Swayne, he should be anxious to see her again. Was the invitation in the nature of a challenge? Well, she was not the sort of person to refuse such a thing, if it was. She would most certainly go; there was always the chance of learning something, and she was pretty confident of her ability to prevent this man Cartwright learning anything from her. And then her eyes fell upon the box of chocolates. That little problem, at all events, was solved. She would take them with her. Mrs. Cartwright was just the sort of person who would adore chocolates.

Vivienne spent the morning in an expedition to Stourminster, not because she was interested in that not very inspiring town, but because she wished to keep out of Austin's way. She was convinced that Swayne had an eye on her movements, and there was no point in her being seen too much in his company. Shortly before four o'clock, she was seated in the drawing-room at White Lodge.

Mrs. Cartwright was effusive in her thanks for the chocolates. "That was really a very sweet thought on your part, Miss Perrin. I love chocolates, especially these. You got them at Birdley's, I see. They are famous for their chocolates. They always fill their boxes with these two kinds, the round and the square. I simply adore the round ones, they're delicious. Anne loves the square ones; we often buy a box between us and share them. You won't mind if I put the square ones aside for her?"

"Oh, I shall be only too delighted. Mrs. Wynter was very kind to me yesterday."

"You made quite an impression upon Anne, my dear. She could talk of nothing else after you had gone. In fact, she asked me if I would take you to tea with her to-morrow. I promised I would ask you, but I feel that you must be far too busy to come out to Fordington every day like this."

"I usually manage to finish what I have to do by tea-time," replied Vivienne evasively. "I should very much like to come to-morrow, if I may."

"Of course, Anne will be so pleased when I tell her you'll come. Ah, here is Frank, I knew he wouldn't be late as you were coming."

Frank Cartwright entered the room, and, at the sight of him, Vivienne felt a return of the vague uneasiness which she had known on the last occasion that she had met him.

CHAPTER XX

VIVIENNE need have had no uneasiness on the score of what Mr. Cartwright's attitude towards her might be. He seemed determined to make himself as pleasant as possible. There was no reference whatever to the reasons for Vivienne being at Yatebury. In fact, the murder of Gilbert Wynter was not alluded to, even remotely. Mr. Cartwright seemed to concentrate his efforts upon making his visitor seem at home.

His wife frankly abandoned herself to the chocolates. "Do you know, Frank, Miss Perrin brought me one of those lovely boxes of chocolates from Birdley's," she said. "Wasn't it sweet of her? I can't think how she could have guessed that I was so fond of them."

Frank Cartwright glanced at Vivienne. "It was very clever of you to discover Birdley's chocolates so quickly," he remarked. "They're by way of being famous locally, but they don't advertise them at all. I should have some while you get the chance, if I were you, or Ursula will eat them all."

"Miss Perrin declares that she doesn't like chocolates," said Mrs. Cartwright. "Besides, don't be so silly. I couldn't possibly eat them all. There's another layer under this one. And, anyhow, I'm putting the square ones aside for Anne. You know how she loves them."

Again Vivienne felt a queer twinge of annoyance. She had let it be understood that she had bought the chocolates. She had no wish that Austin's name should be mentioned at White Lodge. For one thing, she knew the coolness between him and the Cartwrights, and, for another, she felt a natural reluctance at admitting that the box was a present from him. And yet Mr. Cartwright, with that uncanny penetration of his, had clearly guessed that she had not bought them herself.

In spite, therefore, of his efforts to make her feel at home, she was distinctly relieved when the time came for her to go. But Mr. Cartwright refused to consider the idea of her going back by 'bus. "Nonsense!" he said. "I've got the car outside, I haven't put her away yet. It won't take me more than a few minutes to drive you back to Yatebury. Besides, I'm nearly out of cigarettes, and I can't get the kind I like in the village."

Vivienne accepted his offer with the best grace she could. While he had gone to bring the car round to the door, Mrs. Cartwright stood talking to her in the hall. "You won't forget about to-morrow, will you?" she said earnestly. "Anne will be so delighted if you'll come. If you'll meet me here, I'll take you across to her."

Vivienne assured her that she would not forget, and at that moment the car appeared. She got into it, beside Mr. Cartwright, and they started off towards Yatebury.

Neither spoke until they were clear of the village. And then, without warning. "Do you see much of young Austin Wynter?" asked Mr. Cartwright.

The question struck Vivienne as a blow. It seemed to take her so utterly for granted; her professional status, the fact that Austin had called in Perrins to his assistance. Once more Mr. Cartwright had shown that beneath his pleasant and easy-going exterior there was a shrewdness equal to her own.

Her mind was made up in a flash. She had already placed herself in a false position by trying to evade the truth. It would be foolish to do so again, especially as Mr. Cartwright was evidently in touch with Superintendent Swayne.

"I've seen a fair amount of him since I came down to Yatebury yesterday morning," she replied carelessly.

"Queer chap, isn't he?" said Mr. Cartwright. "Neither Ursula nor Anne have ever cared for him. I don't know why. I think his trouble is that he keeps himself too much to himself, and doesn't rub up against other people enough. It seems probable that I shall be more closely associated with him in the future than I have been in the past. He's very clever at his job, there's no doubt about that. But he's apt to think that his own opinion must necessarily be the best, and I anticipate some little difficulty in dealing with him. At the present moment I'm afraid that he wishes Anne, and me as her representative, at the bottom of the sea."

Vivienne made no comment, and Cartwright continued. "I feel I can talk quite freely to you, Miss Perrin, since we are both of us equally anxious to solve the mystery of poor Gilbert's death, you professionally, and I as perhaps his best friend. I don't know what theory you may have formed, and I am not sufficiently impertinent to ask you. I have my own ideas, which, if occasion arises, I shall confide to the police. But, I think you will agree that for the present the utmost discretion is called for. You will forgive my saying that I greatly admired your tact in disguising the real cause of your visit to Fordington last week. We're just coming to the 'King's Head.' Shall I drop you there, or is there anywhere else you would like to go?"

"I'll stop here, Mr. Cartwright, if you don't mind," said Vivienne curtly.

"Very well. I hope we shall meet again before you leave Yatebury, Miss Perrin. Good night."

Vivienne descended from the car, and Cartwright drove off without another word, leaving her more mystified than ever. What was the man's game, she asked herself angrily? Had he been trying to convey a warning, and, if so, what was the nature of it? That he suspected Austin, and had grounds for his suspicions? It had sounded very like it, and Vivienne shuddered slightly as she recalled the tone in which he had spoken.

The thought of Mr. Cartwright and his strange words haunted her all through the evening, and well into the following day. She wished that she had never promised to go to Fordington that afternoon, and she felt very much inclined to ring up Mrs. Cartwright and make some excuse. She was only dissuaded from doing so by her eager wish to see more of Mrs. Wynter, and by the thought that she could leave Fordington before Mr. Cartwright returned from his mill. But it was not without some slight feeling of trepidation that, for the third afternoon in succession, she rang the bell of White Lodge.

She found Mrs. Cartwright waiting for her, in a great state of flurry. "My dear, isn't it maddening!" she exclaimed, as soon as Vivienne came in. "I meant to take Anne the rest of that box of chocolates you gave me yesterday. I knew you wouldn't mind, and Anne would be so pleased. But I can't think where I can have put them. I ate a few more after you left yesterday, but there were still lots left. I hadn't even finished the top layer. And now I can't find them anywhere. Frank must have hidden them somewhere. He always says that I eat too many chocolates if they're left about."

She was bustling about the room as she spoke, looking in all sorts of unlikely places. Vivienne smiled as she watched her. She could not help liking this rather ineffective woman, thoroughly good-natured in spite of all her shallowness. She was about to help in the search, when Mrs. Cartwright uttered a sudden exclamation.

"Why, here they are, in this bureau! I should never have thought of looking there, would you? And I haven't eaten so many, after all. Look, there are still six left in the top layer, and the bottom layer hasn't been touched yet. Three round and three square. I put the other square ones away for Anne somewhere, but it doesn't matter now, there'll be plenty more in the bottom of the box, Birdley always packs them in alternate rows. Shall we go over to Monk's Barn now? I told Anne that we would turn up soon after four o'clock."

They left White Lodge by the side door, crossed the village street, and rang the front-door bell of Monk's Barn. The door was opened by a stranger to Vivienne, evidently Phyllis's successor, and they were shown into the drawing-room.

Anne Wynter rose to greet them, a gracious smile upon her face. "So here you are, Ursula," she said. "And I see that you have persuaded Miss Perrin to come with you. It is really very good of you to come all the way from Yatebury to see me, Miss Perrin."

Vivienne wondered whether it was a trick of her imagination, or whether she really detected a note of irony in Mrs. Wynter's last words. But before she could reply, Ursula Cartwright was speaking, with her usual fluency.

"Miss Perrin is the kindest-hearted person in the world, my dear. She took all the trouble to come to tea with us yesterday, just because I said that Frank would like to see her again, and, you know, the only day he is home to tea is Thursday. And what do you think she brought with her? One of those lovely boxes of chocolates from Birdley's! I've been dreadfully greedy and eaten nearly all the top layer. Only the round ones, of course. I kept the square ones for you, but I put them away somewhere and can't find them. So I've brought the box with me, as Miss Perrin said I might."

"How very good of you, Ursula," replied Anne, "I shall love one or two after tea. I haven't tasted Birdley's chocolates for a long time."

Tea was brought in, and the conversation became more general. Vivienne soon found that Anne was a woman of a much wider outlook than Ursula. She talked about books, plays, and other subjects in which Vivienne could take part. She seemed particularly anxious to lead the conversation away from Fordington and its associations, and, despite several incursions on the part of Ursula, she succeeded.

It was not until tea was over that the chocolates were mentioned again. Then Ursula, during a momentary pause in the conversation, put in her word again. "Do bring out those chocolates, Anne," she said, "I'm dying for one or two of them. Do you know, I believe I should have eaten them all this afternoon, if I hadn't lost them. I only found them again just before we came over."

Anne opened the box and offered it to Vivienne, who shook her head. "Not for me, thank you, Mrs. Wynter," she said. "I'm one of those depraved people who don't like chocolates."

"It probably shows a much more depraved taste to like them," replied Anne. "Never mind, I'm quite sure that Ursula and I shall be able to account for your share. *Come along, Ursula, you won't refuse, I know."

She held out the box as she spoke, and Mrs. Cartwright select-ed a chocolate from among the half-dozen or so that remained on the top layer. "They are good!" she exclaimed, as she put it in her mouth. "I don't believe that anybody in the world makes chocolates like Birdley, do you, Anne?"

"No, I don't," replied Anne, as she, too, put a chocolate in her mouth. "I haven't had any for a long time. They always remind me of Austin. He's my brother-in-law, Miss Perrin. We never saw much of one another, but he always used to come over on my birth-day and bring a box of these chocolates with him. I always ate the square ones, and passed the round ones on to Ursula. We always shared like that when either of us got a box. Come on, Ursula."

The chocolates remaining in the top layer very soon dis-appeared, and Anne, who held the box on her lap, began to re-move the paper and packing above the bottom layer. Vivienne glanced from her to Ursula, who had become unusually silent during the past few seconds. To Vivienne's concern she had all at once become pale, with a sickly greenish tinge beneath the pallor. As Vivienne glanced at her, she dragged herself from her chair, apparently with some difficulty.

"I'm awfully sorry, Anne," she muttered thickly. "I must run away for a moment. I feel deathly sick—"

Anne jumped to her feet. "I'm so sorry, dear!" she exclaimed. "Shall I come with you?"

"No. It's all right," replied Ursula, in a voice which sounded as though each word were dragged from her with difficulty. "I know my way. I shall be all right in a moment—"

She tottered towards the door, dragging herself as though stricken with sudden paralysis. Then, before Anne or Vivienne could reach her, she uttered a deep groan, and fell full length upon the floor.

Vivienne, utterly horrified, sprang across the room and knelt beside her. As she did so, she heard a wild cry of utter anguish from Anne, who sat collapsed in her chair, her hands clasped across her face as though to shut out the sight. Vivienne realized that she would have to take charge of the situation.

She rose to her feet and ran across to the bell, which she pressed feverishly. Then she returned to Ursula's side, and put a cushion under her head. Her whole body was stiff and rigid, and though, from her agonized expression, it was clear that she was conscious and trying to say something, no words came to her dry lips. There was something terribly menacing about her appearance, and Vivienne, who had a slight knowledge of nursing, knew instinctively that her case was desperate.

The door opened, and a maid appeared. "Ring up Doctor Palmer at once," said Vivienne sharply, "tell him to come here without any delay. Mrs. Cartwright has had a sudden attack, and is very ill. Then go across to White Lodge, and leave word for Mr. Cartwright to come over as soon as he gets back."

The maid, after one horrified glance at the figure on the floor, took to her heels and ran. Vivienne turned once more to Ursula. It seemed to Vivienne's horrified mind that Ursula was dying rapidly beneath her eyes.

CHAPTER XXI

IT SEEMED to Vivienne that for countless ages she knelt by the side of Ursula's prostrate body. A feeling of utter helplessness and isolation descended upon her. It was as though she were alone in the world, watching the life ebbing from a woman to whom she felt strangely attached, powerless to do anything to help her.

The mystery of this sudden attack was beyond her. In a confused way she imagined that it must be due to heart trouble, and that, if only she knew what to do, the awful rigidity and speechlessness would pass. In desperation she turned to Anne. "Mrs. Wynter!" she cried, "have you ever known Mrs. Cartwright like this before?" Anne did not appear to hear her. She had buried her face in the cushions of her chair, and was sobbing hysterically. It was perfectly clear that no assistance could be expected from her.

A sudden terror seized Vivienne, and only by a desperate effort could she restrain herself from leaping to her feet and dashing out of this accursed house. For she remembered that it was a fortnight, almost to the hour, since Gilbert Wynter had fallen with a crash in the room above, a bullet through his head.

She was still struggling with her insane desire to fly from the spot when the door opened and Doctor Palmer came in. He took in the whole scene at a glance, Ursula lying in that horribly unnatural posture on the floor, Anne collapsed in her chair, Vivienne pale and wild-eyed, but still retaining command over herself. He knelt over Ursula, and examined her with deft and rapid movements. Then, with a muttered exclamation, he opened the bag which he had brought with him, and took out a hypodermic syringe and a tube of tiny tablets.

"I want some warm water," he said sharply. "If there's any left in the jug on the tea-table, that will do."

Vivienne rose to her feet and fetched the jug. The very fact of having something to do pulled her together. She watched Doctor Palmer as though fascinated, while he prepared the solution and injected it into Ursula's arm.

"We must try to make her swallow an emetic," he said. "And you might get some hot coffee made. No, I'd rather you didn't leave the room, please. Ring the bell and tell the maid to make the coffee at once. As strong as possible, mind."

Vivienne obeyed. Not until she had given the order did Doctor Palmer speak again. "Were you here when Mrs. Cartwright was taken ill?" he asked sharply.

"Yes, I was having tea with her and Mrs. Wynter," Vivienne replied.

"Were you? Do you feel all right? Yes, there doesn't seem to be anything wrong with you." He walked swiftly across the room and examined Anne Wynter, who made no resistance as he felt her pulse, and raised her head to stare fixedly into her eyes. He left her abruptly and came back to Ursula. "Help me to lift her on to that sofa," he said.

Between them they lifted her. She remained as rigid as steel, and Doctor Palmer frowned as he looked at her. "How long is it since she first appeared to be taken ill?"

Vivienne hesitated before she replied. It seemed to her that she had endured a lifetime since Ursula had tottered and fallen before her horrified eyes. She glanced at the clock, and saw to her amazement that it was only half an hour since they had finished tea. She thought for the moment that the clock must have stopped, but its solemn tick, loud and insistent in the silent room, showed that it could not be so. "About twenty minutes," she replied.

"So short a time as that? She must have had a very large dose! We must risk another injection."

Mechanically Vivienne handed him the hot-water jug. One word was ringing through her head. A very large dose! Dose of what? What intolerable meaning lay beneath Doctor Palmer's words. The horror of it overcame her. "What —what is it, Doctor?" she asked, in a trembling voice.

Doctor Palmer looked at her critically. "I don't want you fainting on my hands," he said roughly, with a glance in Anne's direction. "I've enough to do already." He seemed satisfied, however, from his inspection of Vivienne, that she was not of the type to faint easily. He lowered his voice and continued. "Mrs. Cartwright is suffering from poisoning by one of the alkaloids, I don't know which, as yet."

Vivienne could scarcely repress a cry. Poisoning! The idea was incredible. A cold wave of fear ran through her, and for an instant she swayed upon her feet.

"Steady!" exclaimed Doctor Palmer. "You're all right, you'd have shown symptoms by now if you'd taken any. So would Mrs. Wynter. You're a stranger here, aren't you? I haven't seen you before."

"My name is Perrin," replied Vivienne. "I was staying in Fordington last week for a few days, and that's how I met Mrs. Cartwright."

"Oh, you're Miss Perrin, are you?" said Doctor Palmer. "I've heard about you, of course. I shall have to ask you a few questions, if you don't mind. Ah, here's that coffee. Hold the cup, will you, and I'll try to get a little down her throat."

The attempt was only partially successful, and Doctor Palmer shook his head gloomily. "I don't like the look of it," he said. "But there's nothing more we can do. She's almost completely paralysed."

He took off his overcoat and arranged it over her. "When did you first see her this afternoon?" he asked.

"A few minutes before four. I met her at White Lodge, and we came across here together."

"She seemed all right then? Quite well and normal? She hasn't been out of your sight since?"

"As far as I can tell, she was quite well and happy. We have been together ever since I arrived at White Lodge."

Doctor Palmer glanced at the clock. "Hm!" he said. "It's nearly half-past five now. That's to say she was taken ill about five, according to you. She couldn't have taken the poison before four, or she'd have felt the effects sooner. That means to say that she must have taken it in your presence. What has she had to eat or drink, since you've been with her?"

"We all had tea. You can see the remains of it still on the table. And Mrs. Cartwright brought a box of chocolates with her. The box is on the floor now, beside Mrs. Wynter's chair."

"Chocolates, eh!" muttered Doctor Palmer. He strode across the room towards the box, which had fallen from Anne's lap. It lay on the floor, its contents scattered over the carpet round it. Doctor Palmer picked up the box and looked at it. "Birdley's chocolates," he said. "Do you happen to know when Mrs. Cartwright bought them?"

"She didn't buy them. I brought them to her yesterday. She ate some of them then, and brought the rest over here."

Doctor Palmer bent over his patient with a quick gesture. Vivienne could not see his face, but there was a subtle change in his voice when, after an interval, he spoke again. "Did you eat many of these chocolates yourself, Miss Perrin?" he asked.

"I didn't eat any," Vivienne replied. "Mrs. Cartwright ate several yesterday. She told me that she liked the round ones, and would keep the others for Mrs. Wynter. And Mrs. Cartwright and Mrs. Wynter ate about half a dozen between them after tea this afternoon."

"Hm," said Doctor Palmer again. He seemed clearly uncertain as to what was his best course to take. He glanced again at Anne, who seemed gradually to be recovering herself. Then he turned to Vivienne. "Do you think you could persuade Mrs. Wynter to go upstairs to her room?" he asked. "And I think perhaps that it would be as well if you went with her to look after her. There is very little more to be done here, I am afraid. I must ask both you and Mrs. Wynter not to leave the house. It is possible that either or both of you may have taken a small dose of the poison, and I must keep you under observation for an hour or two."

Vivienne nodded, and after a last shuddering look at the distorted form of Mrs. Cartwright, she walked across the room and touched Anne on the shoulder. "Doctor Palmer says that we should be better upstairs," she said.

Rather to her astonishment Anne rose obediently, like a child, and allowed Vivienne to lead her towards the door. She averted her eyes from the sofa, walking like one in a dream. Doctor Palmer opened the door for them. "Better see if you can get hold of Cartwright," he whispered. "Try the Mill at Stourminster. He may still be there. Tell him that his wife has been taken suddenly ill, and that he had better come here at once."

Vivienne nodded, and having led Anne upstairs, she came down again and went to the telephone. Mr. Cartwright's number at Stourminster was written on a slate by the instrument, and she put a call through, only to learn that he had left the mill half an hour earlier. Thinking that he should be home by now, she tried White Lodge. The servant who answered her said that he had not yet arrived. Leaving a message that he was to come over as soon as possible, Vivienne rang off, and made a third call. This time the number was that of Wynter & Son at Yatebury.

It seemed an age before she was put through. Time was getting on, and any moment Austin might leave the office and be out of her reach. A voice replied to her at last, and to her inquiry replied that Mr. Wynter was just going. A few seconds later Vivienne heard his voice at the other end of the line.

"Is that you, Mr. Wynter?" she asked hurriedly. "This is Vivienne Perrin speaking. I'm at Monk's Barn. I want you to do something for me, at once. Will you?"

"Of course," replied Austin. But some trace of her anxiety must have been apparent in her voice. "What is it?" he continued anxiously. "Has anything happened? Are you all right?"

"I'm all right. I can't talk to you now. Will you put a trunk call through to my brother, and tell him from me that I want him to come down to Yatebury at once? Better try the flat, Kensington 177460."

She waited until Austin had repeated the number, and she was sure that he had understood the urgency of her message. Then, before he could ask any further questions, she rang off. Not a sound came from within the drawing-room, and, with a heavy heart, she went upstairs again to Anne's room.

Anne was lying dry-eyed, staring vacantly at the fire that flickered in the grate. The shock of Ursula's sudden collapse seemed to have paralysed her faculties. She looked at Vivienne, as though trying to recall who she was. Then a sudden light dawned in her eyes, and she spoke feverishly.

"You've seen Ursula again? How is she? What does Doctor Palmer say?"

"I haven't seen her again," replied Vivienne quietly. "I have been to telephone for Mr. Cartwright."

A slight shudder seemed to run through Anne's frame. "Frank? Yes, of course. He should be here to look after her. But she—she'll be all right, won't she, Miss Perrin?"

There was an eagerness in her tone, a pleading to be convinced, that Vivienne could not resist. "We can't do more than leave her in Doctor Palmer's hands," she replied as brightly as she could.

"I hope you don't mind my staying here like this, Mrs. Wynter. Doctor Palmer doesn't want either of us to leave the house. You see, he thinks that Mrs. Cartwright may have—have eaten something that has disagreed with her, and he is afraid that we may show traces of it, too."

Anne's eyes took on a queer look. "I don't think he need be afraid," she said. And then suddenly she burst into tears once more. "Not again!" she moaned. "Not again! I can't bear it, I shall go mad!"

She buried her face in the pillows, and Vivienne, trying to collect her scattered wits, stared at her sob-shaken figure. It was, of course, a terrible shock to Anne that one of her best friends had been taken suddenly ill in her drawing-room, so soon after the tragic death of her husband. But was this shock sufficient to account for the extraordinary state in which she seemed to be? She had been remarkably self-possessed until the moment of Ursula's collapse, almost remarkably so, Vivienne had thought. But from that very moment she had seemed convinced that some terrible tragedy had occurred.

Yet, Vivienne reflected she could not possibly have overheard Doctor Palmer's words. Only Vivienne herself and the Doctor knew as yet that Ursula Cartwright had been poisoned. Was it accidental, or by design? Was this some new mystery, or merely a second manifestation of the horror that seemed to brood over Monk's Barn like an inescapable curse?

Like a prisoner Vivienne sat in a chair beside the bed, fighting the numbness that seemed to have crept over her mind. Strive as she would, she could not control her thoughts, could not force herself to look at the tragedy impersonally.

It was as though events of which hitherto she had been only a watcher had suddenly thrust out a tentacle and drawn her into their power.

Outwardly calm, but her brain a seething mass of incoherent thoughts, she sat and waited for she knew not what. Hours seemed to pass, and she strained her ears for any sound of movement from below. She heard the front door open, then, after a short interval, the sound of heavy footsteps in the hall. This was followed by a murmured conversation, and then the sound of a man's deep voice at the telephone, speaking words she could not catch. A little later, the door opened again, and she recognized Frank Cartwright's voice, speaking in agitated tones.

Shortly after this she heard a car draw up at the front door, and the sound of voices in the hall. Followed a long silence, so long that it seemed to Vivienne to stretch into eternity. And then, at last, footsteps in the corridor, a tap on the door, the white, scared face of a maid.

"Please, Miss Perrin, Superintendent Swayne would like to see you in the dining-room."

CHAPTER XXII

AUSTIN Wynter succeeded in getting Christopher on the telephone, and gave him Vivienne's message.

"All right," replied Christopher. "There's a late train which gets in about eleven, isn't there? I'll come down by that. You don't happen to know why she wants me, I suppose?"

"No, I don't. She rang up from Monk's Barn. I gather that it's pretty urgent. Miss Perrin assured me that she was all right, herself."

"Very well, if you see her, tell her that I'll be at the 'King's Head' soon after eleven."

Christopher rang off, and set about making preparations for his journey. He was very puzzled to know the reason for this sudden summons. It could hardly be that any danger threatened their client, or he would have known of it. Vivienne must have come upon some piece of information upon which it would be possible to act, he concluded.

He felt ill at ease, in spite of his efforts to reassure himself, throughout the journey to Yatebury. It was with a feeling of acute anxiety that he got out of the train and hurried along the platform towards the exit. He had almost reached it, when he felt a touch upon his shoulder, and turned to find Austin Wynter by his side, his face drawn and harassed in the uncertain light of the station lamps.

"Thank God you've come!" exclaimed Austin in a low voice. "I've got my car outside, and I'll drive you to the 'King's Head.'"

"Vivienne?" inquired Christopher sharply.

"Miss Perrin's all right, she's waiting for you. Come along."

Christopher nodded, and followed his client without further question. He realized well enough that a railway station was no place in which to exchange confidences. They reached the car, and as soon as they were safely in it, Austin spoke. "Ursula Cartwright is dead!" he remarked, tersely, as he let in the clutch.

Christopher uttered a sharp exclamation. "Dead! How did it happen?"

"I don't know. There's something horribly mysterious about the whole thing. She died after being taken suddenly ill after tea at Monk's Barn this afternoon. Miss Perrin was there at the time. Superintendent Swayne told me that much."

"Superintendent Swayne! Then it's a matter for the police?"

"I'm afraid so. This is the second time something awful has happened at Monk's Barn. I don't know the details. I was rather anxious about Miss Perrin's message to you. She didn't tell me anything, but I knew from the sound of her voice that it was deadly serious. So I went to the 'King's Head' and waited for her. She didn't come in till after nine, and then she appeared in Swayne's car. He'd driven her back from Monk's Barn. She just nodded to me, and went straight up to her room.

"Then Swayne drew me aside. He said he knew that Miss Perrin had rung me up from Monk's Barn this evening, and asked me what it was about. I saw no harm in telling him, and he seemed quite pleased. He told me then that there had been a tragedy, and that Mrs. Cartwright was dead. And he also said that he would communicate with you after you arrived, if he could find time."

Christopher had no time to reply before the car drew up at the door of the hotel. He jumped out, with a word of thanks to Austin, and rang the bell. The night porter appeared, and he asked for the number of Vivienne's room. Within a few seconds he was knocking at the door. Her voice bade him come in. As he entered the room Vivienne rose from her chair and flung herself into his arms, all her hitherto restrained emotion finding vent in a flood of uncontrollable tears.

He comforted her as best he could. "Poor old girl!" he murmured. "You've had a rotten experience, I know. Austin drove me from the station, and told me something about it. It's all over now, and I'm here to help you if I can."

The storm of weeping ended as suddenly as it had begun. "Sorry, Chris," she said, with a pathetic attempt at a smile. "I don't often behave like that. It was dear of you to come. The time has seemed so terribly long alone. An awful thing has happened, and I don't know what to do."

"Never mind. Hadn't you better go to bed now, and we'll talk about it in the morning?" She shook her head violently. "Go to bed!" she exclaimed. "Do you think I could sleep? No, I'm all right again now. Just having you here makes all the difference. Sit down, and I'll tell you about it."

Christopher obeyed her, thinking it best to humour her. Vivienne gave him a full account of her visit to Monk's Barn, and of the tragic suddenness with which Ursula Cartwright had been taken ill.

"Everything devolved upon me," she continued. "Anne Wynter simply collapsed as soon as it happened. She seemed to know instinctively that something awful had taken place, and was completely overcome by the horror of it. I sent for Doctor Palmer, who gave it as his opinion, almost as soon as he saw her, that Ursula Cartwright had been poisoned."

"Poisoned!" exclaimed Christopher, in a tone of horror. "How on earth did it happen?"

"I don't know. That's the dreadful part about it. After a bit, Doctor Palmer sent me upstairs to look after Mrs. Wynter. I tried to get hold of Mr. Cartwright, and then I thought of asking Austin to send for you. I waited upstairs for ages, and then I got a message that Superintendent Swayne wanted to see me.

"I went down, and found Swayne in the dining-room. He was quite nice to me, but I could see from his expression that the worst had happened. He told me that Mrs. Cartwright was dead, and asked me to describe exactly what had happened. I told him all I knew, as I have just told you. Then he asked me if she had eaten or drunk anything that I or Mrs. Wynter hadn't."

"Presumably she must have," remarked Christopher, "That is, if neither you nor Mrs. Wynter felt any symptoms."

"I didn't, and, to the best of my knowledge, Mrs. Wynter didn't either. Of course, I couldn't remember exactly what Mrs. Cartwright had had for tea. There was bread and butter, and cakes, and all that sort of thing. But I feel pretty certain that Mrs. Cartwright didn't take anything that either Mrs. Wynter or I didn't have too. And we all took tea, milk and sugar. At least, I think so."

"There have been cases where one particular lump of sugar has been poisoned," said Christopher thoughtfully. "Who poured out tea? Mrs. Wynter, I suppose?"

"Yes. But there's another thing. Yesterday I was given a box of chocolates. Now, as you know, I never touch chocolates, so that afternoon I gave them to Mrs. Cartwright. This evening she took them with her to Monk's Barn, and she and Mrs. Wynter each had some after tea."

"Did they finish them?" asked Christopher quickly.

"No, they only finished the top layer. They were going to begin the bottom one when Mrs. Cartwright was taken ill. The box was upset, and the rest of the chocolates fell on the floor."

"You told Swayne about them, I suppose?"

"Yes. When he had asked me a lot more questions, he said that Doctor Palmer would like to see me. Doctor Palmer asked me if I was sure that I felt all right, and then told me that any danger of my having been poisoned too was past. He gave me something to take to soothe my nerves. I've got it in my bag now. And then the Superintendent drove me back here. He made me promise that I wouldn't leave Yatebury without letting him know."

"Quite right. Now, look here, Vi, we shall want all our energies to-morrow, I can see that. Have you got the stuff that Doctor Palmer gave you?"

Vivienne produced it, and Christopher insisted on her taking it. Then, seeing that she was greatly relieved by the knowledge that he was on the spot, he left her and returned to the lounge.

He had not been there many minutes before the night porter appeared. "Mr. Perrin, sir?" he asked. "Superintendent Swayne would like to speak to you on the telephone."

Christopher went to the instrument and answered the call. "That you, Mr. Perrin?" came Swayne's voice. "It's a bit late, I know, but I'd be very grateful if you'd come along to my office and see me."

"I'll come at once," replied Christopher. He left the hotel, and, within a few minutes, reached the police station. The Superintendent was waiting for him, and greeted him warmly.

"It's very good of you to come at this time of night," he said. "You've seen Miss Perrin? Austin Wynter came round and told me that you had arrived, and that he'd driven you to the 'King's Head.'"

"Yes, I've seen her," replied Christopher slowly. "This is a very terrible thing, Superintendent."

"It's ghastly. It almost seems as though there were a curse upon that house. I suppose Miss Perrin told you what happened? She's a wonderful girl, that sister of yours. She was naturally very much upset, but nobody could have given a clearer account. And Doctor Palmer says that she kept her head wonderfully. How did you find her?"

"A bit overwrought, as one might expect, but I think she's better now. I hope she'll sleep. How did you come into this, Superintendent?"

"Doctor Palmer. He got the ladies upstairs, then ran across and fetched Burden, who telephoned straight to me. I drove over, and the first person I ran into was Frank Cartwright. I had a very bad quarter of an hour with him. Of course, I'm ready to make every allowance for his feelings. Mrs. Cartwright had died within a few minutes of his reaching Monk's Barn, and the shock was enough to unnerve anybody. He doesn't seem in any way excited. He was just wildly desperate, if you know what I mean."

Christopher nodded. "I think I understand," he said.

"He turned on me as soon as he saw me," continued Swayne. "He said, quite calmly, that he'd take the law into his own hands if I didn't bring the murderer to book. He had reached the limit of patience. First his best friend had been murdered, and now his wife. I had bungled the first case, and if I bungled the second he would see that I lost my job. I tried to pacify him, but he simply wouldn't listen to anything I had to say."

"He jumped to the conclusion that his wife had been murdered, then?"

"It wasn't much of a jump. Doctor Palmer has no doubt of it, and I don't see any other alternative myself. Of course, I've taken immediate steps. The drawing-room at Monk's Barn has been sealed up, and everything eatable or drinkable found in it has been sent away by special messenger for analysis. Doctor Palmer and the police surgeon are going to make a post-mortem to-night, and the contents of the stomach will also be sent to the Home Office expert for analysis. We'll know something by to-morrow afternoon at the latest. Till then, I'm keeping an eye on everybody concerned."

"Your theory being that the same person murdered both Gilbert Wynter and Mrs. Cartwright?" asked Christopher.

"Well, it sounds probable, doesn't it? There's no evidence to connect the two yet, of course."

"Any motive suggested for the murder of Mrs. Cartwright? From what my sister has told me about her, I should have imagined that she was a particularly inoffensive sort of person."

"It's the motive that has been puzzling me," replied Swayne. "Look here, Mr. Perrin, this conversation is absolutely confidential, of course. I think we both understand, though we may not have said so outright, that the murderer of Gilbert Wynter was either Mrs. Wynter or Austin. Now, I refuse to believe that Mrs. Wynter is guilty in this case. If she wanted to poison Mrs. Cartwright she would have done so at any time. I refuse to believe that she deliberately staged the crime in her own drawing-room, and that she went out of her way to ask your sister to be present as a witness. It doesn't sound sense to me."

"Nor to me. Yet, on the other hand, can you suggest any conceivable reason why Austin Wynter should have wanted to murder Mrs. Cartwright, a woman whom he scarcely knew?"

"He disliked the Cartwrights intensely," replied the Superintendent, rather weakly.

"Quite. I dislike plenty of people myself, but I have no intention of trying to murder them. If I might make a suggestion, Superintendent, it is this. It seems to me not entirely beyond the bounds of possibility to imagine a motive for the murder of both Gilbert Wynter and Mrs. Cartwright."

CHAPTER XXIII

ON HIS way back to the "King's Head," Christopher's mind was full of the suggestion that he had just let drop in the Superintendent's office. If there was anything in Croyle's vague hints, in Mintern's account of what he had seen in the garden of Monk's Barn, there might be two people who had excellent reasons of their own for desiring the deaths of Gilbert Wynter and Mrs. Cartwright.

Christopher was the last person in the world to fly to conclusions. He knew very well how utterly misleading any theory founded on motive alone was apt to prove. Yet, even allowing for all that, the possible existence of such a motive undoubtedly gave food for thought.

But there was no denying that the facts did not fit in as they should have. In such cases it was nearly always the man who carried out the murder, either with or without the assistance of the woman. And yet, from his knowledge of the facts, Christopher found it very difficult to see how Frank Cartwright could have murdered either Gilbert Wynter or his wife. Leaving the second murder out of account, since nothing was yet known of it, the shooting of Gilbert Wynter was as puzzling as ever it had been.

A gun was a man's weapon, rather than a woman's. On the other hand, while the facts did not preclude the possibility of the woman having fired the shot, they did unquestionably prove that the man had not fired it. Cartwright must have been in White Lodge when the gun was discharged, or he could not have appeared at the side door immediately afterwards. Nor could there be any doubt that the gun had been fired from the shrubbery, or, at all events from some point within the wall enclosing Monk's Barn. The direction which the bullet had taken proved that, altogether apart from the finding of the gun itself.

Since, then, Cartwright had not fired the shot, the only alternative, if Christopher's assumption of motive was correct, was that Mrs. Wynter had fired it. So far nothing had transpired to disprove this. But Christopher could not rid himself of the conviction that it was not in the least like a woman's crime. It would have required very strong nerves, which Mrs. Wynter, from Vivienne's account of her behaviour when Mrs. Cartwright was taken ill, did not appear to possess. Besides, that amazing accuracy of aim!

He reached the hotel, still wrestling with the intricacies of the problem. Having peeped into Vivienne's room, and ascertained to his satisfaction that she was sleeping peacefully, he too went to bed.

Christopher and Vivienne met for a late breakfast on the following morning. It was perfectly clear to them both that nothing could be done to elucidate this new mystery until the results of the analyses were received. They got through the day somehow, going over and over again through all the possibilities, without being able to reach any satisfactory conclusion. Until at last, about six o'clock in the evening, Christopher was once more summoned to the telephone.

It was Superintendent Swayne speaking. "I've got some news that will interest you, Mr. Perrin," he said. "I'd very much like you to come along. And it would be a great help if you would bring Miss Perrin with you, that is, if she feels equal to it. She can help to check some of the facts I've collected."

"Oh, Vivienne has quite recovered from the shock," replied Christopher. "We'll come along at once."

They started immediately, and found Swayne sitting at his desk, on which lay a sheaf of papers.

He thanked them warmly for coming, especially Vivienne, to whom he showed every possible courtesy. When they were all seated, he began to speak.

"I've got the results of the analyses," he said. "We'd better take the medical one first. Let me see, now. I'll spare you the details as much as possible. In Mrs. Cartwright's body there were found quantities of a drug called hyoscyamine, considerably more than necessary to cause death. Associated with this drug were smaller quantities of hyoscine and atropine. Now, I don't suppose that conveys anything more to me than it did to you. But the analyst goes on to explain. He says that the proportions of the drugs found suggest that the poison was administered in the form of a concentrated extract of the leaves of the common henbane.

"Well, that's that. Now for the analysis of the various eatables found in the room. Nothing out of the ordinary was discovered in anything that was on the tea-table, the cakes and so forth. They were all perfectly harmless. The same thing applies to the tea, sugar and milk. But you will remember, Miss Perrin, that there was a box of chocolates spilt on the floor. I collected these myself, put them in the original box, and sent them off with the rest."

The Superintendent paused and glanced at Vivienne, who nodded silently.

"I think I had better read you the report on those chocolates," Swayne continued. "Here it is: 'The cardboard box, marked as Exhibit D, upon being opened, was found to contain twenty-eight chocolates. These chocolates contained a centre of some creamy substance, flavoured with two distinct fruit extracts, distinguished by the shape of the moulds in which the chocolates had been made. Fourteen of the chocolates were round in horizontal section, and these were flavoured with one extract. The remaining fourteen were square, and were flavoured with the other extract.

"'The round chocolates were examined first, and were found to be made of ordinary ingredients, containing nothing deleterious. Each chocolate was examined in turn. The square chocolates were then examined in the same way. Of these, six were found to contain quantities of the alkaloid hyoscyamine, associated with other substances, in varying quantities. The average quantity of alkaloid in each of these six chocolates was approximately half a grain. It may be pointed out that the maximum dose usually prescribed is one-hundredth of a grain.

"'Examination suggested that alkaloid had been introduced into the chocolates after manufacture. The method employed seems to have been to prepare a highly concentrated tincture of various parts of the henbane plant, and to inject this tincture into the chocolates with a hypodermic syringe. The orifice made by the needle was subsequently closed by melting the chocolate round it, and allowing it to harden." The Superintendent put aside the paper from which he had been reading. "There," he said. "I think that's the gist of the matter. It seems pretty clear that Mrs. Cartwright died through eating poisoned chocolates, doesn't it?" Christopher was about to reply, when Vivienne interrupted him. "There's a mistake somewhere, Superintendent," she remarked. "The report says that some of the square chocolates were poisoned, but that the round ones were all right. Isn't that so?"

Swayne glanced at the paper once more. "Yes, that's right, Miss Perrin. Why?"

"Because Mrs. Cartwright didn't eat any of the square ones," replied Vivienne deliberately.

Both men stared at her in astonishment. "Are you quite sure of that, Miss Perrin?" asked the Superintendent incredulously. "You didn't watch every chocolate she took, I suppose?"

"No, but she said several times, in my presence and in the presence of her husband and Mrs. Wynter, that she only liked the round ones. The square ones she kept for Mrs. Wynter. I gather that this preference was well known, and the two of them frequently shared a box of these particular chocolates in this way."

"If that can be established, it seems to alter the case entirely," said Swayne slowly. "There's no mistake, Miss Perrin, you can be sure of that. The kind of people who drew up this report don't make mistakes. You're quite sure that it was the round ones that Mrs. Cartwright preferred?"

"Quite sure. I saw her eat several of the chocolates on Thursday afternoon, when I took her the box. She chose the round ones in every case, and put the square ones aside for Mrs. Wynter."

"Put them aside, did she? Do you know what happened to them?"

"I don't, I only know that she couldn't lay her hands on them on Friday afternoon."

Swayne sat silent, plunged in thought. Then he turned to Christopher. "Well, what do you make of that piece of information, Mr. Perrin? Seems to upset the theory you hinted at last night, doesn't it?"

"I'm bound to confess that it does," replied Christopher. "If the poisoner knew that Mrs. Wynter had a preference for the square chocolates—and that he or she knew that a preference existed seems to be shown by the fact that only one sort were found to be poisoned—it looks very much as though Mrs. Wynter, and not Mrs. Cartwright, were the intended victim."

"It does, very much. Mrs. Cartwright must have taken one of the square ones inadvertently, and it happened to be a poisoned one. It is a miracle that Mrs. Wynter did not hit upon one of the poisoned ones as well. However, we can only be thankful that she didn't. The point is, how did the poison get there?"

"Have you had an opportunity of tracing the box of chocolates?" asked Christopher anxiously.

"I have. I'll tell you all about it, and Miss Perrin will correct me if I am wrong. They were bought at Birdley's, a confectioner in the High Street here, on Wednesday. Mr. Austin Wynter went into the shop during the afternoon, and asked for a box. As it happened, they had none ready at the time, but informed him that a box would be available about six o'clock. Mr. Austin asked them to send it up to his rooms. Birdley did so, and the box was delivered between six and seven in the evening. It was taken in by Mr. Austin's landlady, who placed it on the table in his room.

"Mr. Austin spent the same evening with Miss Perrin. I know that, for I happened to see them together. Miss Perrin may remember that we had a short conversation together. Mr. Austin then returned to his rooms, where he remained until he went to the works on Thursday morning. When Mr. Austin was called on Thursday morning, he gave his landlady a parcel, addressed to Miss Perrin at the 'King's Head.' He asked her if her son, who works nearly next door to the hotel, would leave the parcel on his way to work. The boy did so. Perhaps Miss Perrin will tell us if she received the parcel, and, if so, what was in it?"

"I received the parcel, and it contained the box of chocolates," replied Vivienne faintly.

"Well, it's pretty certain that they were not poisoned when they left Austin Wynter's hands," remarked Christopher. "Or, at all events, if they were, he didn't know it. You're not going to suggest that his object was to kill my sister, are you?"

"Most certainly I am not. But he knew that there was very little risk of that. You see, on the previous evening, when they went to the cinema together, he bought Miss Perrin a box of chocolates in the entrance hall. I happened to be standing close by—I suppose I may as well admit that I have been interested in Mr. Austin's movements lately. I don't think either of them saw me, just then. And I happened to overhear Miss Perrin tell him that she never ate chocolates."

Vivienne nodded. "That's quite true," she said in a low voice. "I did tell him so."

"But we'll let that pass, for the moment. Now, I haven't been able to trace the box from the time that Miss Perrin received it until she took it to White Lodge on Thursday afternoon."

"It never left me all day," said Vivienne. "I took a 'bus to Stourminster in the morning, lunched there, and came back to Fordington in the afternoon. I had the box with me all the time."

"You went to Stourminster? Did you by any chance meet Mr. Cartwright there?"

"No, I only went there out of curiosity, to see what sort of a place it was."

"I'm afraid that you can't have found it very attractive, Miss Perrin. I have spoken to Mr. Cartwright, and he confirms your having given the box to his wife. He was afraid that she would eat too many at once, and he hid the box inside the lid of a bureau that she never used. At that time there were about half a dozen chocolates left in the top layer. Did you notice if these were still there when you saw the box on Friday?"

"Yes, they were. I remember seeing about half a dozen on the top of the box. Mrs. Cartwright could not find the box until she opened the lid of the bureau. I was there at the time."

"That certainly goes to show that the box was there from the time that Mr. Cartwright hid it on Thursday evening until then. The bureau was not locked, I suppose?"

"I think it was locked, but the key was in the lock. I couldn't be sure of that."

"It looks as though the only occasions on which the chocolates could have been tampered with were on Wednesday or Thursday night," remarked Christopher thoughtfully.

"Yes. By someone who wished to contrive Mrs. Wynter's death," replied the Superintendent. "As I said just now, your theory will want a bit of revising. We've got to look for somebody who would benefit by the deaths of both Gilbert Wynter and his wife. And, entirely between ourselves, I don't think we shall have to look very far. If the plot had been successful, Austin Wynter would, at this moment, be the sole owner of the business of Wynter & Son."

CHAPTER XXIV

THE Superintendent's words pierced Vivienne's heart like a dagger. That such a construction could be placed upon the mysterious murders at Monk's Barn had not occurred to her. Yet now, in a flash, she saw it clearly enough.

Yet, knowing that the eyes of the two men were upon her, she strove to restrain any display of the emotions which surged through her. She merely nodded wisely, as one who appreciates a wholly impersonal point. She sat there, apparently listening to their further conversation, but, actually, her mind was filled with the roaring torrent of her own thoughts, striving to evolve some reason from their headlong rush.

Hitherto, she had regarded the danger in which Austin stood as, at the most, an awkward circumstance. So convinced had she been in her own mind of his innocence, that she had been more amused than otherwise at the police having suspicions that he had murdered his brother. But now she realized that the death of Mrs. Cartwright had entirely altered the state of affairs. There was no denying the fact that everything pointed to the unfortunate woman having been an accidental victim; that the murderer's hand had been pointed at Mrs. Wynter. And she could not combat the logic of Swayne's deduction. Who but Austin could have desired the removal of both Gilbert Wynter and his wife?

And yet, in spite of logic, her faith in Austin never wavered for an instant. Proof might be piled upon proof, but that, she knew, would never shake her in the least. For, amidst the swirl and eddy of a thousand conflicting emotions, one incontrovertible fact arose like a beacon, bright and firm in the heart of the troubled waters. She knew at last that she loved him, and that, beside that love, the logic of circumstances was powerless to shake her faith.

She sat there, in the drab environment of the Superintendent's office, only half hearing what her brother and Swayne were saying. She felt impelled to cry out, to show them the obvious folly of wasting time over the discussion of Austin, since it was impossible that he could have had anything to do with it. It was like listening to two children, arguing about things which they could not understand. But she managed to control herself, and their words came to her, as though from a great distance.

"There's no question of accident, in either case," Swayne was saying. "And it's obviously more than coincidence that both deaths took place at Monk's Barn. It's a perfectly safe assumption that they were both the work of one and the same person. I think you'll agree that, Mr. Perrin?"

"Yes, I'm with you there," replied Christopher.

"It's hardly likely that two distinct people would choose the same scene for their crimes."

"Well, then, let's examine the first murder in the light of the second. I never concealed from you the fact that I thought that Mrs. Wynter might have had something to do with killing her husband. Put it this way. His will was in her favour. They didn't get on together; she may even have known or suspected his affair with Phyllis. Local gossip suggests that she was more or less in love with Cartwright. It was always possible that she may have come to the conclusion that murder was a more satisfactory way out of her difficulties than divorce. We're agreed there, too, I think?"

Christopher nodded, and Swayne continued. "Against it, as I said before, was the fact that it was utterly unlike a woman's crime. And, now that Mrs. Wynter herself has only escaped being murdered, by a miracle, I think we can definitely rule her out from any suspicion of complicity in the first crime. And, if the person committed both, then all outside people like Mintern are ruled out as well. The same argument applies to Cartwright. We know he couldn't have committed the first, and we may assume therefore that he didn't commit the second. Apart from that, I can't imagine any possible reason for his attempting Mrs. Wynter's life. Remains only your client, as you're bound to admit."

"No. I won't go so far as that. The world isn't so small that there may be someone else in the case, who has so far contrived to keep in the background. We mustn't lose sight of that possibility."

Swayne shook his head. "I'm not losing sight of it, but the possibility is exceedingly remote. I'm not saying that some person may exist who might conceivably have a motive for wishing to murder Gilbert Wynter and his wife. Motive is always a desperately difficult thing to discover, and there may be some obscure story which we have not heard of. But look at the opportunity. Honestly, Mr. Perrin, can even your imagination produce any person who could both have shot Gilbert Wynter and poisoned the chocolates, selecting only those which Mrs. Wynter favoured? Frankly, mine can't."

"Without a much wider knowledge of the Wynters' friends and acquaintances, I can't," replied Christopher. "But, I repeat, it isn't altogether impossible."

"I admire your optimism. Now, let's look into the history of that box of chocolates, quite impersonally. They were ordered from Birdley's on Wednesday afternoon. They were delivered to Austin's rooms that evening, where they remained for the night. On Thursday morning they were taken to the 'King's Head,' and given to Miss Perrin. Miss Perrin had charge of them all day, until the afternoon, when she passed them on to Mrs. Cartwright. Throughout Thursday night and the greater part of Friday they were at White Lodge, until Mrs. Cartwright took them to Monk's Barn and handed them on to Mrs. Wynter. At what stage was the poison introduced into them?"

Christopher shrugged his shoulders. "The opportunity seems to be pretty wide," he remarked.

"It is. Let's examine it. Remember, I'm speaking of possibilities only. They may have been poisoned when they left Birdley's. They may have been poisoned while they were in Austin's rooms, by anybody who had access to them there. They may have been poisoned by Miss Perrin. Finally, they may have been poisoned while they were at White Lodge, by Mr. or Mrs. Cartwright or any of their servants. That's about all, I think."

"Well, if we are going to arrive at the poisoner by a process of elimination, we can begin with Birdley's," remarked Christopher with a smile. "I know nothing of the shop, but I don't imagine that a respectable confectioner would be likely to sell poisoned chocolates. And I think we might strike out Vivienne, too. She may have had some motive for trying to kill Mrs. Wynter that I don't know of, but I doubt it. Besides, if the theory that the same person carried out both murders is correct, she's absolved anyhow. She has a perfectly good alibi in London covering the time when Gilbert Wynter was shot."

The Superintendent allowed himself a hearty laugh. "Yes, I'm quite ready to eliminate Miss Perrin," he replied. "Remember, I warned you that I was only stating the possibilities. Seriously, I think we can limit the tampering with the chocolates to Wednesday and Thursday nights, when they were at Austin's rooms and White Lodge respectively."

"There is just this about it, Superintendent," said Christopher thoughtfully. "There's a difficulty about the chocolates having been poisoned on Wednesday night. Mrs. Cartwright ate several of them on Thursday without feeling any ill effects."

"Yes, but she only ate the round ones," said Swayne significantly. "You remember what Miss Perrin told us just now. The square ones she put aside for Mrs. Wynter. I shall make it my business to find out what became of those, of course. I've already warned Mr. Cartwright that no chocolates found at White Lodge are to be eaten under any circumstances whatever. If Mrs. Cartwright had kept to her usual habit on Friday evening she would be alive now. She must have taken one of the square ones inadvertently, and hit by chance upon one of those which had been poisoned.

"Now, about the poison itself. I had a chat, in confidence, of course, with Warburton, our local chemist. He's a clever chap, and, what's more, I can trust him to keep his mouth shut. I asked him about this henbane stuff, and he told me that it is fairly extensively grown for medical purposes. He doesn't know of its being cultivated anywhere about here, but it grows wild in North Somersetshire, and he's often seen a stray plant or two in wild places close round here. He gave it as his opinion that anybody who wanted henbane and could recognize it when they saw it would have no difficulty in collecting as much as they wanted."

"Well, I'll accept Warburton's word for that. I'm no botanist myself. But, having collected the henbane, some knowledge of pharmacy would be required to extract these drugs you speak of from it."

"Very little," replied Swayne. "I asked Warburton about that. It seems that anybody who had a book of reference and some simple apparatus could do it. Of course, it wouldn't do to boil down the leaves and so forth and make a sort of tea out of them. It's a bit more complicated than that. A man would want some sort of laboratory to get the drugs sufficiently concentrated. But it wouldn't require a skilled chemist."

"I see what you're driving at. The murderer wouldn't risk trying to buy the drugs already prepared. He'd run too much risk of being traced, even if he succeeded in procuring them at all, without a doctor's prescription. If he knew how, he would naturally produce them himself from the henbane plant."

"Exactly. Now, let's approach the question from that point of view. Is there anybody in the case who possesses the necessary knowledge, both to recognize the henbane plant and to extract the drugs from it? I think there is. Austin Wynter is a man who has studied science in very nearly all its branches. Of course, he has concentrated upon the electrical side, since that is of most use to him in his business. But I happen to know that, incidentally, he is a bit of a botanist. And it's also a fact that there is a laboratory of sorts at the works, which he often uses for experiments, chemical as well as mechanical."

"Possibly. But a knowledge of botany and chemistry is not confined to our client."

"Certainly not. Don't think I'm prejudiced, Mr. Perrin. I'm only trying to be fair with you. Look here, I've jotted down a few notes on a piece of paper, and I'll read them to you.

"Here they are. I'll say nothing about motive, merely opportunity. First of all, circumstances connected with the murder of Gilbert Wynter. No witnesses have been produced who can testify to Austin Wynter's actions between six and twenty to eight that evening. Austin admits that he had an argument with his brother that afternoon. Since his brother's opposition has been removed, he has put his own ideas into execution. Croyle admits that he took the key of the yard gates on the night of the murder. Croyle was to some extent under an obligation to Austin. If Austin could have obtained access to the Monk's Barn garden, it would have been possible for him to go there, fire the shot, and return to Yatebury between six and the time he returned to his rooms. Austin is said to be a very good shot.

"That's the first list of notes. Now we come to the second. Circumstances connected with the murder of Ursula Cartwright. The fact that only the square chocolates were poisoned points to the attempt having been directed at Anne Wynter. Anne Wynter, through her representative, Frank Cartwright, has been questioning Austin's actions at the works since his brother's death. Austin presents a box of chocolates to Miss Perrin, knowing that, even if they were poisoned, she would run no risk, since she had told him the previous evening that she did not eat chocolates. Austin knew that Miss Perrin had been invited to tea with Mrs. Wynter in the near future, and may well have thought that she would naturally take the chocolates with her. Austin has considerable botanical and chemical knowledge. Under the terms of their father's will, Gilbert's share of the business reverts to Austin on the death of Gilbert's wife."

Swayne laid down the paper and looked Christopher squarely in the face. "That's my summing up of the facts," he said shortly.

Christopher rose from his chair, and beckoned to Vivienne, who, pale and anxious, followed his example. "It's very good of you to put your cards on the table like this, Superintendent," said Christopher gravely. "In return, I can only promise you this, that if any scrap of evidence comes my way, you shall have it at once. Come along, Vi, we mustn't waste the Superintendent's time any longer."

They walked to the door. But, as Christopher was leaving the room, he stopped, as though struck by an afterthought. "By the way, Superintendent, there's one fly in your carefully prepared ointment," he remarked casually.

"What's that?" inquired Swayne.

"Why, how on earth could Austin have known of Mrs. Wynter's preference for the square chocolates?"

Without waiting for a reply he shut the door, and, taking Vivienne's arm, hurried her away.

CHAPTER XXV

VIVIENNE kept silence as she and her brother walked back from the police station. An utterly unaccustomed despair had fallen upon her, its dark folds enveloping her as in a pall. She felt overwhelmed by the strength of the case against Austin, ridiculous as she knew the accusation to be. Her mind steadfastly refused to contemplate the awful possibilities of the future.

She could find no spark of consolation even in her brother's parting shot. There was a reason, she knew, why Austin should have known of Anne Wynter's preference for the square chocolates. Anne herself had said that he was in the habit of bringing her chocolates on her birthday; a formal tribute, no doubt, a sort of conventional rite carried out for his brother's sake, and having no real meaning. On those occasions, would he not have noticed that she picked out the square ones for herself? She prayed fervently that this little fact should never become known, even to Christopher.

When they reached the hotel, Vivienne went straight up to her room, pleading a headache. Christopher, probably for the first time in his life, was relieved at her departure. He guessed something of her secret, and was appalled at the situation which it involved. For the present, at least, he could find nothing with which to comfort the sister to whom he was so devoted. Until he could find some convincing alternative to the theory of Austin's guilt, he was helpless. And he felt that he could review the situation better alone, unracked by the sight of Vivienne's white and piteous face.

He selected an inconspicuous chair in the smoking-room, and picked up an evening paper, which he made a pretence of reading. Actually, his trained mind was intent upon the varied aspects of the tragedies which had taken place at Monk's Barn, testing the Superintendent's theories, and seeking the weak spot in them. The attitude he tried to take up was one of sheer impartiality. He liked Austin Wynter, and he guessed that his sister felt for him something far stronger than mere liking. He could not bring himself to believe that Austin could be a brutal and callous murderer. Yet, as he told himself bitterly, this in itself was no proof of Austin's innocence.

There was no denying that Swayne's case was a very strong one. It was almost certain that the same hand had both killed Gilbert Wynter and attempted the life of his wife. The only person at present known with a motive for both was Austin. Opportunity, though fairly wide in the second case, was greatly narrowed in the first. And yet, in spite of all this, there must be some other explanation, could he but hit on it.

Meanwhile Vivienne was sitting in her room, staring wide-eyed into the fire. All her usual spirit, her brilliant powers of deduction, had deserted her. She was nothing more than a loving woman, faced with a situation which numbed everything but the agony of her heart. Hideous pictures passed through her mind; the arrest of Austin, his trial, his conviction. And, more awful than these, the thought that she might never see him again.

The resolve came to her suddenly, and, once taken, she acted upon it unhesitatingly. She left her room, furtively as a hunted thing, and slipped out of the hotel unobserved.

She knew the address of Austin's rooms, he had mentioned it in the course of conversation a day or two previously, and by this time she had a sufficient knowledge of Yatebury to find her way there without much difficulty. She rang the bell, and waited in an agony of apprehension on the step. Was she too late? Had the thing which she dreaded already taken place?

At last, after what seemed an age, the door was opened and an elderly woman confronted her. "Is Mr. Wynter at home?" she asked, in a faltering voice.

The woman glanced at her, rather curiously, she fancied. "I think so, Miss. Will you come in?" she replied.

Vivienne entered the little hall, walking as though in a trance. Indeed, it seemed to her as though she were in a dream, which was shortly to dissolve, to give way to natural things once more. She was vaguely conscious that the woman opened a door, and said something to her. Then she walked in.

Austin had been sitting at a desk, writing. He had looked up as the door opened, and still sat gazing at her, as at some marvellous and unexpected vision. Then, slowly, he rose to his feet and stretched out his arms towards her. As though impelled by some irresistible force, outside her own volition, she floated across the floor until she was held fast within his embrace.

Neither seemed to feel the need of words. For Vivienne, the ecstasy of those precious seconds left no room for any other feeling. She was rapt in transcendent happiness, lifted from earth into a heaven of overpowering love. The world was forgotten, far beneath her feet, for one blissful instant the horror that encircled them both loosened its deadly grip and allowed her to soar into the heights. Then at last, with a long sigh of happiness, she gently disengaged herself, and sank into a chair beside him. "I—I had to come," she whispered.

He stood looking down upon her, strangely inarticulate. It seemed as if he had nothing to say, if just her presence alone fulfilled all his desire, all his longings. And then at last he found words, strange conventional words, utterly inadequate to express his love. "I didn't mean to tell you until—until everything was over."

"Do you think that I didn't know?" she replied, without looking up. "I knew, I wanted you to tell me. But it wasn't until this evening that I knew, too."

He fell on his knees beside her and kissed her once more. "Vivienne!" he exclaimed softly. "You don't know what this means to me. Ever since I first saw you I have been longing for the moment when I could tell you that I loved you. I never dared believe that you could care for me. And then, when the door opened, and I saw you standing there. . . ."

"Care? I think I must have cared all this time, but I didn't know it," she replied. And then suddenly as though reality had swept back upon her in a devastating wave, she leapt to her feet, a look of stark terror in her eyes. "Austin!" she cried. "It's not true! Tell me it isn't true, or I shall go mad!"

He tried to catch her in his arms, but she evaded him by a quick movement. "No, listen, you must listen to me!" she continued. "I must know, before they take you from me. You didn't do it? You don't know anything about it?"

She gazed at him supplicatingly, and he returned her gaze with eyes as steadfast as her own. "I couldn't lie to you now, in this most wonderful moment of my life," he replied steadily. "I know no more than you who murdered my brother or Ursula Cartwright."

"Thank God!" she exclaimed, with a deep sigh of content. "I knew it, but I had to hear it from your own lips. Silly of me, wasn't it? But I felt as if I'd been caught in a trap, and only you could release me."

She smiled at him in the relief that his words had brought her. But her smile faded as swiftly as it had come, and the old look of urgent terror took its place. "Austin, I'm afraid!" she continued. "They think you did it, that's why I came here. We must do something . . ."

Very tenderly he took her in his arms, and this time she made no resistance. "Darling, I told you long ago that as long as you believed I was innocent, I did not care who thought me guilty," he whispered. "Let them think that I did it. What does that matter to us now?"

She tore herself away from him impatiently. "To us, nothing," she replied. "But, don't you understand. The police. They will arrest you and take you away from me. And after that—Oh, I daren't think about it!"

"I have thought about it," he said calmly. "I haven't said anything to you, but I know that Swayne's men have been watching me for the last few days. It wasn't by accident that the Superintendent ran into us after the pictures the other night. I have been expecting to be arrested ever since Mintern was released, but I have realized that I can do nothing to avoid it. I am not afraid of what may happen, for, since I am completely innocent, there can be no evidence against me."

The unruffled tranquillity with which Austin spoke seemed to restore Vivienne's confidence somewhat. "Yes, I suppose that's so," she agreed, rather reluctantly. "But I was with Chris in Superintendent Swayne's office just now, and he made out a horrible case against you. It's all circumstantial, of course. But it's terribly difficult to answer until we can find out who really committed the murders."

"Yes, I suppose it is," said Austin. "I haven't the slightest idea who killed Gilbert. It seems utterly impossible that anybody could have fired that gun, except Anne, and, though I have never liked her, I can't believe that she could have brought herself to do such a thing. I know that she and Gilbert didn't altogether hit it off, of course. But, on the other hand, I haven't much doubt who killed Ursula Cartwright."

"You haven't?" exclaimed Vivienne eagerly. "Who was it? Tell me, Austin."

"Why, Cartwright. He's always been in love with Anne. I could see that for myself, and, as you know, I didn't go out to Fordington much. As soon as I heard that Gilbert had been murdered, I thought that he had done it, until I found from the evidence that he couldn't possibly have been in the shrubbery at the time. But I haven't the least doubt that, finding Anne a widow, he made away with Ursula so as to be free to marry her." Vivienne shook her head despondently. "I'm afraid that won't do," she replied. "You haven't heard the whole story as I have. There isn't any doubt that the poisoned chocolates were meant for Anne, not Ursula. And the very fact that Mr. Cartwright was in love with Anne goes to prove his innocence."

"Meant for Anne!" exclaimed Austin. "How do you know that?"

She told him of the examination of the remaining chocolates. When she had finished, he took her hand in his. "I don't understand it, any more than you do. The whole thing is horrible, especially the fact that that poor woman was poisoned by eating chocolates out of a box which I gave you. There is only one thing I am devoutly thankful for, that you did not allow yourself to be persuaded to eat any of them."

"Tell me one thing, Austin. Why did you send me the box after I had told you that I never ate chocolates?"

"Why did I send them to you? I don't know. I very nearly didn't. And then I thought that they had been bought for you, and I wanted to show you that I was thinking about you. And, at that time of night, I could find nothing else to send. I almost ventured to believe that you would understand."

"I did understand, I think. But we're wasting time. Can't you make any suggestion, Austin? You know that both Chris and I shall leave no stone unturned to find out the truth, but I simply don't know where to begin. I'm no nearer finding out who murdered your brother than I was when you first came to us. And as for poor Ursula, I'm utterly in the dark. It must have been somebody at White Lodge, but who, if not her husband? And if he'd wanted to kill her that way, he'd have poisoned the round chocolates, not the square ones. It's like an awful riddle."

"Never mind, sweetheart," said Austin cheerfully. "Whoever did it, I didn't, and there isn't the slightest chance of my having to suffer for it. You can make your mind quite easy about that. I may have to put up with a good deal of unpleasantness, that can't be helped. My only regret is that I ever dragged you into it all."

"I don't regret it. We shouldn't have met, if you hadn't. But, Austin, it's going to be very hard for me to have all the world suspecting you, when I'm so proud of you."

"Poor little woman, I know. The burden is going to be all on your shoulders, not mine. You have brought me too much happiness this evening for me to care in the least for anything else. At the worst, it's only a temporary shadow. The truth will come out in time, you see if it doesn't."

Vivienne was about to reply, when the insistent note of the front-door bell pealed through the house. She made an instinctive gesture, as though to protect the man she loved from the danger which threatened him, then stood motionless by his side, her hand in his. Thus they heard the shuffling steps of the landlady as she went to the door, then a few murmured words. Then the door of the room opened.

Vivienne uttered a sharp exclamation of relief as she saw Christopher, but the expression on his face caused her to start forward anxiously. "Chris!" she said. "What is it?"

"Hullo, Vi, I thought I might find you here," he replied, with a rather poor attempt at cheerfulness. "That's what I came for. It's time you went home to bed, you know."

"You had better know why I came here," she said steadily. "I came to tell Austin that I loved him."

Christopher betrayed no astonishment. Instead, he looked gravely and searchingly at Austin. The result of his inspection seemed to satisfy him, for he stepped forward and laid his hand on the other's shoulder. "I'm glad," he said simply. "But there are other things that must be thought of at the moment. Off you go,

Vi. You can find your way home all right. I shan't be more than a few minutes, but I want a word with Austin first."

Slowly Vivienne turned and walked to the door. But there she paused for an instant. A brave smile flickered for an instant about her lips as she turned her eyes upon Austin in farewell. Then the door closed behind her, and the two men were left alone.

CHAPTER XXVI

NEITHER spoke until the dull sound of the front door closing behind Vivienne came to their ears. Then Austin turned to Christopher. "Why did you send her away?" he asked quietly.

"Because on my way here I met Superintendent Swayne," replied Christopher equally simply.

Austin nodded with an air of comprehension. "I thought that was it," he said. "When will he be here?"

"In about ten minutes, I should say. I asked him to wait a quarter of an hour, till Vi had gone. We both want to spare her as much as possible, I take it?"

"Naturally. I'm afraid she will suffer far more than I shall. I can't ask you to believe me on my word alone, in face of appearances. But, if it is of any use to you, I give you my assurance that I am innocent."

"I believe that," replied Christopher steadily. "The thing to do now is to make arrangements for your defence. Have you any instructions to give me before . . ."

Austin interrupted him before he could finish the sentence. "Before I am arrested? No, I think not. It's no use asking you to do what you can to find the real criminal, for I know you'll do that in any case. I've been expecting to be arrested for the last day or two. Swayne's a very good fellow, but the workings of his mind are a trifle transparent. I saw my solicitor this afternoon, and he's taking all the necessary steps to retain counsel, and all that sort of thing."

"There's nothing here that you'd rather the police didn't see? There'll be a search, of course."

"Only this," replied Austin, going to the desk and picking up a couple of sheets of paper that lay upon it. "I was writing to Vivienne, when she came in as though my longing for her had caused her to materialize before my eyes." Deliberately he tore up the closely written sheets, and placed them almost tenderly upon the fire. He watched them till they were utterly consumed, and then turned abruptly to Christopher. "I should like you to believe that I had no intention of saying anything to your sister until I had been cleared of the suspicion that hangs over me," he said.

Christopher smiled. "The fact that she came here to-night proves that she knew already what you had to tell her," he replied. "I don't think Vi would have been happy if she had not been certain, though."

Austin made no reply. In the silence the clock upon the mantelpiece seemed to tick with ever-increasing loudness, the only sound which disturbed the utter stillness of the house. Christopher fidgeted impatiently. The intolerable strain of waiting was clearly getting upon his nerves. His ears were strained for the first sound which should announce the inevitable.

It was Austin who broke the silence. "Swayne's a man of his word," he remarked, as he glanced unconcernedly at the clock. "His time's nearly up. He'll be here any minute now." He paused, and then continued in a slightly changed tone. "I'm not going to indulge in heroics," he said, a slight smile playing about his features. "I'm not going to say that the consciousness of my innocence supports me, or anything like that. I know that I've got to go through a very bad time, but—well, the prospect just simply doesn't appall me. I look upon it as one of those unpleasant episodes of life which have got to be gone through as cheerfully as possible. It's difficult to explain."

Christopher nodded, rather absently. His whole attention seemed to be concentrated, not upon what Austin was saying, but upon the road outside. He stood by the window listening, fingering the curtain nervously.

"I suppose there's a strain of mysticism in me," continued Austin quietly. "I've always imagined that one never attained supreme happiness in this world without undergoing some corresponding misery. It isn't jealousy on the part of Providence, which ordains that the scales of good and evil should be evenly balanced. It's something far deeper than that. I think that Providence knows that happiness is, in a sense, as great a test as misery, and that we require a period of self-discipline before we are fit to enjoy it. And surely no man knows greater happiness than I."

Christopher glanced at him curiously, without, however, relaxing his attitude of watchfulness. Austin was sounding depths of feeling of which he had never thought him capable. If he had subconsciously retained the slightest doubt of his innocence, these doubts were completely swept away. "You can trust me to look after Vi until you are released," he said, rather awkwardly.

"I know, and that relieves me of the only anxiety I have," replied Austin. "So long as you and she believe me innocent, I am completely indifferent as to what the rest of the world thinks. I've never cared much for other people's opinions, and I care less, now. I can go through this ordeal with a perfectly peaceful mind."

Again the profound and deadening silence fell. The clock ticked out a few long-drawn seconds. And then, with a sigh almost of relief, Christopher turned suddenly from the window. "They're coming!" he exclaimed, scarcely above a whisper.

"Punctual almost to the minute," commented Austin. With a sudden gesture he held out his hand. "Good-bye, Perrin," he said. "I can't thank you now. That will come later."

Christopher took the outstretched hand and clasped it warmly. "Good-bye," he said. "You know that your friends won't spare themselves working for you."

The bell pealed once more, and the two men waited, their eyes fixed upon the door. They heard the shuffling step of the landlady, the few words spoken without. Then the door opened, and

Superintendent Swayne, accompanied by a constable, appeared on the threshold.

"Good evening, Superintendent," said Austin, in a conversational tone. "I was expecting you. Come in."

Swayne entered the room, and closed the door carefully behind him. He glanced round the room, and his face assumed an expression of relief as he saw that its only other occupant was Christopher. He advanced swiftly, until he stood facing Austin. There was a second's pause, dramatic in its intensity, before he spoke. "Austin Wynter, I arrest you on the charge of murdering Ursula Cartwright," he said solemnly. "I have to warn you that anything you may say may be used in evidence against you, and also that a second charge may be preferred."

Austin bowed his head in acknowledgment. "I understand, Superintendent," he replied quietly. "I am quite ready to go with you. I've got a suit-case here, ready packed with a few necessaries. I suppose that there is no objection to my taking it with me?"

"None at all," said Swayne. "You will understand that it will have to be examined at the police station. We will walk straight there now. There is nobody about in the streets so late as this. You will, of course, give me your undertaking not to attempt to escape?"

Austin smiled. "I have no intention whatever of attempting to escape," he replied.

Swayne nodded. "Very well," he said. Then he turned to Christopher. "I shall have to ask you to leave the house as well, Mr. Perrin. I am leaving a constable in charge here."

They went out in procession, Swayne and Austin side by side, Christopher following them. The road without was dark and deserted, the infrequent lamps dulled by a fine rain which was falling. At the gate Christopher paused, looking intently after Swayne and his prisoner until their footsteps died away in the distance. Then, with a shudder which he could not repress, he turned and walked swiftly back to the "King's Head."

As he went up to his room, he tapped quietly at Vivienne's door. Her voice immediately bade him come in, and he opened the door, to find her sitting by the fire. She looked up as he entered, a smile upon her face. "Well?" she inquired, without a tremor in her voice.

Christopher sat down beside her before he replied. "Swayne came a few minutes after you had gone," he said, watching her anxiously.

"Of course. That was to be expected. Oh, Chris, you don't know how glad I am that I saw Austin first. I've been so utterly miserable, so terrified, and now, since I've seen Austin, I know that everything will be all right. You didn't mind my running away like that without telling you where I had gone?"

"Mind? No, I guessed where you were as soon as I found you weren't in your room. Vi, dear, I'm so glad. I shall miss you terribly; in fact, I don't know how I shall get on without you. But it had to come some day, I suppose, and you've chosen well. Austin's a real good fellow."

"Thank you, Chris," she replied, putting her hand under his arm. "It's very good to know that you think that, too. Don't go away for a minute, I want to talk to you. I want to share my happiness with somebody."

Christopher made no reply. He was marvelling at the potency of love, which had the power to make these two regard the ominous future with such supreme confidence. His own heart failed him as he dwelt upon the possibility which both Austin and Vivienne so steadfastly refused to consider, that Austin, in spite of his innocence, might be condemned. What then would happen to the sister he loved so well?

Vivienne's voice broke in upon his thoughts. "You mustn't think it selfish of me," she said. "I just can't help loving him. I shall hate leaving you, after we've done everything together for so long. But, after all, Yatebury isn't so far away, and you'll come down and see us whenever you can, won't you?"

"You know I shall, Vi," he replied gently. But his mind was elsewhere. Did Vivienne realize all the horrors that lay before her until her dreams of the future could be realized, even if they were not to fall to pieces in disastrous ruin? Did she realize that Austin was accused of the murder of Ursula Cartwright, and that, at his trial, she would be one of the principal witnesses, forced to stand in the witness-box and be browbeaten by opposing counsel before the anguished eyes of the man she loved?

"Look here, Vi!" he exclaimed suddenly. "Don't you think that as soon as possible you had better go back home for a bit? I shall stay down here, of course, and watch the case."

She glanced at him, a look of genuine amazement in her eyes. "Go back home!" she repeated. "Why, whatever can you be thinking of, Chris? Naturally, I shall want to stay as near Austin as I can. Besides, our job now is to find out who really committed the murders. The sooner we do that, the sooner Austin will be released. You don't imagine that I shall leave you to do that by yourself, do you?" Again Christopher looked at her searchingly. "You're sure you're up to it?" he asked.

"Of course I'm up to it. I was a bit shaken this evening, I admit, but then I've been through a good deal in the last couple of days, one way and another. I'm perfectly right again now, you can see that for yourself. It was the fear that Austin mightn't have the chance of telling me that upset me."

Christopher could only pray that her present mood might last. Perhaps it would be better for her if she were fully employed, instead of eating out her heart in idleness. Meanwhile, if they were to act together, discussion could not be delayed.

"Austin was arrested for the murder of Ursula Cartwright," he said. "Swayne dropped a hint that he might subsequently be charged with the murder of his brother as well. You know that Swayne's theory is that the same person committed both crimes, and I think it's pretty certain he's right. But, since the second murder is the substance of the present charge, I think we ought to concentrate on that."

But Vivienne shook her head. "I don't agree," she replied. "To my mind the two murders are so closely connected that for our purposes we can look upon them as one. I've already got the fragments of a theory which would account for them both, but at present it's full of apparent contradictions. I'm quite sure that the clues we want lie under our very eyes, but that we don't see the significance of them. I want to go over every single detail of what we've seen and heard since we've been on the case, and see if I can't fit things into their proper places."

"That's what I've been trying to do, but so far I haven't got a hint towards the solution of the puzzle."

"Never mind. We can't expect to succeed at the first attempt. Isn't it time we went to bed, Chris?"

Christopher took the hint. He rose to his feet, then bent down and kissed Vivienne's hair. "Good luck, old girl," he murmured.

As he left the room, Vivienne rose and gazed intently into the mirror. Then, apparently satisfied with her inspection, she began slowly and deliberately to undress.

CHAPTER XXVII

VIVIENNE remained in the seclusion of her room for the greater part of the next day, which was Sunday. To Christopher, who visited her pretty frequently, she seemed possessed by an excitement the cause of which he could not fathom. Her eyes were bright and eager, there was no trace in them either of grief or apprehension. But she replied to his questions absent-mindedly, as though her thoughts were elsewhere.

In the course of the day Christopher received a visit from Swayne. The Superintendent came ostensibly to serve a notice on Vivienne, summoning her to attend the inquest on the body of Ursula Cartwright, which was to be held on Monday. But it was clear to Christopher, from the way that Swayne waited after he had performed this duty, that he was anxious to unburden himself of other matters. He therefore invited the Superintendent to his room, an offer that was eagerly accepted.

"That's better," remarked Swayne, as he settled himself in a chair. "One can't talk downstairs, in a place like this. You never know who's listening. I'm sorry I had to drag your sister into this business to-morrow, but I couldn't help myself, especially as Doctor Palmer certifies that Mrs. Wynter is too ill to attend."

"Ill?" exclaimed Christopher quickly. "What's the matter with her? She hasn't developed symptoms of poisoning, has she?"

"Oh, no, nothing like that. Her nerves seem to have broken down completely, Doctor Palmer says. I'm not altogether surprised. The shock of Mrs. Cartwright's death, following so close on her husband's, is enough to upset any woman. It appears that she's in a very queer state indeed. Won't see anybody, even Cartwright. Just lies in bed and cries."

"It sounds as if she were more distressed now than when her husband was killed," remarked Christopher. "Cumulative effect, I suppose."

"I don't know," replied Swayne thoughtfully. "From what I hear, she wasn't particularly devoted to her husband, at least not in recent years. I don't know whether she suspected that there was anything between him and Phyllis Mintern. You never can tell how women will behave under circumstances like that. And, after all, Mrs. Cartwright was her best friend, outside her family. You can understand her being upset at her death."

"Does she know that Mrs. Cartwright was poisoned?"

"To tell you the truth, Mr. Perrin, I don't know what that woman knows and what she doesn't know. She's a complete puzzle to me. She's been pleasant enough to me, every time I've seen her, but, when you begin to talk to her, it's as though she was surrounded by a brick wall. You can't get inside it. It'll be very interesting to see what counsel make of her, when the trial comes off."

"If it ever does," replied Christopher lightly. "Many things may happen before then."

Rather to Christopher's astonishment, Swayne made no immediate reply to the implied challenge. He lighted his pipe very deliberately, and then stared gloomily into the fire for several seconds before he spoke.

"I've made a good many arrests in my time, although, I'm thankful to say, very few of them have been on such a grave charge as this. I've known men come quietly, and I've known them bluster. But I've never seen anybody behave quite like Austin Wynter."

He paused for a moment, and then continued. "Often enough, you can get a pretty good idea of whether a man is innocent or guilty after he's arrested. I don't mean at once, but after they've been in custody for a night, and have had time to think about it. Take Mintern, for instance. I had a pretty shrewd idea that he would be able to prove his innocence. All the time he was in custody he behaved as if he had a pretty good joke up his sleeve. But, as I say, Austin Wynter's quite different."

"You've seen him this morning, of course?"

"Oh, yes, I've seen him. He's settled down quite comfortably. He brought some books with him in that suit-case, and they're the only things that seem to interest him. When he was told that his solicitor had come to see him, he looked quite annoyed, and then said, 'Well, I'd better see him, I suppose,' as if the whole thing were an infernal nuisance. From the way he behaves, you'd think he was undergoing a rest-cure."

Christopher smiled at the note of indignation in the Superintendent's tone. "He wouldn't behave like that if he were guilty," he remarked.

"Oh, I don't know. He may have made up his mind that it's all up, and decided that the best thing he can do is to get it over as soon as possible. I've known fellows to take their arrest quietly enough, and then, a couple of days later, make a clean breast of things. But Austin Wynter doesn't seem to bother his head about it, one way or the other."

"Is it permissible to ask what your plans are with regard to him?" asked Christopher.

"I don't mind telling you, in confidence. He'll come up before the magistrates to-morrow, and I shall apply for a remand. The defence won't oppose it, as they'll want time to prepare their case. It wouldn't much matter if they did, for the magistrates are practically bound to grant it, anyway. You'll want to be in Court, I suppose?"

"I should like to, if possible, and my sister as well."

"There won't be any difficulty about that. The proceedings won't take more than a few minutes, and then we can go straight over to Fordington for the inquest. The coroner is going to sit without a jury, so we shall save time there, too. Well, I must be getting back to work, I suppose. See you to-morrow, Mr. Perrin."

Vivienne betrayed no emotion as she entered the packed Court on the following morning. The arrest of so prominent a member of the community as Austin Wynter had caused a tremendous sensation locally, and the whole of Yatebury seemed to be thronging the precincts of the Court. Opinion, on the whole, seemed to be pretty evenly divided. Everyone connected with the firm refused to believe that Austin could be guilty, but there were others who shook their heads. The Superintendent, they argued, would not risk a second mistake. If he had gone to the length of arresting Austin, there must be a very strong case against him. You never could tell what these quiet chaps would be up to. It was a queer business, anyway.

Thus far public opinion outside. Within the Court there was an air of gloomy decorum. It was very dark, and even the few electric lamps that were lighted were unable to cast more than a dim twilight. The magistrates entered, in the same solemn procession as before. And then, almost without warning, Austin appeared in the dock.

This was the moment that Vivienne had awaited. He caught sight of her at once, and smiled at her with such complete confidence that her heart leapt, and she could have cried out with joy. She had a vague impression of men rising and saying a few words.

Then the attendant constable touched Austin on the shoulder. One more reassuring smile in her direction, and he was gone.

"Remanded for a week," whispered Christopher in her ear. "We'd better get out of this. Swayne will be waiting to take us over to the inquest."

Within a few minutes Vivienne was sitting in the big club-room at the "Wheatsheaf" at Fordington, where the inquest was to be held. She had a strange, impersonal feeling, as though the proceedings did not concern her in any way. Her glance swept over the assembled witnesses, until they rested upon Frank Cartwright.

At him she gazed with a curiously intent look. Yet, to the ordinary observer, there was nothing remarkable in his appearance. He sat with his eyes fixed upon the ground in front of him, and, when his turn came, gave his evidence in a low but clear tone. Vivienne herself followed him, and was complimented by the coroner on the clarity of her statements.

Nothing that was not already known to Vivienne and Christopher transpired during the proceedings. The coroner, having heard the evidence, announced that, in accordance with the opinion of the experts, the deceased had met her death by poisoning, administered in chocolates. As to how the poison came to be found in the chocolates, he thought it better to reserve his opinion, owing to the police having already taken action in connexion with the case.

As the proceedings came to an end, Frank Cartwright leant across and whispered to Swayne. The latter nodded, and came over to Christopher. "Cartwright tells me that he has found the chocolates put aside by his wife," he said. "He wants me to go to White Lodge with him and take charge of them. Would you care to come, too?"

Christopher glanced at Vivienne, who nodded eagerly. "Yes, go by all means," she said. "I'll wait for you. I don't particularly want to go to White Lodge again."

The Superintendent introduced Christopher to Cartwright, and the three walked the short distance to White Lodge, where they entered the drawing-room. "This is where I found them," said Cartwright, walking across the room to an oak chest on the far side. "I saw a cardboard box which I did not recognize when I opened it, just before the inquest. It had not struck me to look there before."

The chest was nearly full of half-finished pieces of embroidery, and odds and ends of a similar nature. "I suppose Mrs. Cartwright must have put the box here herself?" he asked.

"There can be no doubt about that. She was the only person who ever used this chest. I think I can explain what happened. When Miss Perrin brought the chocolates on Thursday evening, the box was full. I saw it opened myself. After tea, Ursula ate most of the round ones in the top layer. Shortly after Miss Perrin's departure I left the room. Ursula was then still eating the chocolates. When I came back, in half an hour or so, Ursula was upstairs, but the box was lying open on the chair in which she had been sitting. I noticed that there were only about half a dozen chocolates left in the top layer."

Swayne nodded. This confirmed what Vivienne had told him.

"I supposed that she had taken out the square ones and put them aside for Anne, as she had done more than once before, to my knowledge. This supposition was confirmed, I understand, by a remark she made next day to Miss Perrin. I put the box, with the remainder of the chocolates in it, aside in her bureau, for I knew that if it was left lying about she would be tempted to eat more than was good for her. During my absence she must have found the other smaller box, put the square chocolates into it, and slipped them into the chest, intending to give them to Anne. Ursula was inclined to be absent-minded over trifles, and it is characteristic of her that she should have forgotten where she had put them when Miss Perrin came on Friday."

"It is unlikely that anybody else in the house knew where they were?" asked Swayne.

"Most unlikely. I did not know, and had any of the servants been present when they were put away, Ursula would have asked them if they remembered what she had done with them. Now, if you will excuse me for a moment, I will fetch the box. I have thought it best to keep it under lock and key."

Cartwright left the room, to return in a few moments with a small decorated cardboard box, which he handed to the Super-intendent, who opened it. Inside were a few square chocolates, which he recognized as being identical with those he had found on the drawing-room door at Monk's Barn. He pocketed the box, and, having taken their leave of Cartwright, he and Christopher left the house.

"I'll send these for analysis as soon as we get back to Yate-bury," remarked Swayne, as soon as the door had closed behind them. "If any of them have been tampered with, one thing will be proved pretty conclusively."

"And that is?" inquired Christopher.

"Surely you see that for yourself. It is pretty clear that these chocolates lay untouched in the chest from Thursday morning till Cartwright found them this morning. If anything is wrong with them, they must have been poisoned before Miss Perrin gave them to Mrs. Cartwright. And in that event, I think that even you will be bound to admit that my case against Austin Wynter is pretty well complete."

"Oh, I wouldn't go so far as to say that," replied Christopher carelessly. "We'd better be getting back to Yatebury, I suppose. I wonder what's become of Vivienne?"

CHAPTER XXVIII

IT WAS not long before Vivienne appeared, hurrying down the village street towards them. "I hope I haven't kept you waiting!" she exclaimed breathlessly. "I took the opportunity of visiting one or two of my old acquaintances in the village."

"That's all right, Miss Perrin," replied Swayne courteously. "We've only just left White Lodge. I left the car at the 'Wheatsheaf.' If you're ready, we might walk down there and then get back to Yatebury."

Christopher glanced inquisitively at his sister. He could tell by her flushed cheeks and sparkling eyes that something had happened during the brief interval that they had been apart. But he asked no questions until they had reached Yatebury and taken leave of the Superintendent. Then, in the privacy of his room at the hotel, he allowed his curiosity to find expression. "What have you been up to, Vi?" he asked.

She laid her bag, which seemed unusually bulky and heavy, down on the bed before she replied. "After you left me, I walked up the street, and found that the drive gates of Monk's Barn were open," she said. "I wanted a word with Croyle, and I thought I would see if he was about. I looked about everywhere, in the potting-shed, the greenhouses and everywhere I could think of. I even went into the shrubbery at the end of the lawn. At last I found him busy, right at the end of the garden."

Vivienne paused and looked at her brother mockingly. "I wanted to tell him about Austin's arrest," she added.

Christopher looked at her in amazement. This, he would have thought, was the one subject that she would prefer not to discuss. But he contented himself with a laconic question. "Hadn't he heard of it?"

"No, Croyle's a lonely sort of man. He lives by himself, and doesn't hear much gossip. When I told him about it, he wouldn't believe it at first. When I convinced him that it was true, he seemed to think that it was a practical joke on the part of the police. 'Mr. Austin didn't never do it,' was his comment."

"Well, it's comforting to know that others besides ourselves have faith in him. Did Croyle suggest who the murderer might be?"

"I didn't ask him. I went on to say that Austin would probably be charged later with murdering his brother. The old boy thought I'd taken leave of my senses, I'm sure. 'Nobody would be such a fool as to charge him with that,' he declared. How could he possibly have got into the garden that night, without going through the house? I suggested that he might have borrowed the key of the drive gates from Croyle himself. This struck Croyle as being more amusing than ever. When I made him see that I was serious, he swore that the key had never left his pocket from the time that he took it till Burden called for it, and further, that he had not seen Austin that evening or for several weeks previously."

"Well, if he sticks to that statement in the witness-box, it's a point in our favour," remarked Christopher. "He hadn't anything else to say, I suppose?"

"Nothing of any particular interest. But he mentioned that some days ago Mr. Cartwright came and opened that loose-box, where he and Gilbert Wynter had been working on some invention or other. You remember, it was mentioned at the time. The place was still unlocked, and I looked in. Whatever it was they had been working upon had been taken away, but the place was fitted up as a workshop, with a bench and a lot of tools. And, amongst other things, there was a ball of tarred twine there."

Seeing that she paused significantly, Christopher glanced at her. "I don't see anything startling about that," he said.

"Don't you? Well, I showed it to Croyle, and asked him if he used much of it about the garden. He replied that he never used the stuff, hadn't any on the place, in fact. He preferred wire or raffia, since he believed that tar was not good for plants. I waited till he wasn't looking, then slipped the ball into my bag. Then I thought I'd been there long enough, so I said good-bye to Croyle and came back to meet you. How did you get on at White Lodge?"

Christopher told her what had passed between Cartwright and the Superintendent. "You see how it is, Vi," he concluded. "If those chocolates, or some of them, turn out to have been poisoned, it will look rather black for Austin, for it will show that they were doctored before you gave them to Mrs. Cartwright."

"Oh, they'll prove to be poisoned, all right, you see if they don't," replied Vivienne, almost gaily. "I shouldn't let that worry you, if I were you. Now, I want you to do something for me, Chris.

Run out and buy me a tube of seccotine, will you? There's a stationer's almost opposite the door of the hotel."

Christopher obeyed, completely mystified. It was perfectly clear from her manner that Vivienne believed that she had made some vital discovery, but what it was he could not guess. He could only hope that he was not doomed to some bitter disappointment.

He made the required purchase, and returned to her room. She had emptied her bag, and laid the contents upon her dressing-table. At one end was a ball of tarred twine, nearly half-used, and at the other half a dozen broken pieces of red pottery. Seeing her brother's puzzled expression as he caught sight of these, she laughed gaily.

"Exhibit A," she said, pointing to the ball of twine. "We can leave that for the moment. Have you got the seccotine? Good! Now we will proceed to reconstruct exhibit B. It's like a jig-saw puzzle."

She took the tube of liquid glue, and proceeded to stick the pieces of pottery together. Under her deft fingers they slowly grew into the shape of a flower-pot, about six inches high and the same in diameter. "There!" she exclaimed. "Exhibit B, practically complete. There's one little bit of the rim missing, but that doesn't matter. The next thing we do is to pull down the blinds and draw the curtains."

"I give it up, Vi," said Christopher, in a tone of resignation. "What's the answer?"

"I'm not going to tell you, yet. Make the room as dark as you can. That's better." She clapped her hands suddenly. "Oh, Chris, look!" she exclaimed. "I thought I was right. Look at that flower-pot!"

Christopher looked, and uttered a startled exclamation. The room was not by any means dark, a surprising amount of light found its way round the edges of the curtains. But, even so, from the place where the flower-pot stood, a patch of dull and ghostly radiance shone out uncertainly. "Why, good heavens, it's been smeared with luminous paint!" exclaimed Christopher.

"Of course it has. I spotted that long ago, when I was sketching in Monk's Barn garden, but I didn't understand then what it meant. All right, that'll do. Draw back the curtains and pull up the blind. Now, look at the flower-pot again. You can see that nearly the whole of one side has been covered with luminous paint."

Christopher examined the object carefully. It was as Vivienne had said. "That's queer," he remarked. "And, if you look closely, you can see that it has been hit right in the centre of the patch of paint. A chip has been knocked out of it, and it's all starred round the spot, as if someone had hit it with a hammer."

"Not a hammer, I think we shall find," replied Vivienne confidently. "Anyway, you're satisfied that somebody painted the pot with luminous paint, and that it got broken afterwards? I can tell you, I spent a busy five minutes sorting out the pieces in Croyle's potting-shed."

"But how on earth did you know they were there?" asked Christopher in bewilderment.

"I was on the spot when Croyle found the pieces in the shrubbery, and he told me he was going to put them in the potting-shed. I remembered the incident yesterday, when I was trying to fit together a theory I had formed. That's really what I went to Monk's Barn for this morning."

"I may be dense, Vi, but still I don't see the significance of your exhibits."

"You will, all in good time. Do you remember that there's one thing which has always puzzled us about the murder of Gilbert Wynter? That is, that it is absolutely impossible that anybody could possibly have seen him, much less aimed at his head, from the shrubbery. Remember, the curtains of the window looking towards it were not only drawn together, they overlapped."

"But it seems absolutely certain that the shot was fired from the shrubbery. I don't attach any great importance to the finding of the gun there, but the direction taken by the bullet proves it conclusively."

"It is absolutely certain," replied Vivienne enigmatically. "I'm more convinced of that than ever. I'm not going to answer any questions yet. I've a lot of things to do before I'm ready to do that. For one thing, I want to put a trunk call through to the flat, and have a word with Phyllis. And after that, I'm going on a little expedition by myself this afternoon. We'll meet again this evening."

"Well, this is your show entirely. But if there's anything I can do to help, tell me."

"There's only one thing you can do for the moment. You told me that when Swayne showed you the gun with which Gilbert Wynter was shot, it was wrapped up in some old sacking, and tied with a piece of twine. Now, I want you to see Swayne again and borrow that piece of twine for me. Now, for goodness' sake let's go down and get some lunch. I'm simply ravenous."

Christopher noticed with the utmost satisfaction that Vivienne made the best meal which she had done since the death of Ursula Cartwright. Her whole behaviour radiated confidence, as though all her anxieties were at an end and the problem which had confronted her was already solved. Like a wise man, he did not attempt to probe the mystery. He dreaded lest she had built her hopes upon some theory that would crumble to dust under the rough handling to which it must eventually be subjected.

After lunch Vivienne put her call through to London, and returned, looking more satisfied than ever. "That's one little link fitted in," she said. "Now, I'm going to disappear for a few hours. I shall be back in time for dinner, I expect, but, if not, don't worry about me. You won't forget to ask Swayne for that piece of twine, will you?"

When she had left him, Christopher settled himself down to attack the problem once more. He felt that it was no use trying to follow the lines upon which his sister was working. He resolutely put her curious "exhibits" out of his mind, and tried to strike out a new path of his own. Mrs. Wynter, now. Long ago he had thought it possible that she had murdered her husband. Was it also possible that she had murdered her friend, as the second stage of a plot which would leave her free to marry Frank Cartwright? But, if so, how had she obtained access to the chocolates in order to poison them? And again, now that the way was clear, how was it that she refused to see Frank, as Swayne had said?

His meditations were interrupted by a call to the telephone. The speaker proved to be Austin's solicitor, who asked him, if possible, to come round to his office. Christopher complied with the request, and for more than a couple of hours the two engaged in earnest consultation, examining the circumstances from every point of view, and trying to discover the best grounds upon which to base the defence. It was not until past four o'clock that Christopher was able to get to Swayne's office.

The Superintendent admitted him at once. "Come in, Mr. Perrin," he said heartily. "I'm always glad to see you. I hope your sister isn't feeling the strain of the inquest? The way she gave her evidence was splendid!"

"Oh, no, she's all right," replied Christopher. "Vivienne isn't easily upset. Look here, I haven't come to waste your time. All I want to ask is if I may borrow that bit of string in which the gun is tied up."

"The bit of string!" exclaimed Swayne. "why, what on earth do you want that for? Don't they keep any string at the 'King's Head'?"

"I don't know, I haven't asked them," replied Christopher with a smile. "Between ourselves, it isn't I who wants it, but Vivienne. She's got some idea in her head which she won't tell me, and I'd be most awfully grateful if you'll help to humour her. It keeps her mind off—well, off the arrest you've made."

"I'd do more than that to help Miss Perrin, if it were in my power," said Swayne sincerely. "I hate to think that she's taken a liking to Austin Wynter. It'll be rotten for her if—if anything happens to him. Of course she can have the string: it's got nothing to do with the case, anyhow. I'll get it."

He went to the cupboard where the gun was kept, untied the string, and put it into Christopher's hands. As he did so, the telephone bell rang. He went to the instrument, and carried on a short conversation. When he had finished, he turned to Christopher.

"That was the analyst," he said. "I sent a man on a motor-bicycle over to him with the chocolates as soon as we got back this morning. He says that he hasn't completed his report, but he knew I would like to know how things were going. He's got far enough to be able to say that three of the chocolates show signs of having been tampered with, and that he has examined these first. In each case he has found them to contain the same poison as before."

Christopher's expression was grave as he replied. "That's all very well, Superintendent." he said. "But that isn't any real proof that Austin poisoned them. Cartwright can't swear that they were in the oak chest during the whole of Thursday night. Several people might have had access to them, and to the remainder of the box put away in Mrs. Cartwright's bureau."

"Certainly. But it's up to the defence to find out who tampered with them. Unless they can produce the actual person, I fancy that the jury would fall in with my views. In any case, the fact that these chocolates, which are square ones, remember, the kind Mrs. Wynter liked, have been found to be poisoned, shows beyond a doubt that the object was to poison Mrs. Wynter. It's no good, Mr. Perrin. I fully sympathize with your attitude. But you can't avoid seeing that this is another nail in Austin Wynter's coffin."

CHAPTER XXIX

VIVIENNE left the "King's Head" in a state of elation which she strove her hardest to control. She had no doubt in her own mind that she had solved the mystery of the murder at Monk's Barn. But she knew well enough that this in itself was not sufficient. Her solution must be confirmed by tangible and irresistible proof, and this, she knew, might be extraordinarily difficult to obtain.

She caught the bus that ran in the direction of Fordington, and, having alighted at the stopping-place, walked to the village. She went straight to the front door of Monk's Barn, and rang the bell. A maid answered it, but at Vivienne's request that she might see Mrs. Wynter, she shook her head. "I'm sorry, Miss," she said. "But Mrs. Wynter is seeing nobody at present."

Vivienne had been prepared for this. She took a note from her bag and gave it to the girl. "Take this to Mrs. Wynter," she said. "I will wait and see if there is any answer."

The maid disappeared, to return in a few minutes with the message that Mrs. Wynter would see Miss Perrin. Vivienne followed her upstairs, and was shown into Anne's bedroom. Anne was lying in bed, the note beside her, and a look of undisguised terror in her face. Without a word she watched Vivienne as she entered the room, her eyes following her every movement as she took a chair by the side of the bed. Then, at last, she found her voice. "What is it?" she whispered. "I can't bear this horror any longer. I shall go mad, I know I shall."

"I told you in that note that somebody closely connected with you was in grave danger," replied Vivienne slowly. "That is perfectly true. Your brother-in-law has been arrested for the murder of Ursula Cartwright."

Vivienne had her eyes fixed upon Anne as she spoke. She saw her look of terror slowly fade, to be replaced by one of mingled relief and amazement. "Austin! Austin arrested!" Anne exclaimed. "Is that true, Miss Perrin?"

"Quite true," replied Vivienne gravely. "You understand how serious the charge is. Unless Mr. Austin Wynter can be proved innocent, he will suffer for the crime. And the responsibility for this will rest upon those who know who the true murderer really is, and say nothing."

Anne allowed her head to fall back upon the pillow. "Why do you say that to me, Miss Perrin?" she asked querulously. "Surely you don't imagine that I could know anything about it? I should have spoken at once, if I had."

"I do not suggest that you know anything, Mrs. Wynter," replied Vivienne. "But, perhaps, now that you know of Mr. Austin Wynter's arrest, you may be able to think of something that will assist in his defence. It seems impossible that he should have had any object in killing Ursula Cartwright. You, who knew her so well, may be able to clear up the mystery, or, perhaps, to suggest some other person who desired her death."

She heard Anne's sudden gasp, and a rather grim smile flitted across her lips. But she had gained the knowledge she sought, and there was no more to be said. Without farewell she left the room and walked slowly downstairs. She felt no regret for the trick she had played upon Anne. Sympathy for her could come later, if it were justified. Now she was fighting for the life of the man she loved, and in that battle all weapons were fair.

Vivienne left Monk's Barn by the front door, walked along the street, and turned up the drive leading to the stable yard. Croyle was not to be seen, and from the yard she made her way into the garden. She found the old gardener working in the greenhouses, and he touched his cap, as to an old friend, when she came in.

"Good morning, Croyle," she said. "I hoped for the chance of a word with you alone. You want to do what you can to help Mr. Austin, don't you?"

"Aye, that I do, Miss," replied Croyle eagerly. "I've been thinking over what you told me this morning, and I was wondering if somehow I couldn't do something for Mr. Austin."

"Well, you can. We all believe that whoever killed Mrs. Cartwright killed Mr. Wynter too. Now, Mr. Wynter was shot from the shrubbery, wasn't he? Can you explain how his murderer got into the shrubbery and away again?"

"There's only one way, Miss. He must have been there all the time, leastways unless he went in and out of the garden through the house. He couldn't have got through the yard gates after I'd locked them, and he couldn't have climbed the wall without a ladder. And Burden he told me that he'd examined every inch of the place, and there wasn't any sign of a ladder having been used."

"That's what I thought. Now, Croyle, can you find me a ladder? I want to look at the wall behind the shrubbery myself."

"Aye, that I can, and willingly, Miss," replied Croyle. He went into the stable yard and returned with a ladder, with which he followed Vivienne into the shrubbery.

"Put it up against the wall, will you, Croyle?" she said. "That's right, just there."

Vivienne climbed the ladder, examining the face of the wall intently as she did so. Within a foot or so of the top a projecting stone formed a narrow ledge, which seemed to interest her particularly. She took up a position on the ladder until her head was on a level with the ledge, and from this point she looked about her. Through the upper branches of a tall shrub she could see the side of Monk's Barn, and in it the window of Gilbert Wynter's dressing-room. Farther to the left, and clear of the branches, she could see over the wall dividing the lawn from the road. Beyond this wall, and on the other side of the road, stood White Lodge. The greater part of the house was hidden by the trees which surrounded it, but the end of the wing which abutted on the road was plainly visible, and in it the window of the lumber room, where she had stood with Ursula Cartwright.

Once more she turned and examined the wall.

A short distance from the lodge, and a few inches above it, an iron staple had been driven into one of the joints between the stones. It looked comparatively new, and was entirely free from the rust which had almost eaten away a few nails driven into the wall here and there. Evidently it had been put there not so very long ago. She called down to the gardener, who was standing by the foot of the ladder. "What's this staple for, Croyle?" she asked.

Croyle peered upwards short-sightedly. "I can't say, Miss," he replied. "I don't know as I ever noticed it afore."

"You didn't drive it in yourself, then?"

"No, Miss, that I didn't. I can't see no use in a staple up there, out of reach, like."

"I think I can," muttered Vivienne. She produced a tape measure, and measured the distance from the staple to the centre of the ledge. It was exactly seventeen inches. Apparently satisfied with her inspection of the wall, she began to descend the ladder very slowly, rung by rung, keeping her eyes fixed in the direction of the side wall of Monk's Barn. Suddenly she stopped. In front of her was a gap in the shrubbery, through which she could see the window of Gilbert Wynter's dressing-room. The curtains were drawn back, and the objects just inside the window were clearly visible; the back of the shaving mirror on the dressing-table, and the white shade of the lamp above it.

The gap was formed by a fork in the branches of an evergreen, which approached the wall against which the ladder stood so closely that there was barely room for Vivienne to squeeze between them. In fact, as she descended a rung farther, her coat caught in a projection on the wall, and she turned to release it. She found that the projection was caused by a couple of iron nails, which had been driven into the wall side by side. They were as fresh-looking as the staple.

Disengaging her coat, she descended the ladder until her eyes were on a level with the nails. She took one eager look from here, then measured the distance from the staple to the fork in the branches in front of her. The distance was fifty-two inches. This done, she descended the ladder swiftly until she reached the ground. "That's all, Croyle," she said, her eyes sparkling with excitement. "I've seen all I want to."

Croyle shook his head doubtfully. "Well, Miss, if you're satisfied, that's all right," he said. "But that shot wasn't fired from up the wall, Miss, that I'll swear. There wasn't no sign of a ladder when Burden found the gun. Besides, this is the only one on the place, and it was locked away in the shed."

"Never mind, Croyle, I think we've got a long way towards helping Mr. Austin, for all that," replied Vivienne brightly. "You won't tell anybody what we've been doing, will you?"

Croyle gave the required assurance, and Vivienne left the garden by the way of the yard gates.

Her next visit was to White Lodge. She rang the front-door bell, and was admitted by the maid who had let her in on the occasions when she had come to visit Ursula Cartwright. She inquired whether Mr. Cartwright was in, and was informed that he had gone to Stourminster directly after the inquest, and was not expected back until six o'clock, or later.

This never appeared to trouble her. "Dear me!" she exclaimed. "That's very awkward. You see, I particularly wanted to ask him a question. But perhaps you can help me. You remember that first day, nearly a fortnight ago now, when Mrs. Cartwright brought me here and showed me over the house? I had my sketching things with me. I haven't used them since, but when I was looking over them this afternoon I found that I had lost a bundle of sketches. I thought I might have left them here, for I remember showing them to Mrs. Cartwright. You haven't seen them about, I suppose?"

"No, Miss, I haven't," replied the maid. "If Mrs. Cartwright had found them, she would have been sure to have given them to you when you were here last week."

"The only thing I can think of, then, is that I put them down in the lumber-room. Mrs. Cartwright and I were in there for some time, looking at the garden of Monk's Barn. I don't suppose anybody has been in there since, have they?"

"I don't expect so, Miss. Perhaps you would like to look there for yourself?"

"Well, if it isn't any trouble, I should. You see, the sketches, though they are no good to anybody else, are very valuable to me, and I don't want to lose them."

"Oh, it's no trouble, Miss," replied the girl. She led the way upstairs and Vivienne followed her, exulting in the success of her little deception. They reached the lumber-room, and Vivienne began to look about with an air of deep concern.

"I don't see them anywhere," she said. "But, now I'm here, I may as well have a good hunt. Don't let me keep you, though, if you're busy. I'll come downstairs when I've finished, and tell you whether I've found them or not."

The maid left the room, and Vivienne immediately began a swift examination of the litter that encumbered the place. The old air-gun which she had seen on her previous visit seemed to intrigue her particularly. Having made a swift but thorough examination of the shelves, she picked it up, approached the window, and looked out. It was already getting dark, and the village street was deserted. She hesitated for a moment, then opened the window and dropped the gun on to the pavement below. It fell with a clatter which seemed to wake the echoes for miles round.

Vivienne shut the window hurriedly. "It doesn't matter much if anybody does pick it up before I get there," she muttered. "It would still be evidence of where it came from."

She left the room and ran downstairs, drawing an envelope from her bag as she did so. The maid was waiting for her in the hall. "It's all right," said Vivienne. "I've found them. Thank you so much."

Having been shown out of the house, she hurried out of the gate and into the village street. The air-gun was still lying on the pavement beneath the window. Looking about her furtively she picked it up and concealed it as best she could beneath her coat. Then she smiled, rather ruefully. There was nothing for it but to walk back to Yatebury. The gun was far too conspicuous for her to venture to enter a 'bus.

She reached the town without attracting attention, and managed to enter the hotel unobserved. With a sigh of relief she disembarrassed herself of the gun, and put it away in her wardrobe. Then, since Christopher was not in, she went out again, and visited several shops. At one of these, an ironmonger's, she made a purchase, and stood talking for a few minutes with the assistant who served her. Then she returned to the hotel. Christopher had just come back from his interview with the Superintendent, and was sitting in the lounge.

"Hullo, Chris!" exclaimed Vivienne. "Here I am, you see. Come upstairs, I want to talk to you."

They went up to Vivienne's room. She shut the door carefully, and turned to her brother. "Did you get that bit of string?" she asked.

"Yes, here it is," he replied, producing it from his pocket.

"Right, lay it out on the floor," said Vivienne, with suppressed excitement. "Now measure it from the end of one loop to the end of the other. Here's a tape-measure. But, before you measure it, I'll tell what the length is. Sixty-nine inches."

"By jove, you're right!" exclaimed Christopher. "How on earth did you guess that?"

"I didn't guess it. I deduced it. Give it to me. This is exhibit C. Now observe. The twine is exactly the same as the ball I brought from Monk's Barn this morning. In fact, it's pretty certain that this piece came off the ball. Again, do you see how neatly the larger loop fits round the flower-pot we called exhibit A?"

"Yes, I see that," replied Christopher in a puzzled tone. "But I'm blest if I see what you're driving at, Vi."

"You'll see, all in good time. Now then, have a look at exhibit D."

She went to the wardrobe, produced the air-gun, and laid it down before Christopher's astonished eyes. "Don't touch it," she said. "There may be some useful finger-marks on it."

"Where in the world did you get this?" asked Christopher.

"At White Lodge. I didn't know how to smuggle it out of the house, so I threw it out of the window, but I don't think it's done it any harm."

"Sounds uncommonly like larceny. What do you want it for? What's the significance of it, anyhow?"

"It's the gun by which Gilbert Wynter was killed," replied Vivienne deliberately. "Sit down, and I'll tell you a most amazing story of perverted ingenuity. The mystery of the murders at Monk's Barn is solved at last!"

CHAPTER XXX

CHRISTOPHER listened to Vivienne's description with ever-increasing amazement. "By jove, Vi, I believe you've got it!" he exclaimed, as she finished. "What on earth put the idea into your head in the first place?"

"The sheer impossibility of anybody, no matter who it was, having aimed at Gilbert Wynter's head through the closely-drawn curtains. And yet, since the fact remained that he had been shot through the head, by a bullet fired from the shrubbery, it was obvious that there must be some explanation of the apparent impossibility. And then I began to put insignificant trifles together."

"Well, it's a jolly fine piece of work, anyhow. I think we ought to go straight to Swayne and put the matter before him."

Vivienne slipped her hand under her brother's arm. "Chris, dear, this is my show, isn't it?" she asked.

"Rather," he replied readily. "You've done everything entirely off your own bat."

"Then let me finish it my own way. I'm terribly afraid that Swayne won't be convinced, and that he'll bungle the whole thing. I know you promised him to tell of any evidence that came your way, but all this isn't evidence, yet. It only forms the grounds of an unconfirmed theory. I want you to come to Fordington with me, now. We can see Swayne afterwards, if you like."

After some demur, Christopher agreed. They secured a taxi, and Vivienne gave the address of White Lodge. Arrived there, they rang the bell, and asked to see Mr. Cartwright. They were shown into the drawing-room, and after some delay Mr. Cartwright appeared, a stern expression upon his face.

"Good evening, Mr. Cartwright," said Vivienne. "You will understand the reason for this intrusion presently. Allow me to introduce my brother Christopher."

Mr. Cartwright bowed distantly. "I presume that you are here in your professional capacity, Mr. Perrin," he said.

"Quite right. Christopher and I have been consulted upon the murder of Mr. Wynter, as I believe you know;" replied Vivienne. "In connexion with that, we have discovered certain facts, upon which we thought it better to obtain your opinion before seeing Superintendent Swayne."

There was no mistaking the significance in Vivienne's tone. Cartwright glanced at her sharply. "I should be glad to learn these facts, Miss Perrin," he said.

"Well, the first concerns the gun found in the shrubbery. It was in its place in the cupboard on Wednesday. On Thursday you came home from Stourminster early, following your usual custom. You went to Monk's Barn about four o'clock, and had tea with Mrs. Wynter. After tea you let yourself out by the front door. At least that is what Phyllis tells us. You didn't happen to look in the cupboard and see if the gun was there then, did you?"

"Certainly not, Miss Perrin," replied Cartwright with dignity. "I should not be likely to pry in the cupboards of my friends' houses without permission."

"That's a pity," said Vivienne, entirely unabashed. "You see, the gun must have been taken some time between Wednesday and Friday evening, and Thursday seems the most likely time. No other stranger seems to have visited the house after that, except the vicar's wife, and it's not likely that she took it. The only other possibility is that Mrs. Wynter removed it, for some purpose of her own."

The shot told, as Vivienne had guessed it would. An angry look came into Cartwright's face, and he seemed about to make some indignant reply. However, he controlled himself. "It is, of course, ridiculous to suppose that Mrs. Wynter ever touched the gun," he said coldly.

"Oh, hardly ridiculous," replied Vivienne. "Still, we can pass over that point. Somebody must have taken the gun, mustn't they? Well, do you know, Mr. Cartwright, that somebody must have been very familiar with Monk's Barn and its garden. You would never guess what they did with it."

"I should be very glad to know," said Cartwright, with an air of sarcasm which ill-concealed his eagerness.

"I'll explain, as best I can. That somebody, who in future we'll call the murderer, made his way into the garden of Monk's Barn soon after six o'clock, when Croyle had left. I'm not certain how he did it, but I think I can guess. He had a duplicate key to the yard gates. There wouldn't be any great difficulty about that. It's not a very complicated lock. If the murderer knew how to use tools, he could buy a blank and cut one for himself. The original key used to hang on a nail in the garage. If the murderer had access to the workshop fitted up in the loose-box next door, he would have had plenty of opportunity of copying it."

Cartwright shrugged his shoulders. "Really, Miss Perrin, all this is rather hypothetical, isn't it?" he said.

"Entirely," replied Vivienne. "It seems to me the most likely explanation, that's all. The only alternative is that the murderer reached the garden with Mrs. Wynter's connivance. That may be the truth, of course."

Again a dark flush of anger surged into Cartwright's face. "I should be glad if you would keep Mrs. Wynter's name out of this," he said harshly.

"Then we must suppose that the murderer made his way in by some such means as I have suggested. He had the gun with him. Now, as I said before, he must have been very much at home at Monk's Barn, and must have had unlimited access to the garden. You probably know who fulfilled those conditions better than I do, Mr. Cartwright. He had previously made a very careful study of the shrubbery and the wall behind it. I think the murder had long been premeditated, and that the preparations were made well in advance."

Vivienne paused. but Cartwright made no comment. She therefore continued, slowly and deliberately.

"In the shrubbery is a gap, caused by a fork in the branches. From this spot, an excellent view of Mr. Wynter's dressing-room window can be obtained. The murderer discovered this, some time during daylight, when the curtains were drawn back. It occurred to him that a gun rested on the fork of the branches and aimed half-way between the shaving-mirror and the lamp above it would infallibly be pointed at Mr. Wynter's head when he was shaving. If it happened that a couple of nails were driven into the wall behind, to support the stock of the gun, the aim would be all the more certain."

It seemed that Cartwright was feeling the heat. He moved away from the fire, took out his handkerchief and mopped his forehead. Christopher, who was watching him intently, saw that his hand was trembling.

"I don't suppose those nails were there by accident," continued Vivienne. "I fancy the murderer drove them in when he discovered the gap. He had seen the possibilities of it, and, at the same time, he drove in a staple, a little higher up. His preparations were then nearly complete. All he wanted now was a flower-pot, a piece of string, and some luminous paint. To obtain the flower-pot was easy. There were plenty in the shrubbery itself, stacked there by the rather untidy Mintern. There was a ball of very excellent tarred twine in the workshop in the loose-box. And, in the course of this afternoon. I found an ironmonger in Yatebury where one can buy luminous paint. You know the shop, Mr. Cartwright. I heard, incidentally, that you had bought some there yourself, not long ago."

Cartwright moistened his lips, and it was evident that when he spoke he did so with a great effort. "This is all very interesting, Miss Perrin," he said. "But, you will forgive me, I know. I feel hardly up to hearing it to-night. The shock of my wife's death . . ."

"I think I should make an effort to listen to the rest, Mr. Cartwright," said Christopher quietly. "I don't think that my sister has much more to tell you. But, of course, if you prefer it, we can go straight back to Superintendent Swayne, without obtaining your opinion."

Cartwright cowered visibly before the veiled menace of Christopher's words. He flung himself into a chair, and lighted a cigarette with trembling hands. "Very well, I will listen," he said brokenly.

"Thank you, Mr. Cartwright," replied Vivienne.

"Now we come to the night of the murder. The murderer had already provided himself with the flower-pot, painted with luminous paint, and a piece of tarred twine, in which he had made two loops, one large and one small. By the way, those loops furnish a further clue. They were tied by somebody who had some knowledge of the sea. A yachtsman perhaps. A bowline is rather an uncommon knot for a landsman to tie. You'll understand that, Mr. Cartwright, since you used to go yachting with Mr. Wynter."

She paused and glanced at Christopher, who nodded to her to continue.

"The murderer went into the shrubbery, loaded the gun, and placed it in the fork of the branches, with the stock resting on the two nails. He then balanced the flower-pot on a little ledge that there is in the wall. He then passed the large loop in his piece of twine over the flowerpot, led the other through the staple, and then slipped it over the trigger of the gun. His preparations were then finished, and he left the garden by the way he had come.

"You visited Monk's Barn that evening, Mr. Cartwright, shortly before seven, and left the house when Mr. Wynter went upstairs to shave, as you told Burden later. The murderer must also have known of Mr. Wynter's intentions, for here comes the curious thing. He must somehow have made his way into this very house where we are now, and gone straight up to the lumber-room. Now, as you no doubt know, from the window of that room one can see straight across the road into Mr. Wynter's dressing-room. And in that room the curtains of the window overlooking the road are rather narrow, and do not quite meet.

"Mr. Wynter must have turned on the light when he entered the dressing-room. Through the gap in the curtains, the murderer, concealed in the unlighted lumber-room, could see him as he shaved. He could also see, by opening the window and leaning out very slightly, the faint glow of the flower-pot painted with luminous paint. Now, there was an air-gun in the lumber-room; I think the murderer must have known this before he entered White Lodge. He picked this up, loaded it, and awaited his opportunity.

"At that moment he saw a bicycle lamp coming up the street. It was pitch dark, he could not see who the cyclist was, nor would the cyclist see him. As soon as the cyclist dismounted and entered the policeman's cottage, the murderer knew that it was Burden. He saw how useful his evidence might be in his own favour. He waited a minute or two. Mr. Wynter was still shaving. Then he aimed the air-gun at the flower-pot, and fired."

Vivienne paused, and then, with a glance at Cartwright's tense face, continued:

"Everything happened exactly as he had planned it. The slug from the air-gun struck the flower-pot, and knocked it off the ledge. In falling, it jerked the string, and so pulled the trigger of the gun. The pot fell to the ground and was broken, the string falling with it. The recoil of the gun dislodged it, and it too fell, to be caught in the branches of the evergreen, where Burden found it.

"You know the rest, Mr. Cartwright. You, by some curious chance, heard the report and ran out into the street through the side door of White Lodge, Here you met Burden. But see how cleverly the murderer had arranged things. The shot had obviously been fired from the shrubbery. There was no risk of Burden discovering the fragments of the luminous flower-pot, since he searched the shrubbery with his lantern, and the faint glow would not be noticeable in any other light. It followed, to all appearances, that the murderer must have been in the shrubbery when the shot was fired. It could have occurred to nobody to look for him in the lumber-room, of course."

Vivienne ceased, and a deep silence fell upon the room, broken only by the sound of Cartwright's rapid breathing. He sat huddled up in his chair, the ghastly look of a hunted animal in his eyes. Vivienne, stern and pitiless, glanced at her brother triumphantly. Then, after a long pause, she spoke again:

"Now we come to the tragedy of your wife's death, Mr. Cartwright," she said quietly.

CHAPTER XXXI

VIVIENNE paused, but no sound came from the huddled figure of Cartwright. The only sign that he had heard her was a compulsive twitching of his lips.

"The death of Mrs. Cartwright was, of course, the sequel to the murder of Gilbert Wynter, and there is no doubt that it was carried out by the same hand, by that mysterious murderer who had unlimited access both to Monk's Barn and White Lodge.

"This crime, too, had been premeditated, and the murderer was merely awaiting his opportunity. He had collected a supply of henbane leaves, and from these he had prepared a very powerful poison. I am inclined to think that he prepared it in this very house. In the lumber-room upstairs there is a collection of simple chemical apparatus, not in any way suspicious in itself, but rather significant under the circumstances.

"The murderer also provided himself with a hypodermic syringe. And then, last Thursday, when I brought Mrs. Cartwright that fatal box of chocolates, he saw his opportunity. He must have known Mrs. Cartwright's preference for the round ones, and Mrs. Wynter's preference for the square. Some time during Thursday night, after the chocolates had been put away, he obtained access to them, and carried out his deadly work.

"His object was to make it appear that the attempt had been made to poison Mrs. Wynter. For this reason, he injected the poison into several of the square chocolates in the lower layer of the box. But there were half a dozen chocolates left in the top layer, and, naturally, these would be eaten first. Two or three of these were round, and these he poisoned. He also poisoned some of the square chocolates which had been put aside by Mrs. Cartwright. But these he hid in a secure place, so that there could be no danger of Mrs. Cartwright finding them and giving them to Mrs. Wynter. His object in doing this was to prove that the chocolates had been poisoned before they reached White Lodge.

"Everything went as he had foreseen. Mrs. Cartwright took the chocolates to Monk's Barn, and, directly after tea, she and Mrs. Wynter began to eat them. There was no danger to Mrs. Wynter. Only the round chocolates in the top layer were poisoned, and Mrs. Cartwright was certain to be overcome before the bottom layer could be reached. This is exactly what happened. Mrs. Cartwright selected the round chocolates, and was killed by the poison contained in them."

Cartwright stirred feebly in his chair. "There is no proof that any of the round chocolates were poisoned," he whispered hoarsely.

"None whatever, since Mrs. Cartwright had eaten all the poisoned ones before she was overcome. But I was present, and I am certain that she ate none of the square ones. The inference is a matter for Superintendent Swayne. The fact remains that Mrs. Cartwright died from the effects of an exactly similar poison to that found in the square chocolates."

Vivienne's voice, hitherto stern and accusing, changed its tone to one almost of gentleness as she continued: "Mr. Cartwright, I do not know what your relations with Mrs. Wynter may have been, nor do I wish to know. But this I am bound to point out to you. If the facts which I have outlined to you should ever become public, if they should ever be mentioned in Court, those relations would become the subject of the most searching inquiry. How far this would react upon Mrs. Wynter, you alone know."

A long silence fell upon the room, a silence during which Vivienne and Christopher watched Cartwright intently. He seemed to have fallen into a kind of trance, which paralysed all his faculties. At last he spoke, in a weak, uncertain voice, like that of a man at the gates of death. "What do you want me to do?" he asked. "I would give all I possess to shield Anne from the slightest breath of scandal."

"What action you take is a matter for you alone to decide, Mr. Cartwright," replied Vivienne solemnly. "We are not here to blackmail you, only to give you warning of what we have discovered. Within an hour Superintendent Swayne will be in full possession of the facts."

Cartwright made no reply. He uttered a deep groan, and his head fell forward on his breast. Vivienne glanced at him pityingly, then made a sign to Christopher. Silently they left the room, Cartwright giving no sign that he was even aware of their departure.

They entered the waiting car, and drove straight to the police station at Yatebury. Swayne, who had been warned by Christopher that he might expect a visit in the course of the evening, was awaiting them. "Hullo!" he exclaimed. "Come in, I'm always glad to see you both. I'd almost given you up; it's eleven o'clock. I rang up the 'King's Head' just now, and they told me you weren't in."

"I'm sorry we kept you waiting, Superintendent," replied Christopher. "But I think you'll agree that it was worth it. We've got some very extraordinary things to tell you. Vivienne has made some astonishing discoveries, which I think she'd better explain to you in her own words."

Swayne smiled politely. "Fire away, Miss Perrin," he said. "I'm all attention."

Vivienne told her story, in almost the same words as she had unfolded it to Cartwright. The Superintendent, whose face had at first expressed nothing more than a mild amusement, listened with ever-increasing attention. As she proceeded, he nodded eagerly from time to time, sometimes interrupting Vivienne to make a hasty note. She had practically reached the end of her recital when the telephone bell pealed out suddenly.

With an exclamation of impatience Swayne went to the instrument and picked up the receiver. As he listened to the message his expression changed to one of horrified amazement. "What, again!" he exclaimed. "All right, Burden, I'll be with you as soon as I can get out."

He laid down the receiver and turned to Vivienne and Christopher. "Cartwright's committed suicide," he said, with strange and significant curtness.

Vivienne glanced at him, a half smile upon her lips. "I thought he would, Superintendent," she replied tranquilly.

"You thought he would!" exclaimed Swayne. "Well, I shall have to go out to Fordington at once, and I think you and Mr. Perrin had better come with me."

In a minute or two all three were seated in the Superintendent's car, driving furiously towards Fordington. They pulled up at the front door of Monk's Barn. Swayne leapt out and rang the bell. The door was opened by Burden, who led the way into the dining-room. There, laid out on the table, was a body, reverently covered by a sheet. The Superintendent approached, lifted a corner of the sheet, and gazed long and thoughtfully at the dead man's face. Then he folded the sheet back again, and turned to Burden. "Let's have the details," he said shortly.

"At ten minutes past eleven this evening I was sitting in my cottage, sir," begun Burden with official precision. "There was a knock on the door, and I opened it. Mr. Cartwright was standing outside, and he asked me if he might come in. He had a piece of paper in his hand, and asked me if I would witness his signature. He said he was sorry for troubling me, but that it was most important that it should be signed at once. The paper was folded, so that I could only see the last line of writing, 'shortly to appear.' Mr. Cartwright signed the paper, and I witnessed his signature. He then thanked me and left the house, putting the paper in his pocket as he did so."

"Did you notice anything peculiar in his manner?" asked Swayne.

"Well, sir, I thought at the time that he looked a bit strange. But his hand was steady enough as he signed."

"All right, go on."

"I was just thinking of going to bed, sir, when there was another hammering at the door. I glanced at the clock, it was twenty-eight minutes to twelve. I opened the door, and there was the maid from Monk's Barn. She couldn't hardly speak, sir, she just caught me by the arm and dragged me across the road. The front door of Monk's Barn was open, and I went in. In the drawing-room I found Mr. Cartwright lying on the floor, with Mrs. Wynter in her night-dress bending over him and holding him in her arms, sir."

Vivienne uttered a quick gasp, and Christopher put his arm round her protectingly.

"I immediately telephoned to Doctor Palmer, sir, and he promised to come round at once," continued Burden. "Then I turned my attention to Mr. Cartwright. I could see he was quite dead, sir, and I tried to get Mrs. Wynter away. But it was no good. She struggled so fiercely when I tried to lift her up that I thought it best to leave her.

"In a few minutes. Doctor Palmer came, and then I telephoned to you, sir. Then I went to have a look round. I had noticed that the french window in the drawing-room was all smashed to pieces, and that Mr. Cartwright's hands were terribly cut about. I thought he must have burst open the window and come in that way. I went out into the garden and through the stable yard into the drive. The drive gates were open, and there was a key in the lock. That's queer, sir, for I noticed later that the original key was in the usual place in the garage. While I was at the gates, I saw that the side door of White Lodge was open."

Christopher and Swayne exchanged a quick glance. "That confirms the theory of the second key," murmured the latter. "What did you do next, Burden?"

"I came back to the house, sir, and Doctor Palmer called to me. Mrs. Wynter had fainted, and between us we carried her upstairs to her room. Then we carried Mr. Cartwright in here. After that, I found the maid and questioned her. She told me that she was upstairs in her room, getting ready for bed, when she heard a terrible crash. She ran out, and found that Mrs. Wynter must have heard it too, for she was running downstairs in front of her. They reached the drawing room, turned on the lights, and the first thing they saw was Mr. Cartwright lying on the floor, just inside the window. Then she ran across for me."

At that moment the door opened and Doctor Palmer appeared. "Well, Doctor, what is it this time?" exclaimed the Superintendent eagerly.

"Suicide, I fancy," replied Doctor Palmer with a grim note in his voice. "Look here!"

He walked up to the table and lifted up the sheet, exposing the dead man's left arm. Half way up it was a tiny puncture, the skin around it red and angry. "Hypodermic injection of some poisonous alkaloid," remarked the doctor. "It wouldn't surprise me if it proved to be hyoscyamine, the same that was found in the chocolates."

The superintendent nodded, and began to go through the dead man's pockets. At last he produced a folded piece of paper, which he glanced at and held out to Burden. "Is that the document you witnessed this evening?" he asked.

"Yes, sir," replied Burden promptly. "I recognize the last line, and Mr. Cartwright's signature and my own."

Swayne unfolded the paper, stared at it for a moment, then read the contents aloud in a steady voice. "I, Francis Cartwright of White Lodge, Fordington, hereby declare that I killed, alone and unaided, both Gilbert Wynter and my wife, Ursula Cartwright. No other person assisted me in any way, and no other person was aware of my intentions, either before or after the event. And this I swear to be the truth, before the eternal throne of my Maker, before whom I am shortly to appear."

The Superintendent folded up the paper and put it in his pocket. "I think we'd better go across to White Lodge," he remarked.

They trooped across the road, and entered the house through the side door, which was still standing open. A light was burning in the drawing-room, and towards this they made their way. On a small table, conspicuously set beside the lamp, stood a small bottle containing a colourless liquid, and, beside it, a hypodermic syringe.

"I thought so," remarked Doctor Palmer. "I'll bet there's a concentrated extract of henbane in that bottle. He gave himself the injection here, and then went across to Monk's Barn. H'm. Well, I can't stop here; I must get back to Mrs. Wynter. She's in a pretty bad way, I'm afraid. I have the gravest fears for her sanity when she recovers consciousness."

"All right," replied Swayne. "You'd better go too, Burden. Oh, by the way, Doctor, how long would it take an injection of that stuff to kill him?"

"I can't say, without knowing the dose," replied Doctor Palmer. "But, judging by the rapidity of its effect when taken internally by Mrs. Cartwright, I wouldn't like to give an injection more than a few minutes."

He went out, followed by Burden. Vivienne dropped into a chair and covered her face with her hands. "It's terrible!" she murmured through her fingers. "Can't you picture the scene? The knowledge that his guilt had been discovered, and, with it, the frantic desire to save Anne's name at any cost! He must have written that note, gone out and got Burden to witness his signature, and then come back here and given himself the injection. And then, when the fatal step had been taken, the ruling passion of his life proved too strong for him."

She paused, and her two auditors regarded her intently. "Don't you understand?" she continued. "The longing to see the woman he loved once more, to die in her arms! Nothing could restrain him, nothing. He knew that he had not many minutes to live, knew that if he rang the front-door bell the drug might overcome him before he was admitted. There was nothing for it but a wild rush, through the gates to which he possessed the key, and across the lawn. No time to knock on the window, he must already have felt death creeping upon him. He flung himself at the glass, battered it in, and fell upon the very threshold. Did she reach him before he died? Did he have time to realize her presence before the end came?"

"That we may never know," said Christopher solemnly. "At all events, his action has cleared up the mystery."

"Yes, it's done that, right enough," commented Swayne. "What I'm wondering is, just how much he knew of Miss Perrin's discoveries?"

But to this neither Vivienne nor Christopher made any reply.

Next day Austin appeared once more before the magistrates, and, after a short formality, was released. The Court was crowded, and, as Austin stepped from the dock, a tempest of cheers, which could not be repressed, shook the building to its very foundations. It was through Swayne's good offices that he was smuggled out by a back way into a car in which Vivienne and Christopher were waiting, and driven swiftly back to his rooms.

"Well!" he exclaimed in a dazed manner, as he stood once more in his familiar surroundings, "I don't pretend to understand this. Of course, they told me nothing. What's happened? Has the real criminal been arrested?"

"Tell him the whole story, Vi," said Christopher.

"It's up to you, since you're responsible." Vivienne sat down and recounted the events of the previous day, Austin watching her adoringly the while. When she had finished Austin smiled.

"I knew you'd get me out of this somehow," he said simply. "That's why I wasn't in the least perturbed when Swayne arrested me."

With a sudden gesture Christopher took out his watch and glanced at it. "By jove!" he exclaimed. "I promised Swayne I'd go round and see him when the Court was over. I must dash off, or I shall miss him."

He went hastily to the door, then paused, his hand on the latch. "See you and Austin later, Vi," he added. "You'd both better come to the 'King's Head' when—er—when you're ready." And with that he was gone, leaving them to the realization of their new-found happiness.

THE END